ALIENS UNDEAD

SLEEP WRITER BOOK 5

Aliens Undead
by Keith Robinson

Printed in the United States of America
First Edition: September 2019
ISBN-13 978-1695856677

Visit www.UnearthlyTales.com

ALIENS UNDEAD

SLEEP WRITER BOOK 5

KEITH ROBINSON

Part One

TARGET EARTH

Chapter 1

Madison woke to a slant of daylight through a crack in the curtains.

She grumbled and rolled over, tucking the blankets tight under her chin. But the sharp edge of a notepad on her pillow jabbed at her forehead, and she brushed it away, sending it toppling to the floor.

A moment later, she sighed and opened her eyes. The notepad had been on her bedside table when she'd fallen asleep the night before. If it had made its way to her pillow while she slept, that meant only one thing.

Sure enough, the pencil had migrated too, now inches from her face, balanced across the highest curve of her pillow.

Yawning, she rubbed her eyes, focused on the clock— 8:23 AM—and leaned over the edge of the bed to retrieve the notepad. The scrawled message was as untidy as always. She'd been sound asleep at the time, just a small part of her brain wide awake and controlling her twitchy hand like a puppeteer.

She often wondered if it mattered that the room was in darkness when she wrote herself these messages. Did that explain the untidy handwriting? Were her eyes even open? As an experiment, she'd left the lamp on one night, but no message had appeared, so she'd left it another night, then another . . . and after a few restless nights with no messages had given up and plunged herself back into comforting darkness.

Shallows Field, Lunar Eclipse. One of Seven.

Madison stared for a long time. She'd never heard of Shallows Field, but it should be fairly easy to locate. The lunar eclipse part made perfect sense as that was happening tonight—Sunday night, the super blood wolf moon. Liam and Ant had been gibbering about it all week.

But the 'One of Seven' part confused her. She'd never written anything like that before.

She reached for her phone, thumbed to her speed dial, and mashed Liam's geeky face. He answered after four rings. "Mmm?" he said sleepily.

"What time's the lunar eclipse tonight?" Madison asked without preamble.

Liam sighed. "Well, it starts at 9:36, but the bite time is around 10:30, and it'll be a real eclipse from around 11:41 for an hour."

"Bite time?"

"I explained all this a million times yesterday," Liam complained.

"I wasn't listening then. All I heard was *wah-wah-wah.*"

"So what's changed?"

Madison rolled onto her back and held the note high above her head. "A message. It says we should be in Shallows Field during the lunar eclipse."

She could almost see Liam sitting up straight and shaking off his slumber. "Cool! What time?"

"That's what I'm trying to figure out. It's not like the eclipse has a clear start time."

A silence followed. Then Liam said, "Okay, so the bite time is when it looks like a bite's been taken out of the moon."

"Is that why it's called a wolf moon?"

"What? No, that's—"

"And the eclipse starts when?"

She couldn't help smiling at Liam's huffing sound. "9:36," he grumbled. "We won't see much then. That's just a fuzzy shadow thing. Bite time is when it really starts, at 10:34. The bite will get bigger and bigger for the next hour. At 11:41, the moon will be completely red, and it'll stay red for another hour after."

"That's a pretty big window," Madison mused. "Portals stay open for forty-two minutes. Should we assume it'll open sometime during that hour?"

"Or maybe it'll open when the eclipse is at its fullest—at 12:12."

Madison grimaced. "Well, I guess we'll plan to be out from 10:30 onwards, then. It's supposed to be cold tonight, too."

"Better than rain, though. At least Shallows Field won't be a mud pit. I'll call Ant." Liam paused. "Dad said I could stay up late tonight to see it. Hope he doesn't mind if we go off somewhere else. I can hear him now, telling me the moon's *exactly the same* no matter where we're standing."

"Just say we want to get a great view from an open field," Madison said, tossing the message aside. She rolled over again, deciding that another doze was in order. "See you later, nerd-boy."

"Hey, who are you calling—"

She hung up and closed her eyes, thinking of aliens and monsters appearing in the dead of night under a blood moon in Shallows Field—wherever that was.

* * *

"It's not very *red*, is it, this blood moon?" Madison commented.

Liam stuck his lip out as he stared skyward. "There's no pleasing you." He narrowed his eyes at her. "Did you see the solar eclipse two years ago?"

Madison shook her head. "Couldn't see a thing in the darkness."

To her satisfaction, Ant laughed.

It was close to midnight. The three of them stood in the middle of Shallows Field. It was huge and not difficult to find. Though mostly flat and open, clusters of pines made it impossible to see everywhere at once.

Liam's scowl deepened. "Maddy, are you one of those people who only saw ninety-nine percent totality and thought the total solar eclipse was a big fuss about nothing?"

"You mean it wasn't?"

Throwing up his arms in obvious disgust, Liam turned in a full circle and raised his voice at her. "Seriously? If you had even a *tiny* bit of sunlight peeking around the edge, then it was way too bright to look at—"

"Hence the special 3D glasses."

"—which means you didn't see it at all. With a hundred percent totality, you could take the glasses off and actually *look* at it without burning your eyeballs out. And then it was spectacular. Man, you seriously couldn't be bothered to drive an hour north to get into the path of the shadow and see it properly?" He blinked at her. "And they're not 3D glasses."

"I didn't live here then, remember?" Madison said, trying to decide how far she could go to wind him up. "It would have been a four-hour drive south for us."

Liam grunted and shrugged. "Still . . ."

Ant stamped a few times and huddled deeper into his jacket. "Gotta say, Maddy, it *was* spectacular. We viewed it from the highest point on our property, and we had cameras set up and everything. If you want to see some good footage, I have about two hours' worth. Two minutes and forty seconds of totality, plus tons of shots before and after."

She raised an eyebrow at him, and he shut up.

"My events are better," she said, giving Liam a vicious poke in the side below his ribs and making him leap away with a gasp. He hated that. "I challenge you to tell me your silly solar eclipse is better than a portal to another planet."

"No argument there," Liam agreed. "What time is it?"

Madison made no move to pull her phone out. That would involve removing a hand from the warmth of her pocket. There was no need anyway; Liam reached for his own phone about a second later.

"11:52," he murmured. "Do you think we're in the right place?"

"It's a big field," Ant said, squinting into the darkness. "It's pretty bright out here even with the eclipse, but would we see a wormhole if it opened up on the far side? Say over by those trees?"

They each spent a moment turning in slow circles, peering across the flat field. Madison felt sure they'd see a glimmering, shimmering portal if it appeared out in the open, but with so many stands of trees surrounding the place . . .

"Why can't you be more specific?" Liam complained. He shot her a look. "You and your cryptic messages. Why couldn't you give an exact time like you normally do? 'Lunar eclipse' . . . I mean, how vague is that?"

"And 'Shallows Field' is a bit vague as well," Ant chipped in.

"Well, guys, I'm sorry I can't muster a bit more effort when I write to myself *while sleeping*."

Ten seconds later, as they stood there shivering, Ant clicked his tongue and said, "This is stupid. It's fifty below freezing. Let's go back to the car."

"It's not that cold," Madison murmured. "But the car is sounding pretty good right now."

She scoured the darkness for it. The long, black vehicle hulked beyond a rickety fence, parked on the side of the road. If any cops came along right now, they'd think it pretty weird for a stretch-limo to be loitering in such a remote place—and for three kids to be standing out in the middle of a field at midnight in this weather. Lunar eclipse or not, that was strange behavior. Why go so far into the field when they could stand next to the car?

The driver, Lilith, would soon set the officers right. She'd simply raise an eyebrow and inquire as to whether anyone was breaking the law, then shoo them away.

Still, Madison decided the car might be a better place to wait for a portal to open.

"Let's take it in turns," she suggested. "One of us stays here, and the other two wait in the car for a while. Then we'll switch, and that way—"

Liam gripped her arm suddenly, and she knew immediately what that meant. So did Ant. Following his gaze, she strained her eyes to find the telltale signs of a portal.

There.

Chapter 2

The portal opened just like any other, a vertical slit of bright light as though a wizard held aloft a magical, glowing staff in the midst of a powerful spell. Only there was no wizard, so the staff stood alone, poised in midair several feet off the ground.

Then it widened into a circle. The light dimmed as the wormhole formed. Rippling and shimmering, the center of the circle plunged inward, twisting and turning as a tunnel to another galaxy came into being.

"Forty-two minutes and counting," Madison murmured, pulling out her phone to check the time.

Without a word, the three of them hurried closer to the light, veering toward the only hiding place—a single oak tree with a thick trunk. It stood a little too far away for the three of them to get a good look at whatever might come through the wormhole, but they all knew standing out in the open was a bad idea. Being seen would result in the alien visitors turning tail and making a hurried exit . . . or worse, attacking.

Huddled together, Madison and her friends peeked around the trunk, watching and waiting.

It arrived a few minutes later—a dark shape rotating lazily as it sped toward them through the wormhole. Two more followed. They looked roughly humanoid but eerily slender and tall. Two legs, two arms, one head . . . but then Madison squinted and frowned, seeing twin tails that swayed independently side by side, like a couple of serpents had sunk their teeth into their rumps.

Frozen to the spot, she and the boys watched in silence. Her heart hammered. These wormhole events never got old.

The three aliens from a faraway galaxy shot out of the portal and landed in Shallows Field without stumbling. While two immediately began scrutinizing the surrounding field as if checking the place was clear, the third turned and faced back into the swirling tunnel, clearly waiting for a new arrival.

A fourth figure appeared in the shimmering light, tiny at first, growing rapidly, spinning and tumbling but somehow managing to step out neatly at the end. This one wore golden plates of decorative armor across his shoulders, the sign of a leader. He carried a squarish object—a dark-grey metallic box the size of a minifridge.

A machine of some kind? Or simply a container? Once placed on the grass, the four aliens surrounded it, and one twisted something low on the side. The box opened with a *clunk* loud enough to be heard across the field, its top breaking into four triangular pieces that unfolded and pointed skyward.

The visitors stood a moment, studying the container's contents. One reached inside, then withdrew moments later. Something glowed now. The triangles folded back down, shutting out the light.

"They switched it on," Ant murmured.

"Switched *what* on, though?" Liam said in an equally low voice.

Madison shared their anxiety. And when the four visitors bid a hasty retreat into the wormhole and vanished from sight, she felt sure the large crate they'd left behind contained something very bad indeed.

"Could it be a bomb?" she asked, stepping out from behind the tree. "If it is, we need to get out of here—*now*."

Liam gripped her arm. "Hold on. Think about it. If it's a bomb, then it's not gonna be such a small one that we can easily get out of range. What would be the point of that? Why only blow up a field?"

Ant spun to face him. "So it's a nuke?"

"Well, if it is, getting in the car isn't going to help."

"It might if we drive at a hundred miles an hour."

"To where?" Liam argued in a surprisingly calm voice. "And what about our parents? 'Oh, wake up, Mom and Dad—we have to get in the car now and drive really fast, because some aliens just left a nuke in a field, and it's primed to blow.' They won't believe a word."

Madison sighed. "You're suggesting we disarm it."

"No, I'm suggesting we throw it back into the wormhole."

Before he could take the lead, Madison shouldered past him and started running toward the alien artifact illuminated by the swirling wormhole. Liam's idea was brilliantly simple—just pick the crate up and send it back. Behind her, the boys hurried to catch up.

"Oops," Ant grunted. "I see Lilith getting out of the car."

Madison glanced sideways as she ran. The limo lurked in the blackness on the road, but the shadowy figure was easy to see even during a lunar eclipse—especially when she switched on a flashlight and pointed it their way.

Madison reached the crate first. Her hair whipped about in the tug of the wormhole as she put her hands on the smooth, metallic side and tested its weight. The crate shifted easily. She figured it would be simple to lift with some help.

She bent to take one side and waited as Liam positioned himself on the other. Ant arrived and looked like he wanted to take over from Madison, and she muttered, "I've got this."

But just as they lifted the box, the wormhole broke up. The swirling tunnel flickered and fragmented, and silently exploded into a thousand glowing fireflies that zipped about in all directions and faded into the night.

As her hair quit whipping about and fell to her shoulders, Madison stared at Liam on the opposite side of the box. He stared back, wide-eyed. As one, they placed the box back on the grass.

"We'll have to defuse it," he said.

Madison couldn't help noticing the look of excitement in his eyes. "Because you've defused bombs before, right?"

"We should at least open it and see if there's an 'off' switch," Liam persisted. "Or wires. Red ones are bad, I think. Or is it the black ones?"

The three of them looked for a way to open the crate. Madison half expected to see light glowing through cracks on the top, but the X-shaped joins were sealed tight.

"Here," Ant said, reaching for something.

Madison had half a second to see him grasp and yank a narrow lever that turned counterclockwise, causing a loud *clunk* from deep inside. Then the triangles on top lifted, and a flood of yellow light shone upwards. Just like in the movies, a puff of steam hissed out and escaped.

When the glowing steam dissipated, the three of them crowded the crate and peered inside just as the aliens had, each of them at a corner where the triangular lid sections weren't in the way.

"What the—?" Ant said.

Madison stifled a scream by clamping a hand over her mouth. She'd expected a digital countdown clock surrounded by multi-colored wires, all attached to explosive-filled canisters, or blocks of highly volatile C4, or even sticks of bright-red dynamite with sizzling fuses . . . but not *this*.

Inside the crate, a slightly smaller glass-walled container was fixed to the bottom, bathed in a ghostly yellow glow. Inside that, a grey-colored insect almost the size of a cat perched near one corner, its wings vibrating every few seconds.

"That's the biggest dragonfly *ever*," Ant gasped.

Madison fought to hide her revulsion. "I don't think it's a dragonfly."

"Of course it is!" Ant argued in a strangled voice. He pointed with a trembling finger. "Look at the long body."

Madison swallowed. "It only has one pair of wings. Don't dragonflies have two?"

Nobody said anything for a moment. Then Liam leaned closer.

"It's growing."

As if the thing wasn't big enough already! Its legs were splayed wide, but every few seconds it would adjust its stance and spread even wider across the glass-bottomed cell. The ghostly glow throbbed with energy.

"It's half the size of the box," Liam commented. "What happens if it grows too big?"

Madison huffed and stepped back, throwing her arms out. "Who cares? What's the *point* of this? This isn't a bomb. A bomb would make some kind of sense, but this is nuts. Who visits another planet to dump a crate with a giant bug inside?"

The three of them could only watch, puzzled and amazed, as the bug grew to three-quarters the length of the glass box. The soft glow intensified, and the bug itself took on a luminescence, its long, thick body pulsing bright then dimming, over and over.

"It's absorbing the energy," Liam said, his eyes gleaming. "It's like ... like it's being dosed with radiation."

Madison instinctively took another step back.

"Good thing it's behind glass, then," Ant said.

"Close it up," Madison ordered. "I don't know what this is about, but closing the crate seems like a no-brainer."

Ant reached for the lever and turned it clockwise. With the same *clunk* as before, the triangular lid sections dropped into place over the inner glass cell.

Liam scratched his head and puffed out his cheeks before letting out a sigh. "So now what?"

As if in answer to his question, the crate unfolded again. They all jumped back in alarm.

"Okay, I'm calling Lilith," Ant said.

Liam blinked and frowned. "What? Why? How's *she* gonna help?"

But Ant had already dug out his phone and jabbed at the speed dial. Madison heard a tiny ringtone across the field in the distance, and Lilith's flashlight bobbed as she hastened to answer.

"Come get us," Ant said urgently, then hung up.

Liam spread his hands, his question still hanging in the air.

"It's an alien bug," Ant said, gesturing toward the glowing insect. "It's getting bigger, and that box isn't going to hold it for long. We have to get out of here—and fast."

They all turned their attention back to the crate.

In fact the bug had now stopped glowing. Having absorbed all the energy, it pulsed softly, legs and wings pressed up against the glass walls.

"It's gonna break free," Ant muttered, backpedaling. "We have to go."

"No way," Liam said, standing his ground. "Those glass walls are thick."

But Madison agreed with Ant. Besides, why dump a rapidly growing bug on another planet if it died within its own cell minutes later?

It'll be free any second now.

The monster dragonfly suddenly went crazy, and the air was filled with angry clicking and clunking noises as it hammered at the glass from within.

"Run!" Madison yelled.

Ant was already running. To her relief, even Liam sprinted across the field right behind her. Ahead, the limo's headlights were on high beam and turned their way, which meant Lilith had found a way onto the field and was driving across the grass. Madison loved the stern chauffeur in that moment.

Behind them, a sharp *crack* filled the air. Madison glanced back. The crate was hard to see in the darkness, but the glowing bug was not—especially when it lifted into the air.

"It's out!" she screamed.

Chapter 3

Panic ripped through Madison. The idea of a radioactive dragonfly the size of a cat—no, a small *dog* now—tearing after her and sinking its fangs into her neck, or hooking her with a wasp-like stinger and injecting alien poison into her bloodstream, or zapping her with an alien laser ray, or spraying acid venom in her face . . . She had no idea how dangerous this thing was, but she had no intention of waiting to find out.

The car bumped toward them, its engine racing.

"Get in!" Ant yelled, reaching for the door handle long before it arrived.

"No, really?" Madison gasped.

The car skidded to a halt, and the three of them piled into the back. Ant just had time to slam the door shut before the alien dragonfly arrived. It glowed fiercely, lighting up its veined wings. It was beautiful but terrifying.

Rather than tear away across Shallows Field, the limo sat motionless, the engine so muffled it might as well have been turned off. Madison, Ant, and Liam pressed their faces to the glass and peered up at the giant bug hovering just outside.

"It's still growing," Liam whispered.

The chauffeur, Lilith Malvolia, slid the dividing window down and twisted to face them. She had a hard look about her: straight, black hair that hung almost to her shoulders, a thin face, and a glare that could wither a plant. She wore her driver's cap, which always gave Madison the impression she was a Nazi general.

"Why on earth did you let that out?" she demanded.

Ant almost sputtered with indignation. "We didn't! We wanted to throw the whole thing into the wormhole and send it back, but we didn't get to it in time. It opened on its own."

"This is what they wanted," Liam added in a mysterious voice.

"This is what *who* wanted?"

"How should I know?"

Madison listened to the bickering while staring at the giant bug. It seemed to be losing interest. Hovering in place but bobbing up and down, it turned to survey the area. Then it shot away.

She watched the faint glow fade into the distance. "Uh . . . this is bad. We can't let it fly around loose. It might be dangerous."

Ant made a scoffing sound. "No kidding. You think aliens would go to all that trouble to dump a *harmless* killer insect on our planet?"

"So we need to go after it," Madison added.

Nobody responded for a moment.

Then Lilith said, "Even if I could see its feeble glow in the dark, I can't just plow straight through trees and fences." She twisted around in her seat and put the car into drive. "We'll report this to the authorities."

As she turned the limo and headed back to the road, Ant leaned forward to talk to her. "And say what? Giant killer dragonfly from another planet on the loose?"

"Of course not, you ridiculous boy."

"And who would you report it to, exactly? Are we going to the *police*?" Ant scoffed openly. "Yep, let's head on over to the Brockridge Police Department. There's probably one officer on duty this late at night, bored out of his mind and waiting for his shift change. I can see him now, calling in SWAT and the FBI and Homeland Security and the rest . . ." Ant slumped back in his seat. "Can't see anybody paying much attention to reports of a really big but otherwise completely normal dragonfly, can you?"

"They will when it starts killing people," Liam chipped in. He frowned. "I mean, obviously I hope it doesn't come to that, but . . . Well, I suppose if it does attack someone, then Lilith's story about a giant bug will mean something. And if it doesn't attack, then there's no problem. Right?"

"Maybe it's a scout," Madison said with a burst of hope. "Remember that time on the lake? They sent a wasp thing through. It was just a scout."

"That was a robot with cameras for eyeballs," Liam said. "This one is a real insect—and it's radioactive and growing."

Lilith was silent for a moment. Then she sighed. "I'll take you home, but I'll call the police on the way."

She must have had the Police Department on speed dial, because a second later she was connected and talking into her bluetooth mike as she drove through the night.

Madison, Ant, and Liam listened in on Lilith's conversation. Only her side could be heard, but her frustration and rising anger was enough to paint a picture. "Yes, I did say a giant dragonfly. And yes, it's the size of a small dog. It's still growing, and— Excuse me? No, I am a respectable chauffeur. My name is Lilith Malvolia, and I work for Frank Carmichael of Carmichael Industries . . . Yes, *that* Frank Carmichael . . . Please do. He'll confirm my credentials. In the meantime, I suggest you contact the appropriate wildlife control experts and start scouring the neighborhood for—" She tutted. "You'll need more than butterfly nets, officer. And I'll thank you to curb your sarcasm . . ."

The conversation went on, but Madison tuned her out. She nudged Liam and Ant so they turned their attention to her, their faces heavily shadowed in the darkness.

"I'm worried," she whispered. "My message this morning said 'One of Seven.' Does that dragonfly count as one?"

Both boys' eyes widened. "Oh, man," Liam groaned. "Yeah, that's not good. I guess we'll have to be prepared next time."

"With our butterfly nets," Ant added.

* * *

Though it was late when Lilith dropped Madison and Liam off at home, the lunar eclipse meant the evening was far from over. On occasions like this, staying up past their bedtime was almost a requirement.

Madison climbed out of the limo, followed by Liam. She leaned back inside. "Thanks, Lilith."

The chauffeur tipped her cap.

Madison wanted to be respectful to the surly woman so that, in return, Lilith's attitude toward their midnight trips might be a few degrees warmer, and she wouldn't put up so many roadblocks when it came to driving them. She might simply sigh with disgust and only drag her feet a little before agreeing to take Ant and his friends to some random place.

Lilith's heart wasn't exactly overflowing with love, but she did have Ant's best interests at heart—as she often mentioned while tapping the holstered gun at her side.

"See you tomorrow, guys," Ant said from the back seat.

The limo turned around and drove off.

Liam's dad popped outside just then to squint at the giant bite in the moon. Over the hedge next door, Madison spotted her own parents peering out the window, their faces lit only by a softly glowing candle on the windowsill.

"Enjoy your excursion?" Mr. Mackenzie asked as she and Liam walked up the driveway. He pointed at the moon. "You can see it just as well from here. What did you see that was so different?"

"Plenty," Liam muttered.

"Nothing," Madison said, giving him a sharp nudge. She looked around, then tapped Mr. Mackenzie on the arm. "Sir, we heard something about a giant bug on the loose. Might be best to call it a night."

"Stupid name for a bug," Liam muttered.

"Huh?"

Liam smiled. "You said to call it a night, so I said—"

"A giant bug?" Liam's dad interrupted. He raised an eyebrow at her. "Just one? Well, better call out the armed forces, then."

"Actually, Dad, it's pretty serious," Liam said. "Police are warning everyone to stay inside."

His dad laughed. "Where'd you hear this?"

"In the car on the way home."

"Son, do you know what that is up there?"

Liam sighed. "It's a blood wolf moon."

"It's a *super* blood wolf moon. You know what that means?"

"No, Dad. What does it mean?"

"It means, Liam, that all the nutcases are out. A giant bug on the loose? Yeah, sure. Probably a slightly oversized ladybug on somebody's windowsill. Maybe it crawled into a wine glass and was magnified tenfold. Too much wine would certainly help with that illusion."

"It's for real, Dad."

But as his dad laughed again, Madison took Liam's arm and said, "Well, I'm done with the moon anyway. I think we've seen all we're going to see. I'm off to bed."

Mr. Mackenzie looked disappointed. "Really? That's it? A unique event, and you're done halfway through?"

"It's not unique," Liam said, sounding tired. "Not *this* event, anyway."

Before he could blab too much and make his dad suspicious, Madison steered Liam away. "I'm off to bed," she said again, quietly this time. "If there's another message, I'll let you know straight away."

She scoured the news before turning in. The local news channels had nothing, but if they had a story, it wouldn't broadcast until the morning anyway. The internet had nothing either.

The social networks were another matter, though:

OMG! Just saw the BIGGEST bug ever! Got off late shift and went to the car and this thing came right at me and I ducked and it went for this guy instead. I heard him yelling as he went down behind the cars but I didn't stick around. Am I a bad person? Called the police and they said they were sending someone ASAP. Totally freaked out right now.

Madison felt a chill as she read it. This was a friend of her mom's friend's friend. Nobody had responded, but another unrelated post caught her attention:

Is someone having a laugh? Giant radio-controlled bug out tonite. Really cool.

Someone else posted a fuzzy photo of the thing, but it was hard to see. Still, Madison recognized it for what it was—the huge dragonfly monster, probably the size of a sofa by now. If it was still glowing, the photo didn't pick it up.

As she lay there in bed thumbing through her phone, she heard sirens in the distance. She was torn. Should she get up and do something to help find the beast? Or allow herself to fall asleep so she could write a new message? She felt sure there would be another tonight.

Even if she got up, what could she do? How would it help to tell the police or pest control that the giant bug was an alien species? Who would believe such nonsense? And besides, that would put the spotlight on her family. How could a fourteen-year-old girl and two twelve-year-old boys know of such a thing?

She fretted over Lilith's phone call, too. The chauffeur had done the right thing in trying to alert the authorities, but after capturing or killing the monstrous unearthly bug, the police would sniff around looking for answers.

Madison checked that her notebook and pencil were nearby. She fell asleep with her phone clutched in her hand.

Her dreams were filled with nightmarish creatures buzzing about the night . . .

Chapter 4

Madison hurried downstairs clutching a new message. It was only 6:10 AM, but she wanted to catch the local news.

Sure enough, at 6:20, the team reported sightings of a giant-size bug. They said it with a smile because anything out of the ordinary like this was always treated as the "fun stuffer piece" at the end of the show. Madison didn't find it remotely funny. Blurred photos of the bug indicated it was not only bigger than a sofa but would no longer fit in the living room.

She suspected the news was a lot bigger than the reporters let on. What if the FBI had been called in to investigate an alien invasion? They had a paranormal and extraterrestrial division, right? Maybe not exactly the X-Files with an eccentric believer and a skeptical scientist, but something similar.

"Are you seeing this?" she said the moment Liam picked up her call.

"I'm not awake yet."

"Check out the news on TV. That dragonfly is huge now. When's it going to stop growing?"

By the sound of his grumbles and yawns, it would take Liam a while to wake up and climb out of bed, so she told him to hurry and call her back. In the meantime, she called Ant.

"Hey," she said when he answered. "You up?"

"Yeah. Been watching the news. How are we going to stop that nasty critter?"

Madison had given this a lot of thought. "The thing is, just because we know it came through a wormhole from another planet doesn't mean it's up to us to catch and kill it."

"It—wait, what?"

"This would have happened anyway, right? We just happened to see it arrive. And we did what we could to stop it, which wasn't much, but that's not our fault either. Next time we'll do better."

"Next time . . ." Ant repeated.

She felt as confused as he sounded. "I'm just saying we shouldn't beat ourselves up about this. It's not our responsibility."

After a pause, he said, "So did you get a message?"

She held it up and read it aloud. "Shallows Field, 8:35 AM. Two of Seven."

Ant gasped. "Oh man. So they're sending another bug?"

"Don't know for sure, but we'll assume that's what's happening. We need to take something to kill it. Or capture it."

"Didn't you just say this isn't our responsibility?"

It isn't. We could just forget about it. Why should we put our lives in danger? These events will keep on happening whether we know about them or not. And isn't it possible I'm sleep writing just to warn myself to stay away?

Madison sighed. "I guess we should do what we can."

"Have you called Liam yet?"

"He's getting his lazy butt out of bed as we speak. Can you come get us?" After a moment's thought, she added, "Maybe in an hour. Get some breakfast first. Then we'll make plans."

* * *

She was bemused by her parents' reactions to the stories of a giant bug flying around Brockridge. Her dad scoffed about it as Liam's dad had. Her mom watched with wide eyes while another news team delved deeper into the story and sent a reporter to track it down. The footage was dramatic—Nancy Trace riding shotgun while looking over her shoulder at the cameraman, a mike to her chin.

"We're over on Lee Highway where the most recent sightings of the monster dragonfly were phoned in just ten minutes ago. Residents of the Farley neighborhood say the insect landed on several rooftops, then clung to the side of a church, and finally touched down in a backyard—and all before dawn."

Madison couldn't help watching with her parents while she waited for Liam and Ant. Nancy Trace looked pretty cool as she continually tilted her head and touched her earpiece, and when she jumped out of the van and jogged across the road to a crowd of onlookers, she kept looking back at the camera and talking as if she'd rehearsed all night long.

I should be a reporter, Madison thought. *Oh, the stories I could dig up . . .*

Nancy Trace pushed through the crowd, and when she made it to the front and peered over a picket fence, even she was at a loss for words. Not twenty feet away, the gigantic dragonfly was perched on the grass, seemingly at rest, its wings vibrating from time to time.

Madison's parents finally quit trying to explain the story as an elaborate hoax. If it were just one source, one single pre-recorded TV documentary, then there'd be no doubt about the amazing special effects. But this story had been buzzing all morning—almost as loudly as the dragonfly's wings. Seeing it now on the morning news, captured by a simple news camera and witnessed by ordinary people . . . It was hard to rationalize.

A car's horn outside suggested Ant had arrived. Madison, still glued to the screen, huffed with annoyance. His timing! Barely taking her eyes off the TV, she pulled out her phone and texted *Be right out*.

The dragonfly monster left huge indentations in the grass whenever it shifted its footing. The elongated thorax swung around and knocked against a shed, twisting it into a parallelogram. The wings occasionally brushed a tree, and branches jostled violently above.

Sirens in the background meant the authorities had just turned up. Nancy Trace jerked and spun around as if remembering she was live on TV. Rather red-faced, she put on her most professional news voice and spoke like the viewers at home were complete idiots.

"It appears to be a giant dragonfly, and as you can see, it's the size of this resident's backyard. Something that enormous has to rest from time to time, and that's just what it appears to be doing—hanging out on the grass and—"

The police leapt into view, roughly shouldering her aside as they hurdled the fence and drew their weapons. "Stay back, please!" one shouted, facing the crowd and noticing the camera for the first time. "This thing could be very dangerous."

Madison rolled her eyes. "Why do these people have to pretend they know everything when they know nothing at all?"

"Well, it *could* be dangerous," her mom said. "It might bite."

"Dragonflies don't bite," Madison said. But then she realized she had no idea if that was true or not. She was sounding exactly like the clueless people on the TV. "I've gotta go," she mumbled. "See you later."

If her parents had asked where she was headed off to, they probably wouldn't have paid attention to her answer anyway, they were so engrossed with the TV.

Outside, the limo was parked in the lane as usual. Over the hedge to her left, she spotted Liam racing down his driveway. Madison jogged out to meet them and climbed into the car.

"To Shallows Field, Lilith!" Ant announced. "Same place as last night."

"Whoa," Liam said. He lowered his voice as the car pulled away. "We need weapons first. I have a few ideas."

Ant grinned. "Me too. I have a bunch of things in the back."

Madison shot him a skeptical look. "And when exactly did you gather all these things?"

"This morning. Couldn't sleep, so I got to work."

It was 7:45 AM when they arrived for the second time at Shallows Field. It was a lot more inviting in the daylight even with the early-morning mist hanging over the dewy grass. Still, being out at midnight and then back again so soon . . . *Five hours of sleep isn't anywhere near enough*, Madison decided. *I need twice that.*

"Drive across the grass, Lilith," Ant called.

The dividing window slid down with a low whine. "Master Anthony," the driver said, "you do realize that I'm not allowed to drive on the field?"

"You did last night."

"That was an emergency."

"So is this! We think there's another giant bug coming."

Lilith nodded stiffly. "I gathered as much. That's why I'm waiting right here."

"But it'll be so much quicker if—"

"There's nothing in the trunk that a group of healthy children can't carry."

Ant grumbled under his breath.

Madison smiled. "That'll be fine, Lilith, thanks."

Liam glared at her, then leaned forward and whispered, "Why are you sucking up to her?"

"Because we're not spoiled brats." She then added, "And because we need her."

She thought about the gun holstered at Lilith's side. *Yeah, we might need that, too, if things go south.*

Last night's lawn-sized dragonfly might not be too bothered by a few bullets, but a small one would be easier to kill. They just had to get to it before it grew.

It was a crisp morning, and Madison shivered as Ant led the way around to the back of the car. He popped the trunk and gestured.

"One sledgehammer, three butterfly nets, two tennis rackets, some gasoline, and a lighter. I think we're good to go."

Madison and Liam surveyed his arsenal in silence.

"That's it?" Liam said at last.

Ant looked puzzled. "What did you expect? A rocket launcher?"

Chapter 5

Ant reached for the sledgehammer. "So we open the crate first. Then we smash the glass box. Maybe we'll squash the dragonfly at the same time—but if we miss, we can either swat it with the tennis rackets or catch it with the nets and *then* squash it. Or we skip all that and just pour the gasoline in. Set it alight, and . . ." He mimed an explosion with his fingers. "Boom."

"You've really thought about this, haven't you?" Madison said.

Ant hefted the sledgehammer. "Are you mocking me?"

She smiled. "A little."

Liam eyed the sledgehammer with obvious envy. He reached instead for a tennis racket, his lip curling. "Baseball bat would have been better."

Madison absently dug in her pocket for some gum. "And you think you could hit a dragonfly with a baseball bat? I saw you swinging a bat at home. Your dad pitched five times in a row, and you missed every time."

All things considered, Ant had been pretty smart about his choices. Tennis rackets were basically oversized fly swats. Butterfly nets might seem ludicrous when faced with an insect bigger than a cat but otherwise made perfect sense.

Looking across the field, she frowned. "Hey."

Both boys followed her gaze. "What?" Liam said. "Oh!"

Ant was a little slower on the uptake, but finally he got it.

Last night's crate was gone.

"So . . . they came back for it?" Ant wondered aloud.

It was possible. Madison felt sure her sleep writing didn't account for *all* the portals that opened in the local area. If the aliens stopped by to retrieve their crate, it would be a very quick visit, hardly worth adding to her journal.

She became aware of Lilith stepping around to join them at the rear of the limo. She straightened her cap and smoothed her jacket before speaking. "All right, I've just had a call. I think it's time we stopped playing games."

Madison felt a sinking feeling.

"What do you mean?" Ant challenged her.

The chauffeur placed her hands behind her back and lifted her chin so she spoke down her nose at them. "Master Anthony, I understand that the three of you have an *otherworldly insight* into matters beyond my comprehension—supernatural occurrences I find hard to reconcile but cannot deny to be true. That business with all those other kids and the . . . the *mind swap* as you called it. I saw it with my own two eyes, and I kept it to myself, knowing nobody would ever believe such baloney. But after last night, and after seeing that awful flying beast on the news this morning, do you really think I'm going to stand by and let the three of you deal with this matter on your own?"

The game's up, Madison thought. *It was always going to happen someday.*

"You're going to help us?" she asked hopefully. "Are you going to shoot it?"

Lilith scoffed and shook her head. "Don't be ridiculous, young lady. I spoke at length with the police earlier this morning, and they had someone in authority call me back, a Colonel Peterson. Well, he just called. I told him about your planned, uh, *rendezvous* at 8:35 in the field this morning." She looked a little smug as she finished up by saying, "He'll be here shortly."

Ant exploded. "What? Are you *kidding* me? That was our secret!"

"I'm not eight years old," Lilith snapped, "and neither are you."

"He's coming to see the wormhole?" Madison gasped.

Liam was enraged. "You had no right! Do you know what the Government will do to us when they find out everything we've seen? They'll lock us up and question us for months, and they'll experiment on Madison to find out how she sleep writes. We'll never be left alone! They'll use us as a weapon. They'll get the edge on space travel and—" His eyes widened. "Humans aren't supposed to visit other galaxies yet. We're just a Class D planet, so we're told. We're not responsible enough. If this Colonel Pesterton starts—"

"Peterson," Lilith interrupted. She held up an index finger to shush him. "What I saw last night confirmed what I thought I had dreamt—the existence of *wormholes* to other planets. This is far bigger than any of us. We have no right to keep this to ourselves."

"And you have no right to take it away!" Ant yelled.

Lilith crossed her arms. "It's irresponsible to make a game of spying on alien visitors. The authorities must be informed."

"*The authorities must be informed*," Ant mimicked her in an angry, sullen tone. He paced back and forth, red with fury, and finally looked at Madison. "I'm so sorry about this. She had no right."

Madison felt strangely calm. Her own anger hadn't yet erupted. She trembled and breathed hard, but she spoke evenly. "It was bound to happen."

There was nothing to do but wait after that. In an effort to get away from the trumped-up, interfering chauffeur, the three of them grabbed their things from the back of the limo—the sledgehammer, three butterfly nets, two tennis rackets, a can of gasoline, and a lighter—and marched across the field. Lilith said they should stay away from the wormhole, and Ant snorted, and Lilith made a small protest about being ridiculous, and Ant mumbled something like "I'll show you ridiculous upside the head" and ignored her. The driver let it go, obviously deciding this was not a battle she needed to win.

They found the approximate spot where the portal had appeared the night before. Despite the cracking sound they'd heard when the bug had escaped, there was no sign of broken glass.

Throwing the sledgehammer down, Ant resumed pacing back and forth.

"I can't *believe* she did that," he stormed. "She's ruined everything." He paused and gazed at Madison like a puppy dog without a bone. "This was supposed to be your private secret, and now the whole world is going to know. You should never have trusted Liam and me."

"Hey," Liam protested, giving him a poke on the arm. "Speak for yourself. I didn't do anything wrong."

Ant frowned. "So it's *my* fault?"

"It's Lilith's fault."

"Yeah, but she's only involved because *I'm* involved. And I'm involved because *you* are."

"But I didn't blab so loud everyone and their mother could hear."

Ant gasped. "Seriously? You're the big mouth around here, not me!"

"Enough!" Madison snapped, her anger finally erupting. She glared at the two of them, and they dropped their gazes like scolded schoolboys. "I could easily say I never should have told either of you about my sleep writing . . . but the truth is, I'm glad I did. I just wish we'd *all* made the decision not to speak so freely in front of Lilith. We're all to blame—or none of us. Either way, we're in this together. Okay?"

Both boys nodded, finally looking up at her with hopeful expressions.

"So quit your whining," Madison finished as she dug her phone out and glanced at it. "We're ten minutes away. Maybe the colonel won't get here on time."

But he did.

A black SUV pulled up near the limo at the roadside. Madison and the boys watched in silence as a stout, grey-haired man in a U.S. Army uniform and cap climbed out of the back and ambled over to where Lilith waited. Two other men climbed out—a driver and someone in the passenger seat—both wearing the same uniforms. They hung back as the colonel spoke with Ant's driver.

"This is suddenly very real and scary," Madison murmured.

Thoughts of the future tumbled through her mind: soldiers showing up at her house, barging their way inside, arresting her parents, confiscating all her things, setting up a perimeter around the property . . . She, of course, would be whisked away to a secret research laboratory and locked up. They'd give her a notebook and pencil and watch her sleep. They'd never let her visit her predicted events, but she knew the colonel would be there instead, waiting and watching, and one day they'd take the plunge, a squad of heavily armed soldiers with a couple of excited scientists, off to see an alien planet . . . And no doubt they'd bring back all kinds of alien artifacts, perhaps even advanced tech and weaponry . . .

She stood in silence with her friends, watching the interaction between Lilith and the colonel.

Finally, all four adults climbed into the SUV—and started across the field.

"Here they come," Ant muttered.

Stating the obvious again, Madison thought.

Despite everything, she felt reassured by the presence of the sinister black vehicle and the trained soldiers. They would have proper weapons and could easily deal with the alien bug when it arrived. Or, more likely, they'd hoist the entire crate and bug into the back of the SUV and take it off to a lab.

Good luck with that.

She checked the time. Five minutes to go.

Chapter 6

"Morning," the colonel said when the car rumbled to a stop and he stepped out. He was impossibly gnarled, his face deeply lined and weathered. "I'm Colonel Peterson." He glanced at the boys in turn. "Your names?"

"Ant Carmichael."

The colonel nodded slowly. "Your father is Frank Carmichael of Carmichael Industries. I have a great deal of respect for him. Famous for the fluxgate compass. He didn't *invent* the idea, but he certainly improved on the technology."

Ant said nothing. Madison couldn't help thinking the man had slipped in a tiny slur there, suggesting Mr. Carmichael had capitalized on someone else's idea.

"And you?" the colonel said.

"Liam Mackenzie."

"Mackenzie . . ."

After coming up blank, Colonel Peterson turned to Madison.

"And you, my dear, must be the one with the remarkable ability to *predict the presence of wormholes.*" Disbelief practically dribbled from his lips.

"Madison Parker," she mumbled.

"And would you care to explain how you are able to come by such knowledge? Ms. Malvolia here mentioned something about writing messages to yourself in your sleep . . . ?"

His skeptical tone gave her hope. Even with a couple of minutes to go, she clung to the idea that she might convince him it was all crazy-talk. Maybe he'd leave.

"I walk in my sleep, too," she said. "I walked right into a flying saucer one time."

Liam snorted a laugh. "She did. And remember that time you were beamed up into the head of a floating whale?"

Madison smiled. "That was cool."

The colonel didn't look amused. He peered around at the collection of items on the grass. "What's all this?"

"Weapons to destroy giant dragonflies," Liam said with a flourish.

"I see."

The colonel obviously didn't. He looked thoroughly unimpressed.

"You *will* see," Lilith said quietly to the man. "In just a minute, you'll witness something you won't believe."

Madison fidgeted and shuffled. Everything was about to change. When that portal opened, her secret would be out. If only the colonel would just turn around and walk away.

She watched as the officer's gaze paused on a square section of slightly flattened grass. The crate must have stood there awhile before the aliens had collected it. Maybe a *tiny* bit odd to the skeptical man . . . but not exactly X-Files material. Now, if the aliens had left that crate behind, then the colonel would have something interesting to cast his beady eyes over.

One minute to go.

"So am I to understand that a *wormhole* is to open here somewhere?"

The colonel's outright sarcasm hung in the air.

Madison forced a smile. "I think you're wasting your time here, sir."

Lilith sidled closer to the colonel. "8:35 AM, they said. It should happen any minute now, like it happened last night."

Peterson gave her a quick sideways glance, then cast a look at his colleagues who stood off to one side with their hands behind their backs. "Well, I have a minute or two to spare . . . but I will admit, I have my doubts about the wisdom of listening to your story." He stared directly at Lilith. "If it weren't for that giant insect my boys are trapping right now, I wouldn't have given your tale a moment's thought. Your report wouldn't even have reached my desk. Do you know how many crackpots have phoned in this morning?"

Lilith took a step back and lifted her chin. "Are you calling me a crackpot?"

The colonel raised his hands. "Whoa, steady. I'm reserving judgment on this situation for another minute or two."

They all stood in silence, waiting.

Madison stared at her phone. The time changed to 8:35, and she put it away, eyeing the sledgehammer that Ant had picked up again. He returned her gaze and hefted it like he was ready for business.

The seconds ticked by.

Madison was more interested in the colonel's expression than anything else. Despite it all, watching his face change from disgusted sarcasm to wide-eyed wonder should be fun, if only for a second.

After that, everything would change.

The colonel stood like his colleagues, hands behind his back, rocking on the heels of his boots. His jaw looked tight as he stared into the distance. Was his face reddening with anger?

Liam held up his phone to Madison.

She blinked. 8:36 AM.

No portal.

Stunned, she pulled out her notebook message again. She read it four times before letting the boys see it. "It's definitely 8:35 AM, right?"

"That's what it says," Liam agreed, snatching it from her. "Maybe . . ."

But she waved him quiet. "Well, I guess it's a bust," she said to the colonel. *Time to lay it on thick.* "You have to believe me, though. I've seen wormholes, spaceships, aliens . . . a massive whale that floats in the air, a gas beast that has a human face and trailing tentacles, robots—in fact, Liam here actually turned *into* a robot."

"Gah!" the colonel exclaimed, his patience at an end. He spun on his heels and faced Lilith. "You've made a fool of me, but I'll chalk it up to my own stupidity. One abnormally large insect does not mean every crackpot in town is telling the truth about its origins. If I hear from you again, I'll prosecute you for wasting my time."

With that, he stalked away.

Flustered, Lilith went after him, keeping her distance but obviously trying to convince him to stay a little longer. She kept glancing back and pointing, and the colonel barked at her to shut up. His colleagues interceded, taking her by the elbows and slowing her down so he could march off alone. When she finally gave up, the two soldiers left her there and caught up to their leader.

Less than a minute later, the SUV roared away.

"8:40," Madison whispered, staring in disbelief at her phone. "This has never happened before—an event that . . . well, that didn't happen."

Liam was busy scouring the field all around. "The note just says Shallows Field. It doesn't say the exact same spot. We just assumed it would be the same place."

She sucked in a breath. He was right.

"Split up," she ordered. "If it's here, we have to be quick."

They ran off in different directions toward distant stands of trees behind which the portal might be shimmering right now. Madison felt both relieved and terrified—relieved that her huge secret had been totally disregarded by the authorities, but terrified now she and her friends could never rely on Colonel Peterson to come rescue them if the need arose.

They were absolutely on their own.

* * *

Ant found the crate first.

Madison knew it the moment her phone rang and his face lit up the screen. Not bothering to answer, she took off running in the direction he'd gone a few minutes earlier. Shallows Field was huge; he'd vanished into a pretty expansive wooded area well away from the road and halfway up a gentle hill.

She looked over her shoulder for Liam. He'd headed way over to the opposite end, around a line of trees where the old Edward Shallows monument stood, whoever he was.

"It's here," Ant said as she came around the trees and found him in front of the swirling wormhole.

"You really have to stop stating the obvious," she murmured, stepping up beside him.

The aliens had already been and gone, leaving their crate in front of the shimmering portal.

"Help me with it," Madison said, rushing forward.

Together they hoisted the crate off the ground. It was lightweight, just bulky. "Okay, ready?" she said as they moved toward the wormhole. "After three . . ."

They started swinging it from side to side.

"One . . . two . . ."

And just then, the wormhole began to flicker and sputter.

"Three!" Madison yelled.

They lobbed the crate sideways as hard as they could. It flew straight toward the shimmering tunnel—but the suction had already faded, and the walls were busy collapsing. The crate acted like it had been thrown into a pool, an unseen force bumping it off course and tipping it the opposite way.

Then it crashed onto the grass just beyond the wormhole.

Fireflies and sparks exploded in a spectacular display, and the wormhole dissipated.

Ant already had his phone to his ear. "Liam, get over here. But grab the sledgehammer as you come. And the nets. And the tennis rackets. Just grab everything!"

The crate chose that moment to open its lid. The triangular pieces lifted, but the crate was on its side now, and the opening faced directly toward them, revealing the same glass box as before—and another oversized bug.

"It's different," Ant whispered. "It's—what *is* that?"

Whatever it was scrambled to right itself in the confined space. It had a glistening, metallic-green carapace. "A beetle," Madison said with a grimace. "Oh, that's gross."

She stared with revulsion as the critter scuttled around and around, already half the size of the glass box. As with the dragonfly, it glowed brighter and brighter as though absorbing some kind of energy. And as it brightened, it grew inch by inch until its six legs pressed against the glass on all sides.

"At least this one can't fly," she said, looking around for Liam. Where *was* he?

Ant grimaced. "Sure about that? Most beetles can."

Madison looked again. She saw no wings . . . but now that she thought about it, ladybugs and other beetles kept them hidden under their hard shell.

She swallowed. "If Liam doesn't get here soon with the hammer, this thing will break loose and fly away."

Chapter 7

Liam came jogging up at last, lugging the sledgehammer in one hand and the gasoline can in the other. He had bug nets and tennis rackets tucked up under one armpit. He sweated and panted as he threw everything down.

To his credit, he didn't complain. He just picked up the sledgehammer again and advanced on the crate.

He faltered. "So . . . if I break the glass and the bug gets loose, you'd better be ready to swipe at it."

Ant leapt for a tennis racket and did some practice swings.

Madison opted for a bug net. It was a good size, certainly big enough to ensnare the bug.

At that moment, a sharp crack filled the air as the glass lid snapped wide open against the inside of the crate. Madison decided in that split second it couldn't be true glass but maybe some kind of hard plastic.

The beetle spun around.

Liam swung the hammer with all his might.

His aim was mostly on the mark. The glass lid and part of the box shattered into fragments. Unfortunately, his hammerblow glanced off one of the top corners and stopped short of squashing the giant, shiny-green insect.

Before he could draw back for another swing, the beetle scuttled across the grass toward Madison.

Much to her shame, she let out a screech and darted away.

Ant swiped at the monster and let out grunts of terror as the tennis racket bounced off its rounded back. He tossed the racket aside and raised his foot to stamp on the cat-sized bug, but it veered away at the last second. It came straight toward Madison again, and she frantically swept the grass between them with the bug net, causing it to turn and scuttle back toward Ant—who yelled and stumbled away.

Liam tore after it, raising the sledgehammer high. He swung—and missed. By now, Madison and Ant had spread far and wide, and the beetle was making its escape across the field, moving with the speed and agility of a radio-controlled car, surrounded by a faint aura as it soaked up the last of the energy.

"Catch it!" Liam yelled.

Madison knew she'd never live it down if she just stood around letting the thing make off into the distance. She dashed after the beetle and brought the net down around its shiny carapace. It kept on moving and tugged her along with it. The alien pest was *strong*.

But, gasping, she held on. At least she could slow it down—as long as the net didn't slip off the smooth shell. She bore down and dug her heels in. It felt like she had an excited pitbull on a leash.

Liam rushed closer and swung the sledgehammer again. This time his aim was true, and he hit the beetle dead center with a sickening crack.

The critter stopped moving.

Shaking hard, Madison lifted the net. Some of its strings caught on the broken carapace, and she had to tug it free. Liam prepared for another strike—and then paused. The beetle twitched, but clearly it wasn't going anywhere.

Cautiously, the three of them approached.

The beetle's back was caved in. One half of the carapace had dislodged so it was partially open, and underneath Madison glimpsed a delicate wing. Some might call the bug rather beautiful, but she couldn't get past the thick, black legs and vicious mandibles. If that monster had grown bigger than a house . . .

"Imagine how tough that shell would have been at full size," Liam said, gripping the sledgehammer tight. He was trembling. They all were. "Strong as a tank. Nothing could have stopped it."

"So we did it," Ant said, letting out a strangled laugh. "We *stopped* it."

Liam snorted. "Well, Maddy stopped it, and I crushed it. You just ran away."

"So did I at first," Madison said in shame.

"But you came back, so you're forgiven. Ant, though . . . Man, did you see how he squealed when that thing changed direction and came at him?"

Ant couldn't help laughing. "I just about peed my pants!"

Madison let out a shuddering breath and laughed with them. When they finally sobered, she said, "Tennis rackets? Seriously?"

That set Ant off laughing again. "It would have been great if we'd needed to bat the beetle halfway across the field. But yeah, rackets don't work very well as beating sticks."

"Told you a baseball bat would have been better," Liam said. "Live and learn. We'll know next time. Only five more to go."

Madison's elation melted away. *Five more*. "Thing is, it's Monday tomorrow. If there's one a day . . ."

Liam frowned. "Yeah, that's a problem. We can't all skip school at the same time. We'll have to take it in turns. I feel the flu coming on tomorrow. Maddy, maybe on Tuesday you can develop a rash or something."

She scowled. "What? Why a *rash*?"

"And Ant can phone in on Wednesday with a broken leg."

"Yeah, right," Ant said in a scornful tone. "And then how do I explain going back to school on Thursday *without* a broken leg?"

Liam raised the sledgehammer and grinned. "You're right, you can't. We'll just have to break it for real."

The idea of skipping school didn't appeal to Madison, especially Liam's suggestion of taking turns. She wasn't sure what was worse—trying to convince parents and teachers that the three of them being absent one after the other wasn't fishy at all—or having to deal with a new bug *on her own*.

"The next one might not arrive during school," she mused aloud. "Maybe it'll be late one night. Let's just wait and see."

There wasn't much more to be said, so they collected up their makeshift weapons and headed back to the limo. The car was still parked there in the distance. If Lilith had stormed away in a rage, she'd done so on foot!

Madison glanced over her shoulder at the thicket they'd left behind. The crate was now out of sight around the other side. The shattered beetle, too. "When do you think they'll be back?" she wondered aloud, slowing to a stop. "I don't want to miss that. I want to see what they think of their dead bug."

Liam chuckled. "Yeah, that'd be awesome."

"And we have a duty to find out more about these visitors," Madison added.

Ant gave her a quizzical look. "Earlier you said it wasn't our responsibility to—"

"I know, I know. But we just blew off a colonel in the U.S Army, and somehow that means we need to step up."

Both boys stared at her. They seemed . . . *impressed*.

"Doing what, though?" Ant asked. "The aliens might not be back for hours, if at all. I'm not sure I want to hang around. And even if we stay here and they show up, what would we do?"

Madison sighed. "I don't know, Ant. But we can't just walk away. Maybe if we dig a bit deeper *now*, find out more about them, we might be able to stop them coming back with more bugs."

Now they both looked doubtful.

The three of them stood there, undecided. Settle down to wait? But for how long? Hours? Or go home and return a little later with some lunch, perhaps something to do while they waited, like a pack of cards or something . . .

The vagueness of it all was getting on Madison's nerves. "How about we take the crate away and hide it? And the beetle, too."

A smile spread across Liam's face. "You're so smart, Maddy. Yeah, if they come looking for it, maybe they'll find it with a tracking device. They'll come to *us*."

Madison felt a chill. She hadn't considered that, but he was probably right. If the aliens had a way to open a wormhole from a distant planet with pinpoint accuracy, then they could find a missing box when they got here.

Ant grinned. "I like it. We can still keep an eye on the crate and watch out for aliens coming to find it—but we can watch in comfort from my house."

"You want to take it back to your *house*?" Madison exclaimed. "Are you nuts?"

"So where, then?"

The question hung in the air. Where indeed?

"Look," Ant said, "it's not that I *want* aliens showing up in my bedroom. But we can't stand around in a field all day. Anyway, my parents are out—gone to some fund-raising luncheon in New York where my dad'll probably write a check for a few hundred thousand dollars."

Madison always found it strange how Ant spoke of his family's wealth without the slightest hint of conceit. If anything, he found the subject tiresome.

"You know my house is big," he went on. "There's plenty of room to hide, and most of the servants have the day off. If the aliens break anything, I'll get it fixed before Mom and Dad fly back tomorrow. Meantime—we keep an eye on the crate while watching a movie and stuffing our faces with popcorn."

"Works for me," Liam said with a nod.

Shivering, Madison had to agree a stake-out in the comfort of a mansion sounded way better than huddling behind trees all day in a misty field.

With a simple plan in mind, they just had to convince Lilith to help them transport the crate back home. It might *just* fit in the trunk . . .

Chapter 8

"Man, she's a pain in the neck," Liam complained.

The three of them stood looking at the crate. The futuristic minifridge-sized box lurked in the middle of Ant's bedroom floor, its triangular lid sections closed. Inside, the dead beetle lay amid fragments of plastic-glass.

While Liam and Ant stared at the object and talked about how Lilith had complained non-stop for the past forty-five minutes, Madison cast her gaze around the room. She'd never been here before. The first and only time she'd visited the Carmichael residence had been during Liam's transition into a robot. They'd taken over one of the well-appointed rooms in the guest wing.

But this was Ant's actual bedroom, and clearly he was a little different compared to other boys his age. Yes, he had the usual stuff strewn about the place—clothes draped over the end of the bed, socks on the floor, a cluttered desk—but his love of Jules Verne and Victorian-era sci-fi was evident in the extensive Blu-ray collection and huge posters on the wall. She stared with some bemusement at a massive floor-to-ceiling print of *First Men in the Moon* which shouted "H.G. Wells' Astounding Adventure in Dynamation!"

"That's a classic," Ant said, sauntering over.

Madison had never even heard of it. "It looks like a '50s B-movie."

"Close. 1964. It's awful. But it's also fantastic."

She frowned.

Spurred on by her silence, he gestured wildly and spoke with a shine in his eyes. "They go to the moon in the 1960s but find they're not the first. A scientist from the 1890s got there well before them. So the rest of the movie is a flashback to the 1890s, where this guy called Professor Carvor invents some paint that defies gravity, and when he paints it on a spaceship he built, it just kind of floats up into the air and heads off into space—"

"Paint that defies gravity?"

"Yeah, it's genius. Anyway, on the moon, there are these insect creatures called Selenites, which the professor named after the Greek moon goddess Selene . . ." He smiled. "Hey, maybe we should call our giant bugs Selenites as well? Or . . . or Carmichites? Carmites?"

"How about Antites? Or just Ants?" Liam said with a smirk.

Madison snorted with laughter. "Ants! Yeah, that works."

But Ant shook his head. "Calling them Ants would be confusing. They're not ants. No, I like Carmites. Or Antites," he added after a moment's thought.

"Well, *anyway*," Madison said, "clearly you're a nerd of the highest order. How did you get into this stuff, anyway?"

Ant shrugged. "My dad. He grew up on these movies, and it's kind of how he got into his line of work—you know, inventing gadgets."

Liam feigned shock. "You mean . . . your dad has a passion for something other than making money?"

Madison side-swiped him. "Shut up, Liam."

"*Had* a passion," Ant corrected him. "When I was little, he used to play these movies in his office while he was working. It was his idea of quality time with me. He'd sit at his desk, and I'd sit in the armchair in the corner. We never talked much, but sometimes he'd stop working and turn around to watch, then smile and go right back to work. He always had one ear on the movie."

He fell silent, staring off into space. Liam opened his mouth to make some quip or other, and Madison glared at him. Half-watching movies together in silence years ago might be the only real connection Ant had with his aloof father.

She smiled. "Well, being a nerd is fine with me. Just don't ask me to watch old B-movies."

Ant strode over to the crate and wrenched the lever. A loud *clunk* sounded, and the triangular panels opened. "Who needs cheesy giant bugs from B-movies when we have the real thing!"

They peered inside. The cat-sized beetle lay there, unmoving.

The crate had just fit inside the limo's trunk, but Lilith hadn't been happy about it. First, she'd lectured them about giving her the runaround and making her look a fool in front of the important colonel. Then she'd gone on about carting around alien technology and dangerous creatures that might have acid blood. "Have you *ever* been to the movies?" she'd screeched. "Haven't you learned *anything?*" The drive home had been filled with thinly veiled threats suggesting she would tell Ant's parents everything that had been going on. And finally, pulling up outside the door to the guest wing, she'd folded her arms and made it clear she would *not* help unload the crate.

Ant and Liam hadn't needed her help. They'd carried the alien box upstairs just fine without her.

"I'm thinking we might have to cycle to Shallows Field next time," Ant muttered. "Lilith is too much trouble."

"Assuming the aliens come to Shallows Field again," Madison said. "Look, a watched pot never boils and all that stuff. Let's put a movie on—right here in your room, where you have a TV the size of my living room wall, and a sofa for each of us."

Ant beamed. "Yeah. This is a real TV. But what movie?" He turned to face the huge print on the wall. "Hey, how about—"

"No, not *First Men in the Moon*," Madison and Liam protested together.

* * *

They ended up watching *Fantastic Voyage*—"the original 1966 movie with Raquel Welch," as Ant described it, as if there was something about that particular actress that made it all worthwhile. Madison had never seen that one either, and about an hour in, she wished she still hadn't.

"I just don't know what you see in these old movies," she grumbled between mouthfuls of popcorn. "They're painful to watch."

"Raquel Welch isn't," Ant muttered, and Liam chortled. "She was even more awesome in *One Million Years B.C.* That was about dinosaurs."

"Dinosaurs and people," Liam said, nodding. "One million years ago."

Madison thought it sounded just as daft as *Fantastic Voyage*. But she had to admit the idea of miniaturizing humans along with their submersible and injecting them into someone's bloodstream was pretty cool. "This movie isn't exactly Victorian, though," she said. "It's modern. I thought you were all about Jules Verne."

"The original story was set in the 19th century," Ant explained, "but the filmmakers decided to—"

A bolt of lightning sliced through the air from the ceiling to the floor and froze in place. Madison, Liam, and Ant yelled and leapt from their sofas, dropping their popcorn buckets as they retreated from the rapidly forming wormhole.

"Here they come," Ant whispered as the vertical streak widened into a circle and began flickering and shimmering.

Madison side-punched him. "We can see that, idiot."

They ducked down behind the farthest sofa and peered over the top. The wormhole tunnel began swirling, and a powerful draft swept around the room. Moments later, a miniature popcorn tornado formed. Then it was all gone in an instant, sucked into the tunnel.

"Here comes the Popcorn Invasion from Earth!" Liam yelled, shaking a fist at the portal. "Hope you choke on the kernels!"

"They might have choked on a *colonel* if he'd stuck around long enough to see this," Ant commented.

Liam shot him a grin.

Aliens arrived less than a minute later—the same four as before, one at a time, each landing neatly on Ant's bedroom floor and immediately surveying the room.

Madison ducked low, tugging at her friends' sleeves. They waited there, listening hard. The wormhole itself wasn't noisy, but the rushing sound of wind around the room, and the flapping of posters trying to tear loose from the wall, were just noisy enough to mask whatever the visitors were doing.

Liam squirmed across the floor to peer around the end of the sofa. Madison did the same at the opposite end.

All four aliens were gazing into the open crate.

Since their attention was elsewhere, Madison finally had a chance to study them. They were tall. Their silvery clothing was straight out of the movies—a 1950s B-movie, actually—and their knee-length boots were almost comical. She noticed again that one had golden plates across the shoulders. He had to be the leader. Their hands were large, each with seven fingers plus thumbs. *Seems like overkill*, Madison thought. *What's the point of so many?* But then, did humans really need four fingers? Wouldn't three do just as well? What was a perfect number anyway?

The twin tails struck her as odd. She studied the alien whose back was turned directly toward her. In fact, a single thick tail emerged from a short sleevelike opening low on its back, then split in two and became separate entities, curling and flicking independently.

Across the other side of the crate where an alien faced her way, its rather beady gaze was cast downward, but Madison could see a faint yellow glow in its eyes as if the inside of its head were lit up by feeble lamps. She thought of *Fantastic Voyage* and imagined a team of scientists shining their flashlights out of the eyeballs, looking for a way out . . .

The visitors spoke in such low voices she couldn't hear a word they said. Touching two fingers to the middle of her chest, she felt sure her new translator implant would work if only they would raise their voices. The pin-prick wound was still a little sore. It hadn't been at first, when that lizard woman from Glochania had shot her and Ant with the microscopic tech, but a bruise had developed days after. It was fading now, though still itchy.

Whatever the visitors might be saying, she guessed they weren't too happy. Funny how they took Ant's bedroom for granted. She wondered if they'd arrived in Shallows Field to pick up the crate and then realized it was gone and followed some kind of tracker. Or had they come straight here? Either way, they appeared unconcerned.

Madison twisted around and nudged Ant and Liam, who were both flat on the floor peering around the other end of the sofa. "Guys," she whispered. "I'm not normally the one to say this, but . . . I think we should talk to them."

Liam nodded and looked like he was about to jump up.

Ant, though, was horrified. "Huh?"

There was no time to whisper her reasons to him. She shared a glance with Liam and, without a word, they both climbed to their feet.

"Hey," Madison said, her voice surprisingly loud over the rushing wind.

All four aliens turned to face her.

Chapter 9

Madison felt a chill as the four visitors from space glared at her with eyes that now blazed with fire. The one with the golden shoulder armor spoke in an incredibly deep, booming voice.

"You destroyed our test subject."

The words didn't match the movement of the mouth. The lip-sync was off. She heard the booming voice, but her translator implant altered the speech somehow, feeding words she could understand directly into her brain. The nanotech in her chest worked in mysterious ways . . .

"Of course we destroyed it," Madison said as boldly as she could. Yet she trembled. Liam sidled up alongside her, and she was aware of Ant slowly getting to his feet. "You expect us to let it run around *attacking* people?"

"We don't *expect* anything from you," the alien said with a sneer. It—presumably a *he*—advanced on her. "This planet is listed as a Class D. You don't have the right to voice an opinion."

"Don't have the right to . . ." Madison trailed off, feeling a knot of anger in her chest along with the translator. "You think *you* have the right to let giant bugs loose on us?"

"Who do you think are?" Liam cried, stepping forward to meet the visitor. He had his fists balled, but he only came up to the other's chest. "Anyway, I thought you people were supposed to stay away from Class D planets."

The visitor drew himself up even taller, over six and a half feet. His head, and his entire face, loomed even larger now, and his hands had to be twice the size of most. His face was lined and blotched like an elderly person, but he moved like he had the strength of a twenty-something athlete. And with that heavy armor on his shoulders, he would give football players something to think about.

"We are Draduns, from Dradus Mox in the Zutrillon System, and we—"

"Oh, you're from *there*," Liam said scornfully. "I should have known." He looked at Madison, cupped a hand to the side of his mouth, and added in a rather loud whisper, "Never heard of it. Have you?"

Madison shook her head, anger subsiding and giving way to fear again. She had a feeling Liam might land them in very hot water if he kept up with his tirade.

She touched his arm and spoke firmly but a little more respectfully to the visitor. "Whoever you are, you can't just come here and dump your radioactive bugs on our planet. Are you *trying* to hurt us, or do you just not care?"

The alien frowned, then looked back at his colleagues. They seemed equally puzzled. Turning back, the spokesperson for Dradus Mox said, "Radioactive? You are mistaken. And in answer to your question—yes."

A silence fell.

It was Ant who spoke next. "Do you mean 'yes' as in . . . you *are* trying to hurt us?"

The towering alien gave a curt nod. "In a manner of speaking, yes. But you are not our enemy. You are merely . . . collateral damage. A means to an end."

One of the others said quietly, "Enough has been said, Krun. We must leave."

Madison blinked. Though the translator in her chest had offered Krun as a name, the lip-sync was a little off. Interpreting names across galaxies must be a real challenge for a tiny piece of tech. Krun. Was that actually his name, or just a rough idea of what it might be?

The leader, if he was indeed their leader, seemed to enjoy explaining himself. His beady, strangely glowing eyes brightened further the more he spoke.

"If our test subjects are successful here on this Class D planet, they will be successful when we go to war on the forests and wastelands of the Mox."

Madison was getting sick of her home being mentioned in such a sneering, derogatory tone. "Successful how?" she asked through gritted teeth. "What are these bugs supposed to do?"

"We should go now," another of the visitors murmured. The other two had lifted the closed crate easily between them, and they casually tipped it into the swirling wormhole so it spun into the distance.

The one named Krun nodded and started to turn away. But he couldn't resist a last jab. "They are supposed to *destroy*."

Exasperated, Madison yelled, "So destroy your *enemies*, not us!"

"Not until we're certain of our weapon. We must hit the Mox hard and fast with a swarm of the most efficient killers, not poke at them with tests until we get it right."

"And bugs are more efficient killers than you?" Ant piped up.

His question caused the alien to snarl and draw himself up even taller. "No, they are not," he growled. "A handful of our best airborne warriors could exterminate the Mox in one pass. However, open genocide would not sit well with the civilian sector—"

"You think?" Ant muttered.

"—therefore we must quietly *create* an enemy and stand aside while it goes to work. Our people may be suspicious of such a conveniently freak mutation with a single purpose to wipe out the enemy, but doubt and grudging acceptance will prevail. Then life will continue . . . without the Mox."

After a moment to digest this, Ant asked again: "But *bugs*?"

This time Krun had his back to him when he answered. "Bugs are in plentiful supply. They're resilient, tenacious, adaptable, ravenous, and completely expendable. We can wipe out the Mox from afar and feign innocence. And afterward, we can withdraw the Nyx energy and easily restore normality."

"And nobody will wonder where the giant killer bugs came from?" Madison demanded. "You don't think your people will figure it out? What will the rest of the galaxy think? You can't just wipe out a species when you feel like it and expect to—"

"Enough!" the alien snapped. "You speak as though your opinion is somehow *relevant*. It is not. The experiment will continue."

Liam scoffed. "Well, the last two bugs you sent didn't last long." He counted off on his fingers. "One escaped and is being hunted down right now by the U.S. Army. The second—well, you saw it. I hit it with a hammer.

Wham, and dead. Easy. So go ahead, send the other five. We'll stamp 'em out in no time."

Madison winced. *Liam, shut up.*

All four aliens were prepared to leap back into their wormhole by now. But they all paused and looked back at Liam with obvious surprise.

"Interesting," the leader said at last. He squinted at Liam, then at Madison, and finally at Ant. His tails swished back and forth. "The fact that you understand us means you have translators. And it seems you were able to track where we arrived the first time in order to wait for our arrival the second time. That suggests you have possession of somewhat advanced tech."

Liam nodded and folded his arms. "So?"

"But how are you able to predict that we have seven test subjects to send to this world?"

Madison sighed. *Nice one, Liam.*

"Lucky guess," he muttered. "Thanks for confirming it."

The four aliens conferred quietly. Then, one by one, they approached the wormhole and leapt in. Krun, the last one to go, lingered a moment longer. He smiled, and Madison saw nothing but malice in his eyes.

"The experiment will continue. I will be interested to see how you deal with the situation. But I suspect it will end with your deaths. The only question is which of the test subjects will be the most devastating. We will soon have an answer—and then we shall go to war with the Mox and wipe them out once and for all."

"You'll lose," Liam said rather weakly.

Without another word, the alien threw himself into the wormhole and spun away.

Madison stood there with Liam and Ant, not saying anything until the wind died and the swirling tunnel broke up. When silence fell, Madison gave a heavy sigh.

"Liam, you really need to think before opening your trap. You basically just warned them that we know more than we should about their wormholes. Now they're going to up their game."

Liam opened his mouth to protest, but he clammed up again and looked troubled. "I guess. Sorry."

"Never mind sorry. You're gonna be on the front line tomorrow or whenever they're sending the next bug."

"Fine."

Ant went to find a broom while Madison smoothed back her hair and then straightened sofa pillows and whatever else had been swept out of place. Liam quietly messed with posters on the walls where they'd come loose.

After ten minutes of shuffling about, tidying up, and mulling things over, Madison turned to her friends and said what she'd dreaded for some time. "Guys, I think it's time."

"Time for what?" Ant said.

She took a deep breath. "As much as I hate to admit it, I think we have to call for help. Lilith has the phone number for that colonel. He might not be interested right away, but we have to convince him. We need help. We're talking about an invasion of Earth. We're a target, guys— the target of an experiment. They're sending their giant, radioactive bugs to see which one wipes us out the easiest. I mean, we're nothing but lab rats to these . . . these Draduns."

Ant shook his head. "Lilith isn't going to cooperate. And even if she does, the colonel won't."

"We have to try. This situation is getting out of hand. Did they even catch the giant dragonfly yet?" She wrung her hands and paced the room, thinking hard. "So here's what we'll do. I'll wait for the next message. When we get it, it'll tell us when the next bug is coming through. We'll go to Lilith and plead with her, grovel at her feet, whatever—and we'll get her to call the colonel and tell him there's another bug arriving."

"He won't believe us," Ant said again.

"I know—but the bug will come anyway, and then he'll know we were telling the truth. He'll *have* to come see us. Then we can work together. Better late than never, right?"

Watching Liam's and Ant's faces, she could almost see her plan sinking in. They finally caved.

"Okay," she said. "Let's try and relax for the rest of the day. I'll go to bed early tonight."

Liam huffed and threw himself down on one of the sofas. "Can't you just take a nap right here? Get some shut eye, and maybe you'll write a message this afternoon rather than overnight."

That thought had occurred to Madison too, but hearing Liam suggest it somehow made it seem like an actual possibility. It always amazed her how easily he came by solutions. And she *was* tired . . .

"All right," she agreed. "I only got five hours' sleep last night, so I could probably drop off pretty easily. Find me a notepad and pencil." She looked at Ant. "But you guys are going to have to be quiet. A movie will be fine. I can always fall asleep to a movie if I'm tired, especially if it's boring."

Liam grinned. "Let's finish watching *Fantastic Voyage*, then."

Madison rolled her eyes. "Fine. That'll send me off in no time."

* * *

She dozed off about forty minutes later.

The movie continued, and she was vaguely aware of the credits rolling at the end. Liam and Ant murmured to each other, and then the movie went quiet—but a new one started up, and her sleep resumed.

She wasn't aware of writing a new message.

"Maddy," Liam said quietly, shaking her shoulder. "Wake up. It's done."

Blinking and yawning, she struggled to a sitting position. "Huh?"

It had to be mid-afternoon by now. Looking around, she saw the notebook and pencil, but Liam had ripped a page from it. He handed it to her. "It's bad," he said.

Rubbing her eyes, Madison focused on the words.

There it was—another message. The nap had worked a treat.

"Oh," she said, her skin crawling.

3:21 AM. The other five bugs. Stay here.

Chapter 10

"This changes things," Madison said, pacing the room. "If they're all arriving at once, then my plan won't work so well. How are we going to convince the colonel that—" She shook her head and stared out the window across the Carmichael's landscape. "Well, I guess it doesn't make any difference. He's going to find out pretty quickly when the new bugs are in town."

Liam was gazing at the TV screen, which was paused on a scene of an upside-down man's head with spider's legs. Madison had glanced at it a few minutes ago and immediately recognized *The Thing*. What was it with the insect references today? Not that spiders were insects . . .

"I don't understand why you didn't give us all the locations," Liam said, turning at last to give Madison an accusing look. "You just gave a time. Maybe one will arrive here, just because those Draduns will want to punish us for arguing with them, but what about the rest? Or maybe all of them will be in totally different places— heck, maybe not even in this country! Why weren't you more specific?"

Madison felt anger rising. What did *he* know about sleep writing? "If I didn't specify the locations, then I probably don't need to know."

"But we *do* need to know," Ant argued.

"No, we don't." Madison glared at them both. "I have no idea what kind of force is using me as a ouija board, but it knows we can't be in five places at once—and anyway, I think we're meant to do something bigger."

Liam looked doubtful. "Bigger?"

She clammed up, unsure herself what she meant. Something was percolating at the back of her mind, though.

"We could use the echo wand," Ant muttered.

Though Madison shuddered at the very idea of the future-seeing device, she kept quiet about it for the moment.

Liam, however, voiced his opinion quite loudly. "No. We agreed never to dig that thing out of the yard again."

"Yeah, but we could power it up and jump forward a bit just to see where these bugs show up." Ant's eyes were wide with excitement. "I could do it. I'll only be a ghost, but I could float into someone's living room and watch the news, and we'll know instantly where the bugs are, when they arrived, and what happened."

Liam clenched his fists. "And what happens if we find out the world ends?"

Ant barked a laugh. "Except it won't. You know that. You've seen yourself in the future, and—"

"Enough!" Madison interrupted. "How many times are we going to end up arguing over this? Nobody wants to see their own death. Do *you*, Ant?"

He sighed and shook his head. "Not really. I mean, I wouldn't mind if I lived to old age like Liam here. Then it would be worth knowing." He gave Liam a stare. "He won't tell me, though. Did you see me in the future or not?"

Liam opened his mouth, then closed it.

Madison wanted the conversation to end. "Ant, maybe he knows, and maybe he doesn't. But he has no right to change your life by telling you about your death. Or someone else's death. Did you think about that? What if something happens to your parents next month? Or mine? If we can't change it, then I don't want to know about it in advance. How awful would that be, knowing they're going to be killed in a horrible accident but unable to help them?" She took a deep breath. "So let it go. The echo wand is not an option. It stays buried in my yard."

And with that, the topic was abandoned.

She found the remote, switched off the paused movie, and turned to one of the local channels. The news wasn't normally on at this time, but as she suspected, a special bulletin was underway. A harried Nancy Trace jogged along a street along with streams of yelling residents, and as she stopped to continue her report, the cameraman turned to face the source of the panic.

The monstrous dragonfly lifted one tree-trunk leg after another and slowly, ponderously, turned around. Like a runaway crane, the tip of its long, grey body smashed into the corner of a house and took a sizeable chunk out of the structure. The roof on that corner tilted a little, and the gutters came crashing down along with strips of white siding.

Madison, Liam, and Ant crowded together to watch.

"Soldiers are moving into position once again," Nancy Trace said, her face shifting into view. Her eyes shone with excitement mingled with terror. "This monster bug has hopped from place to place for the past few hours, apparently threatened by the approach of Army helicopters. It's now settled halfway along Johnson Road in Brockridge. Residents are fleeing despite warnings to stay off the streets. There's no sign of helicopters this time, because the focus is to surround the creature by troops on the ground without forcing it to take flight again. Tanks are rolling in as we speak."

"Oh no," Madison murmured. "That's less than a few miles from our house!"

"I managed to speak with Colonel Peterson a while ago, and he advised residents all over Brockridge to *stay in their homes.* He said that even though this giant insect is on the rampage, there's more protection inside buildings than out—and let's not forget, folks, that Channel 9 has confirmed the deaths of *four people* this morning, snatched from the street by this unbelievably huge dragonfly."

"A killer dragonfly," Ant said, shaking his head.

Liam snorted. "All dragonflies are killers. Actually, they're *amazing* killers. But usually they just kill other bugs. I was reading about them earlier while you were asleep, Maddy—they snatch mosquitoes out of the air, can hover in place, fly backwards and in all directions—they're really efficient."

"That's good to know."

"But this monster only has two wings," Liam went on, "so it can't be a dragonfly. It's some alien bug that happens to look a bit like one. It could breathe fire for all we know."

A fire-breathing dragonfly, Madison thought with a shudder.

On the TV, the shaky camera showed tanks easing into view from the far end of Johnson Road. The giant bug hadn't noticed yet; it was busy tearing into the side of a house with its powerful mandibles, foraging for food.

"If you're just joining us," Nancy Trace said, out of breath and red-faced as she jogged away from the monster with the cameraman in reverse ahead of her, "the events unfolding here in Brockridge are being broadcast across the nation. Over my shoulder, an insect the size of a house has been hopping across the town and causing widespread damage—and is responsible for the deaths of four people. Where did it come from? Why has nobody seen it until now? How can it exist? These are the questions being asked this afternoon—questions the U.S. Army will not or cannot answer at this time."

Madison felt like her world was unraveling. Watching aliens sneak through wormholes in the dead of night was one thing, a secret she'd shared with her neighbor and his best friend. But this? A gargantuan extra-terrestrial dragonfly attacking the town and picking off its residents while the Army rumbled around in tanks? She'd have laughed derisively had she seen this in a 1950's B-movie, yet here it was, *actually happening right now*.

Nancy Trace kept on, knowing her report was being seen across the country and putting on her very best show. ". . . Experts are saying the giant insect is unable to fly very far due to its size and weight, so it's launching into the air and coming down again, literally hopping from place to place. But those same experts are at a loss to explain how even *that* is possible. Although its legs are as thick as tree trunks, the laws of physics suggest that shouldn't be enough to support the exponentially increased body mass . . ."

"She's right," Liam said, nodding. "Magic has to be involved."

Ant snorted.

Madison turned away from the TV. "I can't help thinking magic *is* involved. That weird light we saw in the crate—and how the dragonfly and beetle glowed as they absorbed it and got bigger—I mean, it has to be some kind of magic, right? Things can't just grow like this."

She almost expected Ant to point out that two bugs had, in fact, grown exactly like that, but for once he refrained from speaking the obvious.

"There's no point chasing after these things," she said at last. "What can we do that the Army can't? Nothing. We need to do something different. Something helpful."

She had Liam's and Ant's attention.

Counting off on her fingers, she outlined the basics of her plan.

"First, we talk to Lilith. She has to convince the colonel more bugs are coming. We don't know where, but we do know when, and the colonel needs to act fast while they're small enough to be stomped on. He needs to send out an alert for people in Brockridge to keep their eyes open."

"That all sounds very simple to organize," Liam said, sarcasm dripping off his tongue.

"Second, we'll be right here in this room waiting for one of the bugs," Madison went on.

"Wait, what?" Ant said, aghast. "Okay, first, how do we know for sure one will come through to this room?"

"Because the Draduns will want to punish us for interfering," Liam offered.

"Or avoid us so we don't mess with their experiment again," Ant argued.

"Well, how about because Maddy's note said to wait here? That's a pretty good indicator at least one bug will end up in your bedroom."

"The note might just be a warning to stay here so we don't get involved."

Liam threw up his hands in defeat.

Madison smiled. "If that's true, Ant, then we'll have a quiet evening. No loss, right?" She paused as Ant digested this. "But I think we should prepare in case a bug *does* come through. Don't you think?"

Ant sighed and nodded.

"And *third . . .*"

Liam and Ant stared at her, their eyebrows raised in an expectant manner. It was rare for them to listen so raptly, to hang onto every word. If only she could enjoy the moment . . .

"Third," she said at last, "we have to do something only we can do. We had the chance to get help from the Army, and we blew them off, so it's up to us."

She swallowed, then continued.

"When a wormhole opens here in this room and a bug comes through, we have to kill it as fast as possible—and then jump into that wormhole and go after them."

Chapter 11

They waited in darkness.

Madison glanced at her phone. 3:19 AM. Two minutes to go. She nervously tugged on one of the long sleeves of her black shirt, grateful to blend into the shadows. The funny thing was, she often wore dark clothing and thought nothing of it. Liam and Ant, though, looked a little weird in their all-black ninja gear.

In comparison, Lilith stood out in her grey chauffeur uniform. Did she ever wear anything else?

The group of four waited side by side facing the exact spot where the previous wormhole had opened. Liam had convinced them all it would form in the same place again—not three feet to the left or in the next room, but *right here*, because the coordinates were already programmed into the aliens' wormhole-opening device.

Unless the aliens *chose* to move it someplace else, which was always a possibility.

Nobody said anything as the minutes marched by.

Their afternoon had been trying, with most of it spent watching TV reports about the monster bug. It had stopped growing and was strengthening instead, and the tanks hadn't balked it. They'd fired on the insect once, but the projectile had glanced off the super-strong thorax and taken out an entire house instead. The bug had staggered, but it seemed unharmed.

An *invincible* giant bug, now?

Colonel Peterson had opted to take the battle out of town, so he'd sent in a couple of helicopters to scare it away. The scene had played out on live TV across the country, and indeed the world. The bug had flown—or rather hopped—all the way to the edge of Brockridge and perched on an overpass, and the Apache helicopters had taken the chance to shoot at it with their side-hung Hellfire missiles. Part of the bridge had collapsed, but the dragonfly had simply hopped away to a nearby Walmart parking lot and started chewing on cars, turning one upside down as though trying to get at the meat under the carapace.

Definitely invincible.

Tanks had rumbled in and faced the insect. But rather than fire and send it hopping away again, the colonel acted with caution and waited for a team of scientists to suggest something more effective than missiles. They came up with plenty of ideas, but trapping the alien creature was their first priority—or at least grounding it.

Out came the flamethrowers. Ten men surrounded the massive dragonfly and unleashed their fury all at once. The bug immediately leapt into the air, but it came down again straight away, fire raging from its wings as they melted in the inferno.

The dragonfly was down but not out. Blackened and agitated, it stamped about the parking lot, smoke pouring off its body . . .

Almost invincible.

Ant's bedroom was in darkness apart from the TV, which quietly replayed endless footage of the bug while messages rolled across the bottom of the screen and reporters interviewed experts. Madison watched the scenes out of the corner of her eye, looking for something she hadn't seen thirty times already.

It had happened around 8:30 PM. The bug's wings, which had been thoroughly melted by the flamethrowers hours before, suddenly repaired themselves and became whole. Afterward, the dragonfly launched and took off—and this time it kept on going, bobbing through the air, almost crashing down but soaring high again, limping through the sky over the woods with Apaches tearing after it.

"Is it true the U.S. Army has *lost sight* of the monster?" a reporter asked a spokesperson for the beleaguered colonel.

"Of course not! We know exactly where it is. The problem is getting to it. It's alighted on a rocky hill in the middle of the woods. We have troops in the vicinity and helicopters overhead."

"And why aren't you blasting it out of the sky?"

"Because if the creature wasn't indestructible before, it is now," came the barked reply.

Madison looked again at her phone. 3:20 AM.

None of them but Lilith had a weapon. She stood there with her gun drawn, clasping it between her hands, aimed at the floor.

When the wormhole crackled into existence at 3:21 AM, the wind buffeted them first, then began tugging at their clothing as the tunnel started swirling.

But instead of a crate appearing exactly as before, tumbling its way toward them, this time they saw a terrifying shape, a wriggling six-legged bug that Madison immediately guessed was a wasp.

Her heart began to hammer in her chest. "They let it out already," she squawked. "Are you ready, Lilith?"

"Ready," Lilith muttered.

The Draduns had upped the ante and thrown them a curveball. No crate, no weird gestation period before the radioactive critter burst loose, just an already growing monster tumbling through the wormhole.

"They can't do that," Liam complained.

"They just did," Ant retorted.

Madison's fear of the wasp was overshadowed by an even bigger risk—the thought of the wormhole collapsing too early. "We have to go," she said in a strangled voice. "Liam, Ant—you ready?"

"Go," Lilith ordered. "I'll take care of the bug."

Madison didn't need telling twice. Even so, leaping into the wormhole now meant rushing toward the wasp, perhaps even colliding with it. But it was better than waiting too long. The Draduns could pull the plug at any moment.

She leapt into the swirling tunnel of light, allowing the powerful suction to pull her along. Glancing back, she saw Liam jumping in after her, then Ant.

Ahead, caught up in its own one-way vortex, the wasp shot toward her. It had to be the size of a pitbull already. Thoroughly appalled and disgusted by the thick black legs and shiny abdomen, and the vivid red stripes that screamed *venomous*, Madison tried her best to twist out of its way . . . but it was like trying to anticipate the trajectory of a falling autumn leaf. She made a frantic last adjustment before slamming into the bug, then tumbled away, shocked and breathless.

Luckily, the wasp-monster seemed confused, otherwise it might have stung her.

A second later, it was Liam's turn to collide with the monster bug. He bounced off and flipped helplessly from end to end.

The spinning wasp shot past a wide-eyed Ant.

Though Madison rushed at great speed through the wormhole to a distant galaxy, the sound of gunshots echoed in her ears—Lilith firing round after round as the giant wasp tumbled into Ant's bedroom back on Earth . . .

She feared for the chauffeur's life. The dragonfly and beetle didn't have stingers that she knew of, though they packed a hefty bite. The monster wasp, though—that much venom would likely kill.

Madison had no choice but to focus on the journey ahead. All she cared about right now was making it to the end of the wormhole before the Draduns pulled the plug on it. She doubted they'd wait long. She imagined their fingers hovering over the "cancel" button, making sure their wasp made it through before deactivating the wormhole.

To her horror, the tunnel began to flicker.

Chapter 12

Madison twisted and screamed at her friends, reaching for them. Liam and Ant began yelling too, looking around wildly as the tunnel stopped swirling.

But the three rushed onward anyway, surrounded by an eerie, muffled silence. Light lay ahead, and Madison swam for it, knowing she must look ridiculous but not caring. And as the light grew larger, she saw motionless figures in a room, apparently unconcerned.

The tunnel flickered and broke apart—just as Madison shot out the end and slammed onto a white-colored, shiny metal floor. A second later, Liam landed on top of her, and then Ant.

Panting, she pushed them off and jumped to her feet. The wormhole dissipated in a shower of sparks. Madison stared in shock. If they'd leapt into the wormhole just a few seconds later, they never would have made it through in time.

She came face to face with the same four Draduns. Krun, the leader with the distinctive gold-plated armor on his shoulders, looked amused. The others seemed a little more concerned. They stood in the center of a circular chamber, a dome some thirty feet across and just as high, with gleaming white walls. Numerous passages led out of the chamber all around.

It took seconds for Madison to cast her gaze over seven all-too-familiar crates spread around the Draduns.

Three of them were open, the triangular lid sections pointing upward.

In the center of the room, a wormhole wand was mounted to the top of a micro-thin telescopic stand with five equally thin legs splayed flat on the floor.

After a moment of staring at each other, three of the aliens suddenly rushed forward to grab Madison, Liam, and Ant, who yelled out and tried to dodge their attackers. None of them succeeded. Captured by the immensely strong Draduns, arms pinned to their sides, she and her friends could only struggle feebly as the smiling leader moved closer to the wormhole wand.

Without a word, he gently twisted the dial on the blue-lit end of the pen-like device, his eyes narrowed. He nodded and pressed the button.

A lightning bolt crackled into existence, and a wormhole spread wide open.

As the tunnel formed, the Dradun stepped over to a closed crate and yanked the lever to open it. The lid sections rose, allowing a ghostly yellow glow to escape from within.

"Stop this!" Madison cried as the Dradun reached inside.

Krun must have unhooked something, because he straightened up holding the glass cell that had previously been firmly fixed inside the crate. Madison grimaced at the sight of the oversized bug inside—a locust, if she wasn't mistaken, bright green and downright ugly. She struggled in the painful grip of her captor.

The Dradun stood in front of the wormhole, his silvery clothes tugged by the draft. He leaned the glass box away from him and clasped one edge of the lid.

Something about the way he hesitated told Madison this method of releasing test subjects was inadvisable. But he wrenched the thing open anyway—and the locust flew straight into the wormhole.

"Three more to go," Krun boomed.

Unable to squirm free, Madison could only share glances with Liam and Ant as the Draduns held them perfectly still and allowed their leader to do his work.

He stood with one finger touched to the end of the wormhole device, his eyes closed. After a minute, he twisted the end, and the tunnel began to flicker and break up. And even before that had finished, he set about opening the next crate.

Liam had a strange look on his face, an intent look of hunger, like he wanted to snatch the device and make off with it. No, more than that—he was fascinated by the Dradun's methods, the weird concentration on the alien's face as if it had programmed the wand by will alone.

Some kind of telepathy, Madison thought.

She shook her head. It didn't matter. What mattered was that more bugs were being released somewhere on Earth while she and her friends literally stood around doing nothing, unable to move a muscle while these hulking brutes held them so tightly.

Fantastic planning, she thought. *Throw yourself into a wormhole and . . . what? Did this plan ever have a Stage Two?*

Truthfully, no. Making it safely to the alien's planet through a short-lived wormhole had demanded most of her attention. But as she stood there watching Krun carry the next glass box to the newly opened wormhole and tilt it forward, an idea sprang into her head. It wasn't a solution by any means, just a single act of revolt. Something to spoil their plans and make these aliens panic.

She watched in horror as Krun flung the glass box open and shook it. A massive red ant flew out.

"There's an Antite for you, Ant!" Liam yelled, thrashing wildly. "Or was it a Carmite?"

"Keep it," Ant said with a grimace.

As they struggled, Madison cast her eyes to the remaining two crates. Both were closed. Both contained monstrous bugs. If a giant, indestructible dragonfly wasn't enough, Earth now had to deal with an oversized wasp, a supersized locust, *and* a gigantic ant. Nobody would know about them until they grew big enough to be noticed, and then it would likely be too late.

At least we killed the beetle, she thought.

What did those last two crates contain? She breathed hard and fast as the Dradun started up a new wormhole and strolled over to the next test subject. He opened the crate, reached inside from one corner, and unhooked the glass box. When he brought it out, Madison could only let out a whimper.

A spider.

"That's not an insect!" she protested.

The Dradun gave her a quizzical look, then held it up high to take a look. "A deadly species. Almost as deadly as the first subject."

Ant scoffed and laughed. "A dragonfly is deadlier than a spider?" he said in a strangled voice.

Krun stood before the shimmering wormhole and paused. "I suspect you are comparing the creatures of our world with your own. Do your *dragonflies* chew through structures as ours do?"

As he tilted the glass box forward and grasped the lid, Madison raised one knee high, then rammed her foot down, making sure her heel raked her captor's shin. It was a valiant effort, and the Dradun grunted and jerked, but his knee-high boots protected him too well, and his grip didn't loosen. Madison thrashed wildly, certain her upper arms were going to bruise.

The leader released the spider. It flew wriggling into the wormhole, on its way to Earth, already growing.

Well, we're just completely useless, Madison thought angrily.

One last box. After a final wormhole crackled into existence, she and her friends watched helplessly as Krun casually extracted the glowing container from the crate and studied the occupant. An eerie, pale-blue scorpion, its stinger arched high and stabbing at the glass.

Madison let out a cry and fainted.

Or pretended to, anyway.

She went utterly limp in the alien's grip. He attempted to hold her upright, but after a moment he simply let her slump onto the stone floor. Madison remained still, listening to Liam and Ant yelling in alarm but ignoring them. Her captor could be standing over her, ready to grab her again. She kept her eyes shut tight, waiting.

Since she lay on her side, hair covering much of her face, she risked a one-eyed peek. Her captor stood inches away, turned toward the swirling wormhole where the alien leader lofted the glass box.

In one smooth action, Madison rolled and leapt to her feet, ducked under her captor's startled grasping reach, then darted toward Krun and slammed into him. She made sure her outstretched hands connected with the glass container as though playing volleyball, punching it sideways.

The impact wrenched the precious vessel from the alien's hands.

Chapter 13

The box crashed down beyond the reach of the wormhole. The glass shattered, and the scorpion tumbled free. It righted itself and scuttled away.

"Restrain her!" Krun roared, his voice thundering around the dome.

But Madison had no intention of being restrained again. She dashed this way and that, faster than the lurching giant, wary of his lashing tails as she dodged around him a third time. Liam and Ant yelled encouragement, struggling in the grip of their own captors.

Meanwhile, the leader kept his eye on the scorpion. But he stayed away.

"Forget her," he barked suddenly. "Let them go. Throw them back in the wormhole. It doesn't matter, just help me catch the subject."

And, just like that, Madison's captor turned away from her. Liam and Ant found themselves free—for a second anyway. One of the aliens shoved Liam hard toward the wormhole, but he dropped and rolled, somehow avoiding its tugging force.

All four aliens spread out around the scorpion. Still glowing, it visibly grew while it stood there with its stinger quivering. It had been the size of a cat a minute before; now it was almost twice as big.

Abruptly, it scuttled toward one of the open passages, pausing in the archway as if to sniff at the shadows beyond.

"No!" Krun growled, taking a few steps toward it. "It must not get loose in the facility. Restrain it!"

None of his colleagues moved. They all stared with wide eyes, their large seven-fingered hands clenching and unclenching, tails undulating back and forth.

"I said restrain it," their leader snarled.

"I suggest we abort this test subject," one replied softly. "May I open the case?"

"You may not!"

Krun's sharp, booming voice caused the scorpion creature to flinch then rotate toward him. It reared up, stinger rising higher . . . then scuttled forward at lightning speed.

Literally *everybody* in the chamber backed up, but the scorpion pursued the alien leader as he danced about in zigzags.

"Stand still!" one of his colleagues barked.

Another picked up one of the crates and launched it at the oversized bug. The crate just bounced aside and angered the scorpion further. It switched targets and went after him instead.

"Abort!" one of the aliens yelled.

Madison edged closer to Liam and Ant, her eyes on the scorpion. "Let's go," she said, gently nudging the boys toward the wormhole.

The tug of the swirling tunnel felt good, like it was welcoming her home. It also felt good to have set one of the Draduns' murderous critters on them . . . not that it would help with the others back on Earth. *One problem at a time.*

With the Draduns torn between running away from the scorpion and blocking its path into the corridors, and the scorpion unable to decide whether to attack or flee, the result was a confused dance around the dome with plenty of hissing and yelling.

Then the scorpion struck Krun, the leader. He gasped as the stinger punched a hole straight through the high boot just below his knee. For a second it seemed the scorpion had lodged itself in his flesh, and the Dradun's jerking movement yanked it across the floor. Then the creature scuttled away, turned, and waited there while its wounded prey hopped around in a circle.

With ragged breath and beads of sweat forming on his head, Krun's shoulders slumped under his golden armor. He wore an expression of defeat. Since the worst had been done, he seemed unafraid now.

Anger boiled up. He pointed and yelled, "Restrain it!"

Oddly, it was like being stung had stripped away his rank. His colleagues simply stared at him, then at each other. One murmured, "Abort?" The others nodded.

"We have to go," Ant whispered.

Madison realized she'd been paralyzed with both fear and morbid fascination. She faced her friends. "Okay. But we should stamp on their wormhole wand as we go."

"Yeah, anything to slow them down," Ant agreed.

The device stood just a little way off, pointing directly at the shimmering tunnel of light. It was needed only to open the wormhole, not to maintain it; the anomaly would collapse in on itself within forty-two minutes. Better still, if they could steal the wand and figure out how to manually force the wormhole's closure . . .

Liam beat her to it. He rushed to the wand and wrenched it free of the micro-thin stand. It wobbled but remained upright as Liam dashed toward the wormhole and threw himself in.

Ant leapt in after him. The two of them spun away.

Madison almost followed, but she paused. The Draduns were preoccupied—three of them staring at the scorpion as it rotated from one to the other—while the fourth knelt to open what looked like a briefcase with a hardened metal shell.

Inside, something glowed—the exact same yellow glow that had surrounded and pulsed through the bugs as they'd been released from their glass prisons. The Dradun squinted in the light and placed a hand across a flat surface within the case. It seemed the energy was contained in a slim box.

"Hurry!" one of the others urged as the scorpion darted forward, jabbed a few times, and scurried away.

Madison stood so close to the wormhole that it threatened to tear her hair out if she didn't leap in very soon. But still she waited.

The alien kneeling by the open briefcase moved his fingers across a tiny touchpad, then quickly stood up and retreated. A thin lid on the flat box opened. The energy within arced outward in streaks throughout the dome. Then, as if it were a sentient being, the glowing tendrils reached for the scorpion.

The effect was instantaneous. The entire bug illuminated and pulsed, then dimmed. It thrashed for a moment and went still.

One of the tendrils then eased across to one of the crates. Madison imagined the dead beetle in there, still glowing faintly. But not anymore. Whatever life force remained in the crate was abruptly sucked out.

Them, in unison, all the tendrils whipped back into the flat box, and the glow subsided.

The scorpion was already dead, yet it continued to shrivel and blacken until it was a dried-out husk.

The four Draduns clustered around the scorpion. Krun was still sweating, and he looked woozy, unfit to command. But for the moment, they were a united and triumphant team.

Before Madison had a chance to second-guess herself, she took five light paces, snapped the briefcase shut, stuffed it under her arm, and ran for the wormhole.

She heard sudden yells from behind her, but it was way too late for them. She was already flying into the swirling tunnel, heading for Earth. She clutched her package with excitement. Whatever it was, could it possibly work again? Could she activate it and suck the energy out of the other bugs?

Glancing back, she grimaced and swore under her breath.

Two of the Draduns were following.

"Switch it off!" Madison screamed long before she reached the end of the wormhole. She could see daylight ahead, a concrete ground, and walls. She tumbled out of the tunnel and staggered forward. "They're right behind me! Deactivate it!"

"I don't know how," Liam said, clutching the wand and fiddling with the end. "I need time to figure it out."

"We don't have time!"

She looked about. An alleyway—in daytime! They'd only been on the Draduns' planet for twenty or thirty minutes, so it *should* be around 3:45 AM . . . but this new wormhole might have opened in another city, another time zone, maybe in another country for all they knew. They could be anywhere.

"Let's just run," Ant said.

After a quick glance into the wormhole and seeing two figures tumbling closer, Madison nodded and clutched the briefcase tighter under her arm. "Go!"

And so they ran.

They took off down the alley, turned left, and tore along an unfamiliar street. Everything looked wrong. It seemed to be the high street of a town somewhere, but everything was close together, the streets narrow. Stores were closed, but people were about, wearing suits and walking fast, heads down. Cars rumbled by.

Even while sprinting, Madison picked up on details. Cars had license plates on the front as well as the back, and the drivers sat on the right-hand side. The signs, the markings on the road, some of the store names . . .

This isn't America, Madison thought in panic.

They crowded around a corner and paused to peer back the way they'd come. It was hard to see the alley from here, but more importantly, they couldn't see any aliens stomping about in broad daylight among the men and women hurrying to work. Maybe they wouldn't dare to—

She gasped. Two Draduns stepped into view from the alley. They might as well have been tourists the way they peered around the place—only these visitors were from another world, and they stuck out like a couple of sore thumbs.

"Go home," Ant murmured to them. "You'll never catch up with us here."

"They don't have long," Madison said. "That wormhole won't be open forever. Maybe they have another wand, and maybe they don't . . . but I doubt they'd risk sticking around. Especially with people about."

Liam made a scoffing noise. "Yeah, this is a Class D planet. You never know about those. If I were an alien flying past Earth, I'd probably roll my windows up and lock the doors."

A woman glanced up from her phone to walk around the two aliens. A second later, she did a double-take and slowed . . . then moved on, glancing back every few seconds. *Some kind of cosplay event*, Madison thought, trying to guess the woman's thoughts. *Or maybe a prank after all the recent news about giant bugs.*

The Draduns took one last look around . . . and disappeared into the alley.

Madison, Liam, and Ant let out cries of triumph and grinned at each other.

Ant punched the air. "The losers gave up."

Liam held up the wormhole wand. "And we have a prize. Finally, we have one of our own!"

Ant frowned. "Maddy, you grabbed their briefcase?"

Hugging it tighter, Madison said, "I'm hoping this is what we need to kill these giant bugs. Let's find somewhere quiet and take a look."

Chapter 14

Staring into the shop window of a TV and electronics retailer, Madison stood there open-mouthed at the scenes unfolding on the silent screens.

The shop had opened a few minutes ago at 9 AM. Her phone had no service, but the time was displayed prominently on multiple TV screens. One news broadcast had the BBC logo, and another read ITV. A third read Sky News. When the weather report came on, a man stood in front of a map of the UK indicating temperatures in Celsius rather than Fahrenheit.

"We're in England," Liam muttered.

It fit. England was just waking up.

Some of the shop fronts had their address printed on the door, and they indicated this was not just England but the capital itself, London, a place Madison had always wanted to visit.

But more importantly right now was what the news teams were reporting—endless footage of the monster dragonfly back home in Brockridge, which was now wreaking havoc at the shopping mall, tearing through the roof and climbing down inside. Helicopters circled the place, their spotlights flooding the area.

On another channel, China was dealing with a problem of their own. It was the middle of the afternoon there, and a terrifying bright-green locust the size of a man had been caught on camera.

And in Melbourne, Australia, a reporter talked about a giant red ant terrorizing a twenty-four-hour gas station. The world was on high alert, and the station's CCTV feed had quickly been patched through to a news team. Madison read the closed-captioning for a while, astonished at how widespread the Draduns' attack was. Their *little experiment*.

Uncaring who might be watching, Madison knelt on the ground and opened the briefcase. Liam and Ant got down beside her, clearly awed at the sight of the slim, glowing box inside.

"He did something with this touchpad," she muttered. "Just ran his fingers over it."

"What's in there?" Ant asked. "Looks like . . . like some kind of *energy*."

Madison raised an eyebrow at him. "Seriously?" She tapped the keys at random. There were only five of them in a row. They had little symbols on, and though her translator was active, the translation didn't help either. They were still just weird little symbols.

They each had a go. When Ant pressed two or three in sequence, the last button lit up. But nothing happened. It was only when Madison took over again that something new occurred—a barely audible hiss that caused the three of them to freeze.

This time, when Madison touched the last button, the slim lid opened, and the whole case lit up with the glowing energy. She scrambled backwards. "Watch out."

Crouching from a safe distance, they watched as tendrils of light snaked outward, searching, sniffing the air . . .

"Well, I'm not sure what we did," Madison whispered, "but if we can get this back home to that shopping mall, I think it'll suck the juice right out of that dragonfly. And once Colonel Peterson sees what it can do, he can fly it out to China and Australia and wherever else—"

She broke off. The tendrils were reaching higher and higher, an endless stream of light that twisted and rose into the air like the fabled beanstalk. The daylight made it hard to see, but it was there, creeping up and up.

Then it jerked and split, shooting off in five different directions.

"Look!" Ant cried, pointing up at the TV screens in the shop window.

In Brockridge, the live feed showed a sudden bolt of light from the sky, a streaming yellow glow that plunged straight through the roof of the mall as if an alien warship was attacking from above.

After a brief flash and pulse, the streak of light vanished—and just moments later, the briefcase flashed as well.

"No way!" Liam yelled.

They watched, awed, as four more pulses descended the beanstalk and flashed inside the briefcase. It dimmed, and the light show ended.

The news teams on TV surely had similar events to report in China, Australia, and wherever else on Earth the alien bugs had arrived. Footage would probably start rolling shortly.

Madison and her friends knelt on the pavement, staring in silence at the briefcase. They didn't need to check the TVs to know it was over. This alien tech—some kind of power that even the Draduns feared and respected—had reached around the world and snatched back its stolen essence.

"I have so many questions," Madison said. She slowly closed the briefcase and rested her hands on it. "This energy . . . What do we do with it?"

"And how do we get home?" Ant said. "Hey, guys, we're being stared at."

A few passersby had seen the beanstalk of light in the sky and traced it to its source. They stood there on the road, looking like they were about to surge forward and demand answers. A car had stopped, and though the driver was leaning out with a frown on his face, the drivers behind had no idea what the delay was and were busy sounding their horns.

Madison snatched up the case and headed off. "Let's get out of here."

"Hey!" a man shouted.

That broke the paralysis. After that, others called out and approached—but Madison didn't stick around. She hurried away with her treasured possession, Liam and Ant at her side.

"It was them!" the man shouted. "Did you see that on the telly?"

Madison tried to ignore the accusing tone in his distinctly British accent. *What, you think we brought the bugs here? You think this is all our fault?*

But as they ran, she couldn't help wondering what kind of stories would arise from this moment. The open briefcase, the huge column of light, the streaks shooting off in all directions, and the simultaneous death of the monster bugs across the world . . .

Madison and her and friends should be hailed as heroes. But more than likely, everyone would assume they were responsible for the giant bugs in the first place.

With the threat of a mob on their tails, Liam waved the wormhole wand around and said breathlessly, "Want me to try this thing?"

"No way!" Madison cried.

Ant looked back at him. "It needs power anyway, right? Like the echo wand?"

"It still has some. Look, the end lights up blue. I don't know how aliens power their gadgets, and I don't know if it's fully charged or half charged or what—but it's got some juice left in it if you want me to get us out of here."

They slowed to a halt on a street corner. They had a moment of peace, but Madison doubted it would last long. She heard a shout.

"And you can get us home?" she asked, unable to keep the heavy dose of doubt from her voice.

Liam pursed his lips. "No. But I can open a wormhole. Opening one is easy—it's just aiming it that's difficult."

"So we could end up literally *anywhere*," Ant squawked. "Like in the middle of deep space, or the heart of a sun, or—"

"No, it'll be a safe place," Liam said. "It'll be a pre-programmed destination. That's how they work. It's like a default setting, to open somewhere that's already programmed in. Trust me, I was a robot once, and I had a wormhole generator built into my system. The problem is, this time I have no way to read the destinations . . . so it'll be random. Safe, but random."

The shouting grew louder.

Madison gave them both a shove. "Let's move."

They ran again, ducking down side streets and tearing around corners.

Giving the mob the slip wasn't so much of a concern as simply getting home. But dealing with the authorities and going through all that rigmarole was still a million times safer than jumping into a wormhole and ending up at some random place in the universe.

Even so . . .

"Open a wormhole," she said as they made it to another alley. This one looked much like the one they'd arrived in, only longer and wider. A box van was parked about halfway along. "Not here, though. Let's find a park or something."

"In the middle of London?" Ant scoffed.

Madison jabbed him. "Yes, Ant, in the middle of London. Have you heard of Central Park in the middle of New York?"

"Well, yeah, but . . ."

They walked. Nobody paid them any attention. Three kids on the busy streets? Perhaps the only thing that looked odd was the fact that Madison carried a sturdy metal briefcase. She caught one scruffy vagrant casting his gaze over it as she passed.

They found a park eventually—a walled area perhaps half a block long. At its entrance, a small cafe offered bacon rolls. Her stomach rumbled. Though only 4 AM or so back in Brockridge, the smell of breakfast in London made her wish they had some British money to spend.

"Do it," she said to Liam.

Ant squirmed, looking like he'd rather take his chances with the authorities. "You know, just one phone call home . . ." He patted his pockets. "If I'd thought to bring my wallet—"

"We can't take this briefcase on an airplane," Madison said, "and I'm not leaving it behind. And now that the bugs are dead, I'm not sure I want to hand it over to the Army. Imagine what they'd do with it. We could end up with all kinds of giant animals, experiments gone wrong." She closed her eyes. "I honestly think we should take this to some other planet and let them deal with it. They're more advanced. They'll know what it is."

They stood in silence among some trees, each contemplating what they were about to do. Ant was the least on board with the plan. Liam looked scared and excited at the same time. Madison, though, felt resigned to the idea—resigned to doing what she knew had to be done despite the obvious danger.

Her sleep writing hobby had taken a serious turn in the last day or two. It was no longer secret. The whole world knew about the giant bugs, and they would soon hear about three kids in London who'd opened a briefcase and sucked up the energy like they were some kind of ghostbusters.

Safely hidden among a densely wooded section of the walled garden, Liam twisted the dial on the wormhole wand and jabbed the button. A streak of light crackled and held in midair, then spread into a perfect circle . . .

"Are we sure about this?" Ant said, licking his lips in the ethereal glow.

Liam grinned. "Nope."

Madison gripped the briefcase's thick handle. "Worst idea ever," she said, forcing a smile. "Who knows where we'll end up?"

Ant huffed and shook his head. "Do we even have a plan?"

Liam gave him a friendly punch. "Yeah. Find some smart aliens and ask them how to use the wormhole wand properly. Then we come home again. Shallows Field is already programmed in. Heck, so is your bedroom. We just need some nice extraterrestrial to show us how to choose a destination."

"Oh, well . . ." Ant shrugged. "Sounds easy. What are we waiting for?"

And, together, they threw themselves into the wormhole.

Part Two

FROZEN CORPSES

Chapter 15

Even before they arrived, Liam knew their random destination was going to suck.

As he twisted through the wormhole with Madison and Ant right behind, he peered ahead at the approaching circle of murky pale-grey gloom. He couldn't tell if it was fog, or clouds, or an expanse of dull water, but it looked pretty dismal.

He shot out the end of the swirling tunnel and landed heavily on a snow-covered hillside under a dusky sky. "Pfft," he said, spitting the cold stuff from his lips as he rolled clear of the portal.

His friends tumbled out in a similarly ungainly fashion. Madison staggered but managed to stay upright, clutching the high-tech briefcase she'd stolen from the Draduns. Ant dropped to his hands and knees, snow up to his elbows.

Liam clambered to his feet and trudged a few paces in the purest, smoothest, whitest wintery landscape he'd ever seen. It had to be a hundred yards or so to the rounded hilltop above—or three times that to the depths of the shadowy valley below. The slope stretched miles into the distance ahead and behind him. The sky was cloudy and ominous, the night closing in, not a star or moon in sight. Mountains loomed in the distance across the valley. A constant frigid wind tugged at his clothes.

It was beautiful—but bleak.

"Well, this is just . . ." Ant said in disgust, stumbling as he turned to take everything in. He threw up his hands. "Perfect. We're at the North Pole. Oh!" He pointed into the distance. "Yeah, that's where Santa Claus lives. I think I see his reindeer."

Liam couldn't help looking. He saw nothing.

Madison put the briefcase down so she could hunch her shoulders and hug herself tight, breath vapors puffing from her nose and mouth. Seeing that, Liam became aware of just how cold it was. All three of them wore dark-colored, long-sleeve shirts and pants—the 'ninja outfits' they'd ended up choosing for their confrontation with the Draduns—but a jacket and scarf would have been far more welcome right now.

He tried not to let his alarm show. "This isn't the North Pole. It's some alien planet somewhere."

"Well, that makes me feel *so* much better," Ant retorted. "Let's just go back to Earth and try again."

They turned to face the wormhole. It hung in midair just above the ground, roughly seven feet in diameter, swirling and glimmering, casting mesmerizing patterns of light on the snow. With its flared rim and long shaft, it was rather like looking down the wide end of a giant, multi-colored, translucent trumpet that strobed light all around.

Pretty, Liam thought.

He patted the pockets of his black cargo pants—and felt a surge of fear.

Madison picked up the briefcase and stepped toward the circle of light.

"Hold on," Liam called, trying to stay calm. He patted his pockets more feverishly. "I, uh . . ."

"What?" Ant demanded, stepping closer to Madison. "Come on, Liam, let's not hang around here. I think it's starting to flicker."

Doubly alarmed now, Liam continued patting his pockets while studying the outer edges of the swirling tunnel. Ant was right—it was stuttering, like fireflies shooting off in all directions. Sporadic pulses suggested it was closing down.

"Why so early?" he exclaimed. "That's not fair!"

"Come *on*, Liam," Madison snapped. Her hair whipped about as she took another step closer to the wormhole. Any moment now, it would yank her in and spin her off back to Earth.

"I-I've lost the wormhole wand," Liam told them. He was already searching the snow where he'd landed in a heap. "It must have fallen out of my pocket when we got here. I kind of just slipped it in there as we were spinning through the tunnel, and—"

"Leave it," Ant said.

"Yeah, it's not important," Madison agreed.

"Not important . . . !"

"Not as important as being *safe*."

Liam threw himself down in the snow, digging his hands into the ice-cold mush and sweeping them around. It *had* to be here somewhere.

"LIAM!" Madison yelled.

But a moment later, Ant muttered, "Too late."

Liam experienced a mixture of emotions—relief that his friends weren't about to head home without him, thankful he wouldn't have to abandon the precious wormhole wand after acquiring it just a short time ago, and terrified that they might be stuck in this depressing place forever.

He paused to watch the wormhole break apart. He felt cheated. Why had it closed so early? What happened to the usual forty-minute time frame? He understood they could be manually closed down early, but that wasn't the case here. He'd simply dropped the wormhole wand in the snow. He doubted that would have deactivated their way back home. Unless . . .

Could it have shorted?

"We're stuck here," Ant said, turning to Liam with a startling look of rage. "Thanks, buddy."

"It was probably too late anyway," Madison murmured, still watching the flickering remnants of the wormhole shoot around in the air.

Liam could have hugged her. He latched onto what she'd said. "Yeah! I saved your lives by delaying you. I *knew* it was too late." Before they could say anything, he gestured at the snow and plunged in again. "Help me find it, guys. We *really* need it now. It's our only way out of this place."

They hurried to help. The three of them worked in silence, almost butting heads and scraping hands as they scoured the snow for the elusive device. Liam didn't want to admit that his fingers had gone numb from the cold, not to mention his toes.

"It's not here—" Madison started.

"Got it!" Ant held up the wand with a triumphant look.

Liam snatched it from him and gripped it tight, shooting Ant a grin. "Thanks, buddy. Man, this thing is literally our only way home—and I dropped it in the snow. It just slid right out of my pocket when we landed."

"You have cargo pants on," Madison said. "How about making use of those velcro pockets?"

"I will," Liam promised.

He held up the slim device. It looked more like a silver pen than ever, especially now that the blue light on the end had faded. But a closer inspection revealed nine slender rings near the tip, each with barely perceptible squiggles that even his translator failed to make sense of. Somehow, twisting those dials programmed the start and end points of the wormhole.

Wait. The blue light had faded?

He was already cold from the snowy landscape, but now an extra icy chill crept down his spine. "Uh . . ."

Madison and Ant stared at him. "What?" Ant growled.

"I think it's drained."

Ant huffed through his nostrils. "The battery's dead? You've gotta be kidding."

Liam's thumb hovered over the small button on the end. "I could press it and see if it has enough juice left to form another wormhole, but . . ."

"So do it!" Ant urged.

"But if it's not got enough power," Liam went on slowly, "we'll end up draining what's left, and then it'll need a full charge instead of a partial one."

Ant held up a clenched fist. "So your suggestion," he said through gritted teeth, "is to freeze up here on this mountain because you don't want to risk draining the battery? What if there *is* enough juice left? Just enough for one more jump? What if you press that button, and it opens a wormhole, and we end up stranded on a nice tropical island instead of this icy dump?"

Liam looked at Madison.

She tilted her head. "He has a point." She patted the briefcase by her side. "And we have power here."

He stared at the case. She was right! That thing was crammed full of the most intense energy he'd ever seen. It was the main reason the three of them had opted to use a wormhole to get back home rather than try to fly home from London. Even with passports, getting through customs would have been impossible without the case being snatched by the authorities.

"Okay," he said. "I just wanted to check with you first, that's all."

Again, he felt the weight of their stares in the subdued light. "You wanted to check with us first?" Madison repeated, a faint smile on her lips. "Since when?"

"Press the button, Liam," Ant said. "Seriously—I'm freezing my butt off, and I'm not in the mood to stand around talking about stuff."

Liam nodded and thumbed the button.

The blue light came on—briefly. Then it dimmed and went out.

He swallowed. "Okay, recharge time."

Madison sighed and bent to open the briefcase. It pained Liam to see her trembling hands, and her puffs of breath snatched away by the wind.

A flat black box was fixed inside. She gently tapped on a small keypad—a sequence they'd chanced upon earlier. When the lid of the box popped open, blinding light flooded out, causing the three of them to flinch.

Gripping the wormhole device, Liam plunged it into the light. He waited, knowing the wand was soaking up the energy. *Hoping* it was, anyway. This aura wasn't exactly normal technology. The Draduns had used it to grow ordinary bugs into monsters. What kind of energy did that? And how had it reached out and plucked that life force back again?

Suddenly nervous, he snatched his hand back. What if the energy had drained the life force from his arm? But everything seemed okay.

"D-d-did it work?" Ant demanded, his teeth chattering.

As Madison snapped the briefcase shut and plunged them into darkness, Liam thumbed the end of the wand again.

As before, the blue light came on . . . and dimmed.

"Nothing. Maybe . . . maybe it's the wrong kind of power?" Liam delved into his pocket. "But we have phones."

He held it close to the wand, watching the screen and expecting to see the battery icon drop to 0% in an instant.

Still nothing. His phone remained fully operational, protesting about the lack of service and continually searching for GPS. The battery showed 72%.

What the . . . ?

He remained kneeling there with the wand held high so they could all see it. The situation was clear. It didn't have enough juice to generate a wormhole, and for some reason it wasn't taking a charge from the contents of the briefcase *or* his phone.

That meant they were stuck.

A dozen terrifying thoughts went through his head then. Primarily, what if this world was utterly devoid of intelligent life? With no technology and no sources of power, the wand would remain dead.

"We're screwed," Ant muttered.

Madison climbed to her feet and began stamping around, hugging herself tighter. "Okay," she said at last, snatching up the briefcase, "first things first. We need to find shelter and get out of this wind."

They looked around once more. "So . . . up or down?" Liam asked.

Ant pointed. "I vote up. I can see it's dark and empty down below, but maybe there's a massive high-tech city just over the hill, waiting for us."

"Sounds good to me," Liam agreed.

They began trudging. The snow was deep enough to make the trek ridiculously hard work, but at least it got their blood flowing and raised their body temperatures. By the time they got to the top, Liam felt warm inside, even though his face and hands were ice-cold.

They stared in dismay. Apart from the ridge they stood upon, the terrain was mostly flat and icy forestland as far as they could see. Not a single light twinkled anywhere—no remote cabins, no campfires, nothing. If anything, the landscape was even darker and gloomier than the valley down the hill behind them.

"Yep," Ant muttered, "totally screwed." He let out a huff of exasperation and glared at Madison. "You should have let me use the echo wand back at the house when I had the chance. I might have seen this coming. I could have brought something to help us—not to change the future or anything, just to *help*."

"Yeah, like some hand warmers," Liam agreed.

To his surprise, Ant gave him a hard shove. "I'm serious. Look, you've seen the future. How about giving us a hint?"

"Guys," Madison warned, clasping her hands over her ears.

Ant pulled at Liam's arm. "Over here. Tell me."

With a sense of doom, Liam allowed himself to be dragged to a safe distance away from Madison. His mind whirled as he tried to figure out what to tell Ant and what to keep secret. He'd done his best to keep a poker face about everything, but maybe it was time.

Liam gave Madison a side-nod and whispered, "She doesn't want to know. She told me . . ." He swallowed. "I saw us, Ant—me and her, in the future. I was an old man. She was an old lady. We grew old together. I saw myself dead in my bed—died of old age. Remember how the echo wand can take you all the way back to your birth and all the way forward to your death? Well, I went forward to the end. I died in my bed, and Maddy was right there in the room with me."

Ant's mouth fell open. It seemed like he actually forgot to shiver for a moment. "You . . . you and *her*?"

"Husband and wife," Liam agreed, nodding.

There. It was out, and it actually felt good.

"Crazy, huh?" he went on, checking to make sure she wasn't listening. She still had her hands over her ears. "When I visited the future, the old Maddy told me not to reveal anything. She said she doesn't want to know. She said she *can't* know, because that would change all that had happened, or what *will* happen."

Ant closed his eyes tight and pinched the bridge of his nose. "Wait—okay, I get it, you saw yourself and her, and you were happily married and lived a long life together. Good on you. So where did you see me? I lived a long life, too, right?"

"I don't know."

"You . . . don't know." Ant clenched his fists. "Come on, man. You must have talked about me when you visited Maddy? You know, like, 'How's old Ant doing these days?' Something like that?"

"It doesn't work like that, buddy. I was just an echo, like a ghost visiting the future. Maddy talked to me only because she could sense I was there. She couldn't see me, or hear me. So I couldn't ask about you. And she never mentioned you."

Ant let out a shuddering breath. "What you're saying is . . . that *you* can't die, because you *know* you live to an old age. And Maddy can't die for the same reason. But me? I could die anytime. I could die right here, today, in the snow."

Liam looked away. "Doesn't mean you will, though."

Ant's breathing had become ragged, mist puffing from his mouth and nostrils. "Liam, the *only* reason I've put up with you leaping into wormholes and dragging us on wild adventures through space is because you've always been so sure about surviving. You *proved* it to us when the Ark Lord kidnapped you and turned you into a robot. You ended up floating in outer space without a spacesuit! Nobody else could have bounced back. Only *you*. But now I know I'm not invincible the way you and Maddy are . . ." He swallowed and shook his head. "This is too much, Liam. I'm done with this."

Seeing an end to the conversation, Liam nodded furiously. "Okay, sure. That's probably a good idea."

"It's just too dangerous for me. When we get home, I'm finished."

"Gotcha. No problem, buddy."

Ant hunched his shoulders, stamped his feet, and trudged back to Madison. "That's *if* we get home," he shot back at Liam.

He didn't seem angry anymore. Now, real terror had set in. Liam felt it radiating off his friends, and he felt it deep down inside, too. It was quite possible they wouldn't last the night out here. They could literally be in the middle of nowhere.

"Okay, so a shelter of some kind," Madison said, her voice shaky. "A cave, *something*. That's what we need, guys."

Nobody argued. They each scoured the landscape, but the dusky darkness was just a little too hard to penetrate. Still, they had to make a choice. Since they stood on the crest of a ridge that stretched for miles in both directions with no end in sight, stumbling the length of it seemed pointless. They'd just have to go down one side or the other.

They chose the valley rather than the flat, featureless expanse.

At least descending the hill was easier than climbing it. They half slid, half tripped their way down through the deep snow, passing the spot they'd arrived, where their deep tracks mysteriously began.

If only the wormhole would magically re-open, they'd be back on Earth in a jiffy—back in that public garden somewhere in London. Suddenly, the prospect of facing dozens of questioning people, the police, immigration officers, then the U.S. Army back home in America, and then their parents . . . all of that seemed so *ordinary* now, so *simple*.

Instead, they were stuck on a stark, snowy landscape, freezing their butts off, with nobody in sight and possibly no way back home.

Chapter 16

Liam was seriously worried about frostbite. He wore a thin shirt, cargo pants, and comfortable but not-quite-snow-proof sneakers. His socks were wet, his feet like blocks of ice.

He huddled with his friends around a small campfire in the shelter of a thick tree trunk and low-hanging branches. Madison's cheeks were bright red against her otherwise pale skin. Ant's teeth chattered noisily. If he hadn't been carrying a lighter as part of his bug-exterminating arsenal, Liam never would have set the twigs alight. *If only we had that can of gasoline, too. We could have made a fire ten times as big.*

Despite the ominous gloom, the evening sky didn't seem to be getting any darker. The smooth hillsides above shone bright in comparison.

"We can't spend all night out here," Madison said at last.

"All I can think about is the next ten minutes," Liam said. "I plan to build this fire up and up until it's a bonfire the size of a house."

Madison let out a small moan and offered a smile. "Sounds good to me."

Ant nodded. "And maybe someone close by will see the fire and come rescue us."

Liam hadn't thought of that.

As the fire crackled away, he placed larger chunks of wood on top, including a piece of branch as long and thick as his arm. He didn't care about the sizzling from the moisture, or the smoke; it just felt wonderful to have some genuine warmth seeping through his clothes to his chest.

"Who brought the weiners?" Ant asked.

Liam slapped himself lightly on the forehead. "I thought *you* packed them."

This brief exchange brought a smile or two. Then silence fell again.

"What are we gonna do, guys?" Madison said at last.

Liam watched her, captivated by the reflection of the flames in her eyes. She absently pushed her black hair from her face.

"We have a wormhole wand, but it's dead," she said. "We have a briefcase full of some kind of alien energy, but for some reason it won't charge the wand. Are we that unlucky?"

Liam unzipped the pocket in his cargo pants and pulled out the device. He thumbed the end. Once more, the blue light came on and faded a second later. "Weird how it acts like it's got *some* power. Normally, when these things run down, they're just completely dead." He shook it, then swatted at it. "I wonder if it's faulty?"

"Is that a good or bad thing?" Ant grumbled. "I mean, if it's just a temporary glitch stopping it from working, then maybe we can charge it later. But if it's permanently busted . . ."

Liam nodded. "Well, obviously *we* can't repair it. So we need to find someone who can."

They pondered for a while. Liam fed the fire and studied his remaining pile of deadwood. He wasn't worried; there was plenty around. Still, it meant someone would have to go hunting and gathering in a little while.

"Okay." He spoke calmly, doing his best to assure them he wasn't about to leap up and run off on some reckless mission. He felt he owed them that—an effort to be a team member and not some runaway train. "How about I make a torch and take a quick walk to see if there's anything around worth finding—a cave, a hidden shack, a millionaire's private mansion, you know? If there's nothing, I'll come back. Then we can try again in another direction."

Madison and Ant were silent. They looked back at him, obviously thinking it over.

At least they're not jumping down my throat for being reckless.

Madison sighed. "Fine. But I'll go."

Liam immediately stood up. "No way. My idea. I'm going."

"How are you going to make a torch?" Ant asked with perhaps just a hint of scorn. "You need tar or pitch or something. You can't just expect a stick to stay lit while you're waving it around in the air."

Liam scowled at him. "I'm open to suggestions, buddy. Did you bring a flashlight with your lighter?"

"Uh, hello? We have phones."

Liam felt very stupid as he instinctively reached for his pocket, but he refrained from fishing his phone out. Instead, he adopted a patient tone. "I know that, Ant, but I'm saving the battery for when we *really* need our phones—like to make calls. It's not that dark anyway."

He said this as he peered out from under the canopy of branches. Perhaps on this world the night never descended into blackness as it did on Earth. It was highly possible. Even on Earth, some parts of the world had days and nights that lasted months at a time.

"I'm all warmed up now," he lied. "I'll be back soon."

They merely stared at him as he turned to leave. Ducking under the branches, he set off through the untouched snow once more.

Behind him, Madison called out in a soft voice. "Be careful!"

* * *

Liam told himself it was a good plan.

It *was* a good plan. It made no sense for all three of them to stumble around in the cold, dark night.

He kept his eyes peeled as he hunched his shoulders and forged ahead. The biting wind was stronger out here in the open—not blizzard force by any means, just icy-cold enough to penetrate his clothes and chill him to the bone. He'd make this quick and get back to the fire as fast as possible.

Glancing behind, he made a note of his tracks in the snow. Easy to see in the wan light, and easy to follow back to base.

Deep down, he didn't expect to find anything. He figured they'd end up spending the night by the fire and setting out in the morning when it was light. But the truth was, he had no idea how long a night was here, or if morning was as bright and sunny as he imagined. For all he knew, this dull, mid-evening sky might be high noon!

He trekked for perhaps twenty minutes, seeing nothing of interest—just scattered trees in an otherwise open field of snow. He could plainly see a sloping hillside to his left, the endless valley wall they'd slipped and skidded down. The opposite wall to his right was just a murky smudge in the distance. He stumbled across a stream, too—frozen solid and buried under the snow, its vague outline meandering through the trees.

Liam sighed and knew he'd have to turn back. He was already shivering and starting to feel numb again, and he had a twenty-minute return walk.

But the moment he stopped—perhaps *because* he stopped—something caught his eye. He squinted, trying to make sense of it. Was it a person? But if so, he or she was motionless, just standing there, facing away. And they were either dressed entirely in thin, grey clothing, or . . .

He clicked his tongue. *It's a statue.*

Still, the discovery excited him. A statue meant *civilization.*

He hurried toward it. Yes, definitely a statue—a rather gaunt, creepy, stooping figure with long arms. It wore rags for pants, which Liam found odd because those pants were real fabric blowing in the wind.

Who puts pants on a statue?

He followed the bent legs down to the snow. *How do you dress a statue when it can't bend its legs and arms? How do you even pick it up to slide the pants on?*

He realized, with a chill, that this was no statue. It couldn't be. It was too realistic, too finely detailed. And too weird. Who would sculpt such a sorry-looking creature?

Liam reached out and touched the figure's shoulder. It felt cold and hard, but not quite stone. It yielded slightly under his touch. *Definitely not a statue.*

It was tall, probably six feet if it stood up straight. Edging around to the front side of the figure, Liam gasped at the sight of its face. It looked like one of those 'greys'—the classic aliens from numerous movies depicting close encounters and flying saucer abductions. But then, so had the Draduns to a certain extent. This particular creature was nasty-looking, with a snarling expression—a heavy brow and deep-set lifeless eyes, a pinched nose like it had melted down to the bone, sunken cheeks, almost no lips, and a full set of bared, surprisingly human teeth.

It's a corpse. It's been here for ages, partially frozen, or maybe in full rigor mortis, rotting away on its feet.

Curiously, the frozen creature wore a thin, faded-red plastic strip around its wrist. The tag had weird symbols on it, which Liam's translator mentally overlaid with the words Ward 13.

He tried to imagine circumstances in which a half-clothed patient, perhaps escaped from a hospital, died upright in the woods with his eyes wide open. How long had it been here?

And why had snow not settled on its bald head and shoulders?

Suddenly afraid, he backed away. The alien appeared utterly lifeless, but . . . what if it wasn't? With a gasp, he noticed for the first time something that should have been obvious before—that the snow around its feet was disturbed. Whatever this creature was, it had left a trail of prints before freezing in place.

Shivering hard, Liam started to turn away. But he paused again, watching the motionless figure, seeing nothing but absolute stillness. Maybe it *was* dead—but very recently.

He could go back to his friends and the warmth of the fire, but what would he tell them? "Sorry, didn't find anything." Or, "Found a scary-looking half-naked person standing there motionless, completely frozen." Either way, he'd go back empty-handed, and they'd spend the night freezing among the trees.

Liam scoured the way ahead, seeking something else to report. What had this creepy frozen creature been out here for?

He pressed on, casting his gaze from side to side. He couldn't fathom why a half-dressed person would be out and about in such a desolate place.

To his surprise, just twenty more paces brought him to a curious mound, a snowdrift the size of a car. Even more curious was the tall, thin metal post sticking out the top. Liam stared at it in amazement, following it up to a slender, pointed contraption. It looked rather like a traffic camera mixed with a harpoon gun. *Maybe a scientific instrument,* Liam thought, chewing his lip. *For recording . . . uh . . . fluctuations in . . . in something or other?*

Or maybe it was exactly what it looked like—a camera.

Or a weapon.

He had no clue. He just knew the contraption was pointing over his shoulder, unmoving.

A tiny red light blinked underneath.

Liam's heart thudded with excitement. Whatever this thing might be, it was *tech*.

"Hello?" he called, his voice cutting through the whistling wind.

He backed up and waved his arms at the camera. Nothing changed, so he circled the mound of snow, looking for a way to climb up and maybe shake the pole a bit. If he could attract the attention of whoever—

A door!

Liam stared in amazement. Around the back of the mound, a steel door was set into an equally steel wall. Judging by the way the snow dipped down in front of the entrance, he guessed this was some kind of bunker poking out of the ground, with a few steps leading down to the doorway. Snow had piled up as high as the handle.

No tracks. Nobody's been in or out for a while.

Of course, 'a while' depended on when it had snowed last. Certainly nobody had been in or out since the last snowfall. That might have been several hours or a few weeks ago.

He dropped down onto the snow-covered steps, feeling three of them underfoot, each narrow and tall. Descending to the doorway, he rattled the handle and sighed with disappointment. Of course it was locked.

Still, a bunker! The excitement of the discovery pumped blood through his veins.

He knocked hard and called out. "Hello? Anyone home? We need help!"

Liam thumped harder and yelled some more, to no avail. What if nobody was inside? But that blinking red light on the camera above suggested *someone* was monitoring the outside world.

His hands were freezing, and now his legs were damp from plunging into extra thick snow. He struggled off the steps and backed away, then sighed and began the return trek to his friends. He wasn't sure if this discovery would help or not, but he had to let them know. And get warm again.

Liam stared warily at the frozen corpse as he passed by.

* * *

"A frozen corpse?" Madison repeated.

Liam huddled by the fire, shivering. Madison had taken his hands and was rubbing them vigorously with her own, which were gloriously warm in comparison.

"Yep," he confirmed. "A dead alien. At least I *think* it's dead. It looks like one of the classic UFO greys. A bit like a Dradun in some ways, only without the double tail. It's just standing there, staring into space, not moving an inch. It has a tag on its wrist that says Ward 13—"

"Never mind that," Ant said. "There was definitely a red light on over that bunker?"

Liam nodded. "The camera is watching, I'm sure of it. Somebody's in there. We need to get them to open up and let us in."

"How?"

"I don't know. Stand there and wave our arms around? I just know we can't stay here. Look, if we can't get into the bunker right away, we'll start another fire right by the door. It's pretty well sheltered on those steps. If someone comes in or out, they'll have to trip over us to get past."

Ant stood up. "Sounds like a plan."

"Whoa, hold on," Liam complained. "Let me warm up a bit first."

Madison continued rubbing his hands, then sat next to him so she could reach around and work on his arms. He smiled at her. "Hey, this is kinda nice."

She rolled her eyes. "Whatever."

When they finally set off, they each held aloft a short branch still hot from the fire, flames licking off the ends. How long they would last was anybody's guess.

They walked slowly, trying to keep the branches alight. Madison's promptly burnt through and fell smoldering in the snow, and she was left with a blackened, smoking end—and no flames. She dropped the branch, leaving her only with the briefcase to carry. Liam's and Ant's lasted a while longer, but it seemed the slightest movement, not to mention the wind, threatened to extinguish them at any moment.

Liam's fizzled out shortly after. He would have tossed it aside in disgust but realized it wouldn't take much to re-ignite once they had a new campfire set up, so he kept hold of it.

By the time they reached the frozen corpse, Ant's flame was flickering sporadically. Still, they used it to light up the creature's face so they could get a good look. It never blinked. It was truly dead.

"Creepy," Madison muttered, stamping her feet. "Where's this door?"

Liam led them to the mound and circled around to the backside. He tried the handle again, then watched as Madison had a go just in case he wasn't doing it properly. It refused to budge, so they hammered on the door and shouted.

Ant went around to the front and gently waved his branch in front of the camera. Doing so instantly caused the flame to die, and he cursed and hurriedly relit it.

"Let's get another fire going," Liam said. "Right here on the steps."

It meant scooping snow out of the way to expose the steps, and fetching fresh twigs and lumps of deadwood from under nearby trees, but they got it organized in short order and added the pre-burnt logs Ant and Liam had brought along. They soon had a fire going on the second of three concrete steps—and this time they had a small alcove with an overhanging roof to shelter them from the wind.

"This is way better," Ant said, leaning back against the wall to one side of the door. "It's luxury compared to the tree we were under."

Perched on the bottom step, Madison smiled as she rubbed her hands over the flames. "Yeah, nice work, Liam. Now, if we can just get the door open . . ."

"What?" Liam put on an aghast expression. "You'd rather be *inside* than out here on the hard steps?"

"Mmm, sorta-kinda."

Liam reached for the door handle again. It was still firmly locked. "There's no keyhole," he commented, peering closely. "I guess it's only meant to be latched from the inside. You have to wonder what happens if some idiot locks himself out."

Ant shrugged. "Maybe it's electronic."

"Could be, could be . . ." Liam took out his wormhole wand and checked it again. Once more, it lit up briefly, then dimmed. On a whim, he offered it up to the door handle and moved it about, not quite sure what he was trying to achieve. Maybe he'd find a power source to charge the device. Or, perhaps the device would unexpectedly unlock the door.

Neither happened. He sighed and put it away.

Madison opened the briefcase, then thumbed the code to access the flat box inside. She eased the lid up, and a dazzling yellow aura lit everything up in a wispy, ghostly glow. The three of them watched the lightshow for a moment. Liam even tried to charge the wormhole wand again, with no luck.

Eventually, Madison closed the briefcase, and everything plunged into shadows again. "I feel like we have the power and the means to leave this place," she grumbled, "but something isn't connecting."

"Like a bad handshake," Ant agreed. "When a network doesn't quite work, or a bluetooth device isn't recognized, or a printer won't print because of a bad driver, or—"

"Yeah, yeah," Liam interrupted. "I just remembered something. That camera above our head has power. I'm going to see if I can draw a charge from it."

He stood and peered up at the post that reached high above—and gasped.

The camera on top was silently rotating.

Chapter 17

"What's it looking for?" Ant whispered.

"Why are you whispering?" Madison said in an equally low voice. "We want them to hear us and let us in, right?"

Liam cleared his throat and spoke loudly. "What's it looking for?"

The camera turned slowly and stopped, pointing off about ninety degrees to the left from its original angle. Moments later, a sudden flash of light emitted from it—a single, dead straight, super-bright bolt of energy that lasted a split-second and vanished again. The only sound was a soft *phut!*

"Whoa," Ant exclaimed. "Was that a *laser* bolt?"

"Just like in the movies," Liam agreed. "But what was it shooting at?"

He turned to go and investigate, but Madison gripped his arm. "Wait. It might be shooting at intruders."

"So?"

"*We're* intruders."

Liam pursed his lips, not sure whether he should argue that point. They were intruders only if the inhabitants of the bunker saw them as such. Since they hadn't been shot at yet, and had been allowed to light a fire on the steps, he figured he and his friends didn't pose a threat.

"I'll be careful," he promised.

He hurried off into the woods, ignoring Madison's protests. Yes, he knew he was being reckless again. But this was an urge he couldn't resist. He *had* to know what the bunker people were shooting at.

Deep in a stand of trees, almost lost in the shadows, another of those grey-skinned gaunt creatures was frozen midstep. Though obviously the same species, this one had a few long strands of white hair hanging down behind its ears, blowing in the wind, and it wore a ragged, threadbare dress that seemed to have adopted the same color as the alien's skin. It, too, flapped about in the constant breeze.

Liam walked around it—her?—with caution, fairly certain the creepy figure had only just arrived on the scene. Her footprints in the snow were fresh as far as he could tell. In fact—

"What the heck?" he whispered.

She was standing on one foot, leaning forward slightly, the other lifted behind her as though she'd just taken a step. Icy moisture dribbled off the bottom of that raised foot. But her pose . . . How could she balance like that? It didn't seem possible.

"Not just frozen," he muttered, "but frozen in *time*. Not your clothes, though. Weird."

He prodded the creature's shoulder. Like the first alien statue he'd come across, its cold flesh yielded under his touch.

A bright flash caught his attention from the direction of the bunker. He watched for a moment, but all was dark and quiet.

Suddenly cold again, he raced back to the others and found them peering up at the camera. No, not just a camera—a space laser ray gun! "What's it doing?" he asked.

"It's turning," Ant said simply. "It flashed again a minute ago, shooting at somewhere off *that* way." He gestured. "Did you—"

Another dazzling flash. The white bolt streaked through the darkness over their shoulders, and they spun around to follow its trajectory.

"What's it shooting at?" Madison demanded.

"Those frozen corpses," Liam said. "Well, they're not frozen until this thing shoots at them. I don't think they're dead. They're just . . . *paused*. Like suspended animation. This laser somehow stops time."

Madison and Ant stared at him. "Stops *time*?" Ant scoffed. But he frowned as if realizing that shouldn't be so unbelievable after everything they'd seen together. "Okay, so it's seeing these aliens coming and freezing them where they stand?"

"Yup."

"And then they die on their feet? They rot away?"

Liam spread his hands. "I don't know."

They turned in a slow circle.

"So that's at least three or four frozen corpses," Liam said. "Maybe more. I don't know how dangerous they are, but I'm guessing they're best avoided. These steps are the safest place to be, then."

Ant shook his head. "The safest place to be is *inside* the bunker."

They returned to their fire and crouched low on the steps. As they did so, the camera-laser-gun fired off another dazzling bolt.

"Five," Madison mumbled.

"Why freeze them, though?" Ant wondered aloud. "Why not just kill them?"

Liam couldn't help chortling. "Bloodthirsty, much?"

"Well, I mean, if they're only frozen . . . do they ever thaw out? Does the effect of the bolt wear off?"

That was a disturbing question Liam didn't want to think about. He stood and thumped on the door. "Hey! Please let us in! You *know* we're out here!" He rattled the door handle again, or tried to. It moved a quarter of an inch at most. "Come on, guys, open up!"

"I have an idea," Madison said, snatching up the briefcase. She marched up the steps and away from the bunker to where the camera was pointing.

"Maddy?" Liam murmured, following her out.

Ant gave a sigh and joined them.

She laid the briefcase on the snow and opened it. Then she tapped the keypad, and the black lid popped up. Once again, a flood of yellow light drifted out like escaping mist.

"We want to trade!" Madison yelled at the camera. "This case of . . . of magical energy has to be worth something. It's yours if you let us in."

Liam nudged her. "Don't forget we need to fix the wormhole wand."

"Oh yeah," Madison shouted, "and we have a wormhole wand—I mean a device—whatever it's called. But there's something wrong with it. If you let us in and help us, you can have this briefcase. It's a fair trade, right?"

There were so many reasons why this might not be a fair trade at all. First, the energy in the briefcase could be far more common than they thought. Maybe these bunker people had plenty of the stuff already. Or, maybe the strange yellow energy was dangerous, in which case letting it into the bunker could be disastrous.

Or these people just might not care.

So it wasn't a complete surprise when the door to the bunker remained firmly locked. The camera eyeballed them in silence, the little red light blinking.

"Well—" Ant started.

The yellow energy suddenly reached outward from the briefcase, tendrils of light going in all directions as though the black box housed a ghostly octopus. Liam gasped when one of the long, translucent limbs encircled his neck and *sniffed* at his face.

The silent phantom moved around his friends, too. They stood quite still, eyes wide, as a soft aura played over their faces.

Then, without warning, all the delicate tendrils twisted together as one and snaked up toward the camera. A laser bolt shot out with that barely audible *phut!* sound, and a patch of snow near Liam's feet puffed into the air.

Then the phantom touched the camera's eye, and the mechanical contraption abruptly tilted forward, its red light dimming.

Its work done, the yellow energy smoothly and silently retracted into the slim black box, where it pooled like dry ice. Madison reached down and gently, shakily locked the lid, then closed the briefcase.

"What just happened?" Ant muttered. "Is that thing in the briefcase trying to help us? Or did it just decide to take out the only protection we have against those corpses?"

Liam spread his hands in answer, not that Ant was looking.

Whatever the intentions of the ghostly energy, it had the desired effect. Moments later, the steel door to the bunker creaked open, and a short man-shaped figure stomped up the steps and came around the giant snowy mound to face them. He put his fists on his hips and stood there looking decidedly angry.

He was plump, about three feet tall with short, stubby legs and arms. Animal furs and leather contributed to his girth. His mouth was no more than a wide, lipless slit, his nose pudgy. Shaggy eyebrows protruded above beady little eyes. Wispy hair hung from under a shapeless hat.

"It's . . . it's *them*," Ant exclaimed in a low voice.

Liam stared in amazement. Of all the worlds in the universe to visit, they had to come *here*—to the home of the gravediggers.

Madison confirmed it for them. "Rock Dwarves—the little munchkins that showed up at Judith E. Chambers' grave," she muttered. "This is the very first alien you guys met."

Well, not this specific one, Liam thought, still gobsmacked. *Although . . . it might be. Who knows? They all look the same.*

"What do you think you're doing?" the stout alien yelled in a gruff voice.

"Uh, sorry," Liam called back.

It occurred to him in a flash that he understood the alien perfectly. Unlike last time, he now had a translator implanted in his chest.

He steeled himself, then started forward.

Ant and Madison grabbed hold of him in unison. "What are you doing?" Ant hissed.

In this matter, Liam knew he was right. "Okay, first, we can't stay out here, especially now that their laser gun is screwed. Second, they're just short little things, like chubby toddlers. Third—"

"Chubby toddlers?" Ant repeated.

"Third," Liam went on, "I know for a fact these guys know how to fix wormhole wands."

He let that statement hang in the air. He could almost hear his friends' brains clanking as they realized he was absolutely right. After a moment, they let go of his arms.

Liam resumed his march toward the rock dwarf. That was Madison's name for them, but it seemed to fit. "Hi," he said, approaching. "Sorry about the, uh, laser gun, but . . . well, it wasn't us, really. It was the briefcase. We don't know what that energy is, but you're welcome to it—if you can just help us out."

The dwarf scowled at him, then huffed and gestured. "Inside."

Hardly able to believe their good fortune, Liam, Madison, and Ant hurried down the steps and into the bunker. It would have been pitch-black except for the flickering candle-lit lamp standing on the floor.

The dwarf followed them in, slamming the door shut as he came. He grunted and struggled with what sounded like a heavy-duty deadbolt. Then he turned and, from the tone of his voice, scowled some more. "No power. Tread carefully." He picked up the lamp and set off ahead.

Liam reached into his pocket. Mobile phones were utterly useless on alien planets except when a flashlight was needed. But it was dead, too. So were Ant's and Madison's. And when he checked his wormhole wand, he found it no longer lit up at all.

They shuffled down a steep, sloping corridor, Liam gazed around with apprehension. Rock walls and floor. That was about it. How far did this passage go?

They walked for maybe three minutes, and then doorways loomed out of the shadows as the light from the dwarf's lamp reached ahead. Here, the rock floor became smooth, shiny metal, and their footfalls turned from dull padding to echoey clangs.

"In here," the dwarf grumbled.

The steel doors to the left and ahead were both shut. The one to the right stood wide open. Inside the small room, tables lined a wall, their surfaces filled with electronic equipment that reminded Liam of air traffic control—bulky square metal boxes with small screens and rows of buttons and switches. All of it was dead.

"Sit," the dwarf ordered, slamming his lamp down on a table. The flame jiggled, causing shadows to dance on the walls.

They sat—on rather short chairs.

"Open the case."

Madison placed it carefully on the table in front of her and opened it. As before, she tapped the keyboard and popped the lid. And as before, the yellow energy spilled out like wispy smoke.

The dwarf leaned closer. "Fix our power," he ordered.

It wasn't clear whether he was talking to Madison or the energy itself. In any case, nobody moved, and nothing happened.

The dwarf slowly turned to face Madison. He had the deepest scowl Liam had ever seen.

"You will restore power to this station," the stout alien growled, "or I'll throw you back outside to face the undead."

Chapter 18

While Ant sat on one of the chairs facing the bank of computers, Madison leaned against the table next to the open briefcase. The smoky energy pulsed and rippled within its box.

Liam figured it was unwise to ask for help fixing the wormhole device while the underground bunker's electricity remained out. "What happens if the briefcase can't restore your power?" he asked the dwarf.

The stout alien paced the room, glaring at the case every time he passed. "It had better. It'll take days to recharge otherwise. The solar panels aren't much good during half-sun."

Liam pricked up his ears. "Half-sun? Like, not quite day and not quite night? How long does that last?"

"Too long." The dwarf studied him. "Where are you from?"

"Earth."

"*Earth*? That's a Class D. How did you get here?"

Liam slipped the wormhole device out of his pocket. "There's something wrong with it. It won't recharge. Or . . . or maybe it just can't take a charge from the briefcase."

The dwarf didn't appear interested. "You'll have to ask Jaxrill. But if it didn't take a charge from that Nyx wraith, I suspect it's because the wraith wouldn't let it."

"The—?" Liam felt a dozen questions pouring through his mind. "Nyx wraith?"

"They're from the Nyx system. These wraiths just float around in space like jellyfish in the sea."

Though Liam heard and understood the analogy, he found it hard to believe the rock dwarf had actually used those words. His lips moved, a growling sound came out, and the translator spoke in Liam's mind—but that didn't mean the translation was a hundred percent accurate.

"So . . . the energy in the briefcase . . ." Madison stood up straight, her eyes wide. "You're saying it's . . . *alive*?"

Ant laughed. "A wraith is a ghost."

"You know what I mean."

The dwarf waddled over to the table and leaned close to the briefcase, holding his hand near it as though it radiated heat. "Where did you find this?" He looked sideways at Liam. "Obviously *you* didn't capture it."

"No! We, uh . . . we stole it from the Draduns. They were attacking Earth."

The dwarf looked at him with a blank expression, but Liam detected a hint of anger in his voice when he spoke. "The Draduns? Tell me more."

Liam went on to explain how the Draduns—"The people from Dradus Mox in the Zutrillon system," Madison chipped in—had been sending bugs to Earth as some kind of weapons test. Not ordinary bugs, though. They'd been doused with the Nyx energy, which had caused them to grow to a colossal size.

The dwarf nodded. "It would. It's highly illegal to trap and use Nyx wraiths. They're sentient beings, completely harmless, but extremely powerful."

"We should release it," Madison cried, leaning over the briefcase again. "I didn't realize it was alive and had *feelings*."

Liam wished she'd stand back a bit. What if the glowing yellow aura wasn't as harmless as the rock dwarf claimed? It was trapped, after all, probably scared. Madison's face was bathed in yellow light as she bent closer. What if it lashed out and . . . and *possessed* her like a demon in an effort to escape? Or melted her flesh in anger, or absorbed her life force and turned her to dust? Anything could happen.

But it remained pooled in the slim black box, its misty tendrils snaking out as if sniffing at the table.

"It needs to be returned to the Nyx system," the dwarf said. "I can take care of that—after it's restored our power." He hastened to explain. "Its energy can be forcibly extracted if you know how and have no conscience, but we won't be doing that. It's taken a liking to you, probably because you rescued it. You need to persuade it to willingly return our power."

Madison pulled up a chair and sat heavily. She rested her head in her hands and looked dismayed. "How?"

The rock dwarf sighed. "They are curious creatures. Some believe them to be highly intelligent, others not so much. It can hear and understand you. Whether it will do as you ask is another matter."

Ant shook his head and sat back. "Great. How do we persuade an intergalactic jellyfish ghost to give back what it stole?"

"Shh," Madison hissed at him.

It was a strange predicament. Everything hung on coaxing a faceless pool of energy to undo what it had done earlier.

Liam warmed to the dwarf and allowed his questions to pour out. "Who are you? What planet is this? What are those corpse things outside? What do they want, and why are you freezing them?"

"Walk with me," the dwarf said, suddenly heading out the door.

He continued talking over his shoulder as they filed along a rock-walled passage with a steel floor. The dwarf, despite his gruff appearance and manner, was surprisingly chatty. With the translator seamlessly interpreting their words, Liam and his friends might as well have been trailing the janitor at school.

His name was Steeg, or at least that was what it translated as, and they were on Kraxis 9. Did that make them Kraxins? Liam wasn't sure, but since people on Earth rarely called themselves Earthlings, he didn't want to ask and make a fool of himself, so he mentally stuck with rock dwarves.

Steeg and a team of thirteen others in the underground base were studying the creatures outside. "They're from the wastelands of Dradus Mox," he grunted.

Liam stopped dead, and his friends bumped into him. "Wait—Dradus Mox? The same place as the Draduns?"

"There are two primary species on Dradus Mox—the Draduns, who dominate the world with their intellect and vastly superior population—and the Mox, a lesser species of lower intelligence and fast-diminishing numbers. It seems the Draduns are seeking to make that a reality as fast as possible."

"But why?" Ant said.

"Because, according to the Draduns, the Mox are savages. They live in the forests and wastelands between cities. That situation has been no more than an inconvenience for a thousand years, but something has changed recently. Now the dead won't stay dead."

Inside the darkened room, someone or something was strapped to a metal gurney, wriggling like crazy. But the glass reflected the dwarf's candlelight, and it was hard to see, so Steeg opened the door and stepped inside, holding the lamp high. Liam, Madison, and Ant crowded into the doorway.

A frozen corpse, Liam thought in horror. Except it wasn't frozen.

The struggling prisoner was gaunt and wearing rags of clothing. It was male with a scraggly white beard and faint tufts of hair on its head.

Unlike those outside, this one was awake and alert. It lay there breathing hard, straining against the tight straps around its chest and thighs, grunting and letting out odd wails from time to time. The room was almost completely bare except for the wheeled gurney.

"As you can see, it's quite strong," Steeg said. "Those straps *should* be strong enough to hold it for a short time. But for an extended period? I wouldn't bank on it." He pointed to a nasty looking probe-like object hanging above. "We normally keep it in stasis, but there's no power, and it's woken. Gasping and breathing, but completely dead. It's safe to touch them while they're in stasis, but do not let them touch you while they're awake. They have . . . shall we say, a death touch?"

"Wait, what?" Ant exclaimed. "Are you saying these nasty-looking things really *are* corpses?" Ant asked. He looked at Liam, his eyes wide. "Zombies, Liam! Real, live zombies!"

The rock dwarf looked puzzled by the word, but he nodded. "They are undead. Not *all* of the Mox are, you understand. The Mox may be savages, but they're peaceful. However, now it seems the dead won't stay dead, and nobody knows why. They're aggressive and dangerous. And this relatively new development has tipped the scales and given the Draduns a very good reason to wipe them out for good—living and dead alike."

Liam could hardly believe it. Walking corpses. *Zombies.* Now he'd seen it all.

"So what does this have to do with you?" Ant asked. "We're not on Dradus Mox, and you're not Draduns."

Steeg's eyes gleamed in the light. "Ah, and that's just part of the mystery, isn't it? How did they arrive here on Kraxis 9? There was a small community not far from here, fifty-two Kraxins. They were overrun by the undead Mox a few weeks ago. No survivors. A horde of Mox still roams this area. We have to figure out how they got here and . . . *cure* them."

"Cure them," Madison repeated. "Make sure the dead stay dead, you mean?"

Steeg nodded. "We can't kill them, so we've been putting them in stasis. Sometimes we go outside and bring one in, like our patient here. But the stasis field doesn't last long, an hour at the most, and they wake. The defense system outside detects their motion."

"It didn't shoot at *us*," Ant commented.

"You have a heartbeat," Steeg replied.

After a silence, Steeg moved on along the corridor, holding his lamp high.

"So," Liam said, going after him, "every time the undead takes a step closer to the station, you shoot them and put them in stasis. Then they wake up and take a few more steps, and you freeze them again . . ."

"Over and over," Madison whispered. "Are they . . . I mean, do they understand what's happening? Are they aware of being frozen?"

Steeg shook his head and arrived at a new room. He paused before entering, turning to hold his lamp in front of their faces. "As far as we know, they have no cognitive senses, just an instinctual desire to reach this station. To kill us."

"For food?" Ant demanded. "To eat our brains?"

"They didn't eat the brains of the nearby community," Steeg answered grimly. "They just killed them all. We don't know why. Maybe we'll find out soon enough."

Liam, Ant, and Madison exchanged glances.

"Because there's no power," Liam said slowly, "and without power, you can't zap the corpses next time they wake up."

"And escape is impossible without a wormhole," Steeg said, surprisingly calm. "We're alone with these undead things."

"But they can't get in, right? The door's locked."

Here, Steeg shifted uncomfortably. "It's not as simple as that. As if being dead and aggressive isn't enough, their strength has increased tenfold . . ."

Footsteps sounded in the room beyond. Another of the rock dwarves appeared, holding up a lamp of his own. He looked just like Steeg at first glance, though wearing a strange necklace of long teeth over his thick fur coat. "Any news?" he complained. "Our work is at a standstill."

"If I had news, Jaxrill, I'd tell you. We are at the mercy of the Nyx wraith that took out our power."

"Well, it had better—"

The newcomer stopped suddenly, staring hard at Liam. His beady eyes opened wide, and then he scowled.

"You," he said at last.

Liam blinked. "Me?"

"It was *you*, was it not?"

"Uh . . ."

Jaxrill stomped closer and grabbed Liam by the collar. Madison and Ant exclaimed loudly, then turned to look at Steeg for help. But Steeg, though puzzled, merely cocked his head to the side.

"In here," Jaxrill snarled.

He dragged Liam through the doorway. The dwarf was shorter, but even holding a lamp in one hand, he was far stronger, and Liam could do nothing to resist. His feet slipped and skidded on the metal floor, the rubber treads of his sneakers squeaking, and he felt his collar tearing. He gasped and panted, trying to get free, while his friends yelled in anger.

Jaxrill marched into a fifteen-foot-high rounded chamber. The cave ceiling had shadowy recesses high above as well as several hanging rock formations. Four small globes hung from wires strung across the room, almost low enough for Liam to bump his head on. They were obviously lamps, but they had no power at the moment. The place—which Liam found strangely familiar—was furnished by a couple of short desks and chairs.

Liam stared at a tripod in the center of the room. It was no different than an ordinary camera tripod back on Earth except for the stubby cylinder fixed between its legs and the wormhole wand perched on top.

In a flash, he recognized where he was.

Jaxrill held the lamp high, watching him closely as though waiting for the penny to drop.

Liam heard Ant and Madison skidding into the room behind him, and he looked back over his shoulder. "Okay, so remember when I jumped into that wormhole next to Judith E. Chambers' grave? This is where I ended up. This is where I, uh . . . borrowed the wormhole wand."

"Stole," Jaxrill corrected him.

Liam shrugged. "I gave it back, right?"

"In exchange for my echo projector."

"True." He swallowed. "I don't have it with me."

"Keep it. Those things are trouble." Jaxrill shoved his face closer. "But be aware that stealing will get you killed. I had an echo projector in one pocket and *this* in the other."

He pulled out what was obviously a genuine alien laser blaster.

Liam licked his dry lips. "So you could have shot me dead and snatched your wormhole wand back," he said, nodding. "Instead, you offered to do a swap. That was, uh . . . nice of you." Swallowing again, he squeaked out one more word. "Thanks."

With his point made, Jaxrill's demeanor softened. He smoothed Liam's collar and stepped back. "Apology accepted. Still, I find it remarkable that you, of all people, should show up here and cause this blackout. It seems you're blundering through space meddling with things you don't understand."

"That sounds about right," Ant piped up from behind him.

Madison nudged him and turned to Steeg, who stood to one side with his arms folded. "Listen," she said, "I know we caused this blackout, and we'll do our best to get the Nyx energy to put things right. But . . ." She eyed the wormhole wand. "Does that still have power?"

"*Nothing* has power," Jaxrill growled. "Your Nyx wraith sucked the energy from literally everything in the station."

Including our phones, Liam thought. *And we weren't even in the station at the time.*

"But if we can get the wraith to restore power," Madison went on, "can you then send us back to Earth? To that graveyard?"

Liam swung back to face Jaxrill. "Yes! Can you? That'd be awesome. Better still . . ." He dug out his wormhole wand and held it up in front of Jaxrill's face. "Can you show us how to program this thing so we can just go wherever we want?"

Jaxrill stared at the wand, then back at Liam. "So you got your hands on another? I won't ask where you acquired *that*. But in answer to your question—no, I can't. You need an implant."

Liam grinned at Ant and Madison. "Well, as it happens," he said, tapping his chest, "we *do* have implants. That's how we can understand what you're saying."

Both Jaxrill and Steeg guffawed.

It was Steeg who finally explained. "Translator implants are basic technology across many galaxies. Everyone has them—except Class D planets, of course. But the implant you need to navigate the universe through wormholes is far more advanced."

Jaxrill tapped the side of his head. "Not everyone has them. I do, but Steeg doesn't. I'm one of three in this research station capable of wormhole navigation. The implant is expensive. The device itself is even more expensive. You shouldn't be playing with it. It will get you killed. Hmm, perhaps I should confiscate it . . ." he added with a frown.

Liam snatched his wand away and slipped it back into his cargo pants pocket. "Well, we'll talk about it later," he said hurriedly. "I guess right now we need to get that Nyx wraith to—"

At that moment, the clang of metal sounded along the corridor they'd just come from. Then, a second later, the resounding crash of glass spilling on the metal floor.

Jaxrill and Steeg exchanged a glance.

"What was that?" Ant demanded.

Steeg shook his head in disgust. "*That*, young human, was our patient breaking loose."

Chapter 19

Liam wanted to snatch up Jaxrill's wormhole wand and give it a try just in case it had some juice left in it. Wherever it took him would be better than here. Instead, he ran with the others along the corridor toward danger— to the room the undead Mox had smashed its way out of.

Luckily, the creature was heading *away* from them, toward the bunker's main entrance—perhaps its *only* entrance. Steeg, in the lead, yelled over his shoulder, "It's heading out!"

"So let it go!" Ant suggested.

Jaxrill, at the rear, raised his voice. "Steeg, don't go after it without a weapon."

"Weapons won't do much good, and you know it," Steeg shouted back. "If it opens the door and steps outside, I can shut it out before it lets others in."

It was only then Liam realized the extent of the problem. For some reason he'd been focused on the corpse escaping, but that wasn't the issue at all.

"It could turn on you," Jaxrill argued.

"I have to try."

"Steeg, we have inner doors we can shut—"

"They're not strong enough. The outer door is three times thicker."

They all stampeded past Steeg's control room and headed up the sloping corridor toward the bunker's entrance—which now served as the exit. All the while,

Jaxrill urged his colleague to slow down, to stop, to *think*, but Steeg ignored the advice and hurried on, muttering, "It's my job."

Liam felt a chill, and it wasn't just the draft rushing down the passage. He wondered how many of the Mox were back to normal, their stasis having expired. What if they were crowded around the bunker steps right now, vying to get inside?

The whole situation reminded him of the Lurkers he'd run from deep under the ground beneath his house. Different adventure, but the same feeling of terror.

"Do you have a plan?" Ant panted. "Do your guns work?"

"No," Jaxrill answered from the back. "Even if we had power, our weapons wouldn't stop them. The Mox just absorb the energy. Stasis is the only effective protection, and it's temporary."

Well, that's reassuring, Liam thought. He would have slowed to a stop if he didn't have Madison on his heels.

"We're too late," Steeg called from ahead.

Abruptly, the entire group came to a halt. The chill from the entrance was more evident now. The door had to be wide open.

"I need to close it," Steeg growled. "I have to try. You know I do."

This time his colleague said nothing. In that moment of silence, it seemed an understanding passed between them. Jaxrill's shoulders slumped.

In the light of his bobbing lamp, Steeg faced them all. "The Nyx energy—"

"I'll deal with that," Jaxrill assured him.

Steeg nodded and hurried on ahead.

Jaxrill faced Liam and the others. "Our power must be restored," he growled through gritted teeth. "We have stasis grenades, but they're no good without recharging. You have to convince your Nyx to reverse whatever it did."

"It's not *our* Nyx," Liam complained.

Jaxrill hissed and one-handedly gripped Liam by the shirt. "*You* brought it here. It drained our power because of *you*." He then turned to glare at Madison. "Get the case. Open it. Tell that wraith to give us back our power. Otherwise we'll die here."

A terrible wail echoed in the darkness. Liam, Madison, and Ant clutched at each other as Jaxrill held up his lamp toward the main entrance—not that its feeble light reached more than a dozen feet.

The scream faded, and silence followed.

"They're inside." Jaxrill sighed and ushered the others to head back. "We'll close the inner door," he said in a trembling voice. "It won't keep them out, but it'll buy us time."

His pain was almost tangible. Guilt crept into Liam's heart. Had Steeg *died* up there? It sure sounded like it. And why? Because of what the Nyx wraith had done. It wouldn't have happened if he and his friends had stayed in London.

On the way back through the complex, Madison nipped into Steeg's room and snatched the briefcase off the table. Then they all tumbled through the doorway that led to the observation room and Jaxrill's chamber. The dwarf slammed the door shut and bolted it. He placed one of his hands on the cold steel, then turned to Madison and held the lamp near his face so they could see his steely expression.

"Do it now," he said.

She dropped to the floor and opened the briefcase. The yellow aura spilled out, brightening the corridor. "We need your help," she murmured, leaning close. "Let this place have its power back—otherwise we all might die."

The energy throbbed and pulsed, and a tendril snuck out. It sniffed at Madison's face, then reached up for Liam's. He stood stock still, wondering just how dangerous this entity was. Could it physically harm him? He imagined it could. Just a small piece of its being had caused bugs to grow!

Maybe I could grow too. I could be a giant and squish these corpses in my hands.

Except that would mean growing to a substantial size within a confined space—not that he wanted the Nyx energy inside him in the first place.

If the Nyx wraith understood what was being said, it refused to cooperate. It simply sniffed around, then retracted into its slim box. Madison looked up at Jaxrill with a look of hopelessness on her face.

The dwarf let out a grunt of anger and slammed a fist on the steel door.

From deeper in the complex, voices called out. Jaxrill yelled to his colleagues in a thunderous voice. "They're inside!"

"So what's the plan?" Ant asked him. "You must have an emergency plan, right?"

Jaxrill's lamp wobbled as he held it in his trembling hand. "Oh yes. We have several emergency procedures in the event stasis fails and the undead break in. One of those procedures takes into account a complete power failure. That's why we have numerous battery backups. But . . ."

Liam groaned. "But you never planned for batteries being drained as well."

"We never predicted some fool would bring a Nyx wraith into the complex."

He stalked off, taking the sole lamp with him and leaving only the soft glow from the wraith in the open briefcase.

Liam, Madison, and Ant stood by the steel door, comforted by its solid presence between them and the outside world. "How bad can it be?" Liam whispered. "This door is pretty solid, right?"

"Poor Steeg," Madison said, shaking her head.

Ant scoffed. "Poor *us*. We have to do something. Maddy, try again. Talk to the Nyx in your nicest voice."

Looking doubtful, Madison dropped to the floor again. "Please," she said softly. The rest of what she said was too muted to hear, so Liam and Ant just glanced at each other before turning their attention to the door. They pressed their ears to the cold steel.

They heard nothing—yet. But a whole horde of the not-so-frozen corpses could be shuffling along the corridor toward them.

Still, the door was thick and strong. There was no way they were getting through.

"I can't believe these guys only have *laser* blasters," Ant said. "What's wrong with a good old-fashioned gun with bullets that doesn't need power?"

Liam nodded furiously. "And stasis grenades? They need power, too! How about a simple stick of dynamite and a match?"

"Some knives and axes," Ant went on. "Bows and arrows! My mom always says there's just too much reliance on electronics these days. One little blackout, and total chaos."

Liam eyed the door's sturdy bolt. "Well, I think—"

But what he thought instantly fled from his mind as something thumped the steel door with tremendous force. He jumped back in alarm.

A second thud. This time the door rattled in its frame.

"Look," Ant cried, pointing.

In the middle of the door, an odd lump had formed. And as they watched, another thud caused that lump to expand outward.

"The Mox can't be that strong," Ant moaned, shaking his head as he retreated. "No way."

"Steeg said they were," Liam muttered.

The next few thuds warped the door so much that it started to bend and twist its way out of the frame.

"We have to go," Liam said, bending down to Madison. She was still mumbling to the Nyx wraith, but she jerked when he placed a hand on her shoulder. "Maddy, we need to find a safer place. They're gonna be through any second now."

"I feel like it's responding to me," she said, gently closing the flat box and then the briefcase. Everything went dark then, but Liam could hear her picking the case up and clutching it under her arm. "It's fluttering like it's . . . like it's enjoying being petted, you know?"

Liam didn't know and didn't care right now. He wished Jaxrill had left them a lamp! He gave Maddy and Ant a shove, and together they stumbled in the pitch-darkness down the corridor.

They found light ahead. A crowd of Kraxin rock dwarves milled about in the chamber, most of them holding lamps, collectively brightening the entire room. Liam, Madison, and Ant stood in the doorway for a moment.

There were thirteen of them, each as short and stout as the next. Seen together like this, the differences stood out a mile: a mixture of thin and fat faces, some with pale skin and others with darker complexions, ages ranging from old to older . . . Three dwarves had longer, far more lustrous hair and rounder body shapes, evidently the females of the group. One senior scientist sported a conspicuous mop of unruly white locks and thick sideburns. Clothing differed, too—mostly dark-brown fur coats, some wearing what looked like smocks, Jaxrill and a couple of others adorned with tooth-filled necklaces . . .

Liam felt quite tall by comparison, though taller didn't equate to stronger; he clearly remembered how strong Jaxrill's grip had been on his collar.

He nudged Madison. "Get the briefcase open again."

Without a word, she navigated around the milling crowd and opened the case on a table. As she bent over the pulsing energy and resumed her whispering, more and more of the Kraxins noticed and fell silent. Soon the entire room was watching her. If she noticed the stares, she ignored them.

Despite the scowls and muttering, none of the Kraxins said anything out loud. Liam guessed they all knew better than to upset the human girl while she was busy doing something crucial. Restoring power was of the utmost importance right now.

But after a minute of watching and waiting, the crowd grew restless. Madison glanced up and said, "I'm sorry. I'm trying. It just . . . it's not working."

Jaxrill threw up his hands in exasperation. "Try harder! Do you hear that?"

In the distance, the sound of thudding and clanging filled the corridor.

"They'll be through any moment." Jaxrill shook his head. "We can't wait here. We need more doors between us and them. Get to the isolation ward. There are three steel doors between here and there. That'll buy us time."

With a lot of grumbling and angry words directed at poor Madison, the crowd filed from the chamber using one of the passages opposite. They took their lamps with them, and as they emptied the ever-darkening room, Liam once again eyed the wormhole wand perched on the tripod in the center—a delicate instrument the Kraxins carefully avoided.

Jaxrill remained with the last lamp flickering at his feet. He stood glaring at Liam, then Ant, then Madison in equal measure. "The four of us will wait here. If we can restore power, then I can freeze them with a stasis grenade." He patted his pocket. "And then I can activate a wormhole and eject them one by one."

"Where to?" Liam blurted, excited by the idea of a working wormhole.

"To the wastelands of Dradus Mox, where they belong." The dwarf nodded as if agreeing with himself. "I'll keep a few back as test subjects, but we don't need them all. The valley is overrun by them anyway. We'll use this disaster as an opportunity to clean up a little and send 'em home. That is"—again he glared at Madison—"*if* you get our power restored."

"I'm trying!" she protested. "You should stop talking. I thought I was getting somewhere just then, but you put it off."

Liam always thought she looked cute when she got flustered and red-faced. On the other hand, she looked cute no matter what.

She resumed her gentle cajoling, leaning over the briefcase and causing the Nyx wraith's glowing tendrils to sneak out and gently encircle her.

Jaxrill spun at the sound of a violent clang back along the corridor. "They're through the door." He pulled out his stasis blaster, stared at it, then put it back with a huff of annoyance. "There's nothing between us now," he said. "I'd hoped . . ."

He stomped over to the tripod and detached the wormhole wand. Then he left the chamber, following the passage the crowd had taken earlier.

"For when power is restored," he said, waggling the device as he went. "Though I hate generating wormholes in tight corridors."

Liam could imagine why. The chamber had plenty of space, but the corridors did not. If misplaced, the swirling wormhole might be half in and half out of a rocky wall, which could block access—and egress, for that matter. The idea gnawed at him for a second. Did that ever happen? What if he rushed headlong down a wormhole only to collide with a wall dissecting the far end? That could *hurt*.

He and Ant waited until Madison had once more snapped the briefcase shut before the three of them hurried after the rock dwarf.

Darkness closed in behind.

Chapter 20

They passed a few more openings on their way deeper into the complex, but finally Jaxrill turned and made his stand at a steel door spanning the corridor.

"Come through," he grunted, gesturing. "Get back to what you were doing. I'll keep watch."

He left the door open for now, squinting into the shadows for approaching corpses, while Madison released the Nyx wraith once more.

Ant knelt by her side. "Maybe it needs to hear from the two of us," he suggested.

She shrugged. "Can't hurt."

So they both spent the next few minutes pleading and reasoning with the mysterious yellow aura. Its tendrils snaked out to caress Ant's face. Liam watched for a while, a little creeped out but also puzzled. Why had the wraith so readily helped them get access to the station earlier but seemed unwilling to save them now?

Maybe it's just too stupid to figure out we need help this time.

That made a certain amount of sense. The three of them had been physically cold and tired, and their dire situation had been obvious. Getting into the station had been impossible, so the Nyx wraith had drained the Kraxins' power, somehow knowing it would force them to open the door and . . . and . . .

Liam frowned. That didn't sound like stupidity. That sounded like pretty astute reasoning, perhaps even cunning. If it could figure *that* much out, why couldn't it understand what was happening now?

Unless it *could*.

He dropped to his knees between his friends, shouldering them aside. "What do you want?" he demanded, leaning over the briefcase.

"Liam!" Madison snapped.

He looked at her yellow-lit face. "Being nice isn't working. This thing wants something. It needs to tell us before it's too late."

She frowned. "What do you mean it *wants* something?"

"It got us inside this bunker. I don't know if it did that for us or for itself, but think about it: If we'd died outside in the cold, what would have happened to the Nyx?"

"It would have been trapped inside the briefcase," Ant muttered.

Liam shook his head. "Maybe, maybe not. We opened it a bunch of times. It could have escaped ages ago, only it didn't. It feels safe in there. But it must want to go home, right?"

"Of course," Madison said. "We all do."

"Well," Liam went on, his thoughts whirling, "we're thinking of it like a dumb space jellyfish when maybe it's more than that. It was pretty smart to get us inside the bunker, but it did that for itself, not for us. So what does it want now? What does it want us to do?"

Jaxrill took a step backward and placed his hand on the door handle. "I think I see them."

Liam, Ant, and Madison jerked around to look. In the darkness of the long corridor, Liam thought he heard a muted shuffling noise in the distance, but he saw nothing at all.

Except . . .

His skin crawled. Were those gleaming eyes? A patch of grey skin in the gloom?

He swung back to the briefcase. "Tell us what you need," he urged.

The yellow aura simply pooled like mist in its slim box, short tendrils sneaking out at the sides.

"You want to go home, yes?" Liam said.

No response.

Liam tried again, louder this time. "Home? You want to go home? Into space? You want to float around in the vacuum?" He leaned closer. "I can make that happen. All I need is a fully charged wormhole wand. Just give us our power back. Make the lights come on, make the stasis grenades work, and charge my wand, and we can all get out of here alive. But if you lie there doing nothing, we'll all die."

Groaning came from the far reaches of the corridor. Liam twisted around again, and this time he saw them—a horde of shuffling corpse-creatures. They moved exactly like zombies in movies and TV shows, slow and unsteady . . . only these ones had the strength to knock through a steel door, so they couldn't be *that* unstable on their feet . . .

"Get the wand out," Madison said.

Liam took it out of his cargo pants pocket so the Nyx wraith could see it—if 'see' was the right word for the way a misty substance viewed things in life. It normally floated around in space, after all.

To his surprise, a smoky tendril emerged and circled the wand and his hand. He felt the faintest of tingles. He held his breath, hoping the familiar blue light would illuminate on the end of the wand . . .

Then the tendril withdrew.

Frustrated, Liam had to restrain himself from shouting at the aura and kicking the case across the floor.

As if sensing the failure, Jaxrill sighed and said, "We need to retreat a bit farther."

The corpses were just thirty feet away now. They shuffled in creepy silence, stooping and swaying as they came, their gazes fixed ahead.

Gently, Jaxrill closed the steel door and bolted it.

About twenty seconds later, a clanging thud made them all jump, even the dwarf. Liam watched, morbidly fascinated, as the second thud dented the door inward.

"How can they be so strong?" he exclaimed.

Jaxrill shook his head. "I don't know. When they first started rising from the dead back in their forests and wastelands, they were manageable. The Mox could tackle them and bring them down. But these are . . . different. Far more dangerous. We shot at them with stun guns, and they barely flinched. We upped the power, but they kept on coming. We resorted to full blaster power—bolts of energy that can kill a Kraxi—and yet they absorbed the impact."

Madison climbed to her feet. "And that's why you've been freezing them."

"Stasis works fine. They're enclosed in a pocket of suspended time—unharmed but incapacitated. That's what we've been doing ever since."

He spoke amid the deafening thumps on the door. The steel gradually warped inward, its hinges, lock, and deadbolt holding but severely tested.

"And these are what the Draduns are wanting to wipe out," Ant stated. "I don't blame them."

Jaxrill turned to him, holding the lamp high. "Not exactly. The Mox are primitive and mostly peaceful. *These* creatures are mutations. Much of their territory is forest, but there are wastelands, too. Maybe they crawled out of some toxic region. How they transported across space to our world is a mystery, but we suspect the Draduns have been—"

"Did they, though?" Liam asked.

"Did they what?"

"Did they crawl out of some toxic region? Why do they wear the same kind of drab, greyish clothing?"

"That's not unusual for the Mox. Most wear animal skins, but some wear discarded clothing from the Dradun cities." He paused. "The dead may not have risen at all. It's said that one Mox clan dabbled in the dark arts of magic. Many think this is a curse gone wrong. It would explain their strength—and their touch of death."

"But *magic*, though?" Ant exclaimed.

"I didn't say I believed in such nonsense."

Another round of savage thumps on the door caused it to pop loose of its frame at the top. Jaxrill inspected it and backed away.

"Okay," Liam said, "but what about the red tag?"

"The what?"

"Around its wrist. Maybe it means something?"

"The red . . . *tag*?" Jaxrill narrowed his eyes, obviously perplexed. But as the thumping increased, he huffed with impatience and pointed at the briefcase. "Close that up. Let's move along to the next door. They'll be through any moment."

But it seemed the aura had brightened considerably all of a sudden. Thick tendrils snaked out and undulated in the air in front of them. Liam couldn't help thinking it looked like an octopus trying to block the way.

Madison knelt to close the case, but one of the tendrils circled her waist—and tightened. Gasping, she reached for it. Her fingers slipped through the incorporeal entity, yet the tendril held her fast. Then it pushed her away, actually slid her backwards across the floor, and let go.

The four of them stood there in amazement between the steel door and the Nyx wraith. Ant tried to dart around it—but tendrils whipped out and blocked his way.

"It's trapping us," Jaxrill growled.

Liam suddenly felt very scared. Not wanting to be Mox fodder, he made a similar dash to get around the briefcase. Again, the tendrils whipped out, and he felt their physical presence on his chest and shoulders as they shoved him back toward the steel door.

Madison, still on her knees, reached out with imploring hands. "Please—why are you doing this? What do you *want*?"

Chapter 21

With the Mox pounding on the battered door, the group wanted to retreat deeper into the facility—but the wraith's phantom tentacles cut off their escape, leaving them only a small space to huddle. The door buckled further. Another few blows and it would be so bent out of shape that it would simply slip free of the lock and deadbolt.

It's steel, Liam thought. *How can they do that to steel?*

The pounding stopped for a moment as fingers slipped through a gap at the top of the door to one side. They grasped and wiggled, and then a hand squeezed through, and a wrist, and a forearm . . . but the door held for the moment.

Liam stared. There was that red tag again. This Mox had to be the very first one he'd inspected outside in the snow. "Look!" he said to Jaxrill. "See? Red tag!"

Jaxrill had the briefest of glimpses before the hand was snatched away. Then the pounding resumed.

"It says Ward 13," Liam told him. "If the Mox are so primitive and living in the wastelands, why would one be wearing a tag like that?"

Madison let out a gasp. "Guys . . ."

The Nyx aura had brightened further. It had emerged from its slim box and now floated in the air, a shapeless entity with at least a dozen tendrils stretching across the corridor from wall to wall and floor to ceiling.

"Ward 13," Liam said loudly.

The wraith pulsed with energy.

Nobody needed to say anything. They just exchanged glances, their thoughts unified. The Nyx was clearly excited at the mention of the red tag.

Abruptly, in a dazzling flash, the wraith released a wave of energy. It fired off in all directions, passing through the walls and ceiling—and a second later, the overhead lights came on.

"Whoa!" Ant yelled as the steel door crashed open.

It teetered and wobbled on one hinge, but it held there as the group backed into the arms of the wraith. The undead Mox advanced through the doorway.

Jaxrill pulled out a palm-sized cylindrical object. He grasped it at both ends and twisted, and it popped open by lengthening half an inch. A red band of light flashed on and off around its middle.

After a shout of triumph, Jaxrill yelled at the others to get back. Liam wanted to argue that they couldn't, that the wraith was blocking their way, but he suddenly found that it wasn't; it had retreated along the corridor a little way, and they were able to step over the briefcase and get some distance from the undead invaders.

Jaxrill tossed the cylinder. It bounced on the floor and hit the ankle of the nearest Mox.

Then it exploded in a flash of pure-white light.

There was very little sound, just the familiar *phut!* they'd heard outside. The cylinder remained in one piece, spinning around and around until it came to rest. But the flash had dazzled them all, and in the aftermath . . .

Liam rubbed his eyes. He saw the creatures leaning forward and reaching out, but they were absolutely still. *Frozen corpses*, he thought with relief.

Not all of them, though. The first half-dozen, maybe. The rest, at the back, still shuffled and moaned. But they didn't try to shove their way through the crowd. Instead, they swayed from side to side as if waiting for the horde to resume its march.

"A wormhole," Madison urged, gripping Jaxrill's arm. "Can you send them away like you said you would?"

Jaxril blinked and shook himself awake. "I think I caught some of the blast," he muttered. "The grenades are short-range, but we were *very* close . . ." He blinked at her. "A wormhole?" Then his face cleared. "Yes!"

He pulled out his wormhole wand. When he thumbed it, the light came on. "Power is restored," he said with obvious relief. "All right. Let's set this to the wastelands of Mox. We'll send these things back to—"

Abruptly, the Nyx's tendrils shot out and weaved between them all. One wrapped itself around Jaxrill's wrist and squeezed, and the wormhole device dimmed.

"No!" Jaxrill yelled. He struggled to free himself from the wraith, but it clung on. "Why did you do that? What do you *want* from us?"

"Is it dead again?" Ant groaned. "What the heck?"

They all stood there, confused. For the moment, it seemed *everything* was frozen in time and not just half a dozen Mox at the front of the horde.

"It doesn't know any other way to communicate with us," Madison said. "It knew we needed power this whole time, but it waited until we did something it approved of—a reward for saying the right thing. And now it disapproves."

Liam nodded. "I swear it's about that red tag."

The moment he said it, a pulse of light throbbed along the wraith's outstretched tendril and engulfed the dwarf's hand. His wormhole wand came back to life, the blue light on the end illuminating.

The tendril let go and eased away—but it hung close, waiting.

"I think that's a pretty clear message," Madison said. "The red tag means something. What is Ward 13?" She touched Jaxrill's arm. "Any ideas?" she added gently.

He frowned at her, then turned his gaze to the leading Mox, who stood frozen with his hands reaching. He was the only one wearing a red tag, at least as far as they could tell.

"Ward 13 . . ." Jaxrill muttered.

He pulled out a knife. Liam glanced at Ant, and a mutual thought passed between them: *So he does carry an ordinary pointy thing, then. It's not all laser blasters and energy weapons.*

Jaxrill carefully cut the red tag off the Mox's wrist. He looked at the outside first, confirming that it did indeed read Ward 13. "There's a chip. We need a chip reader. Unless . . ."

He held up his wormhole wand and frowned as he pointed it at the tag. Then a look of understanding passed across his face.

"Coordinates. For a cloudstation."

"A . . . a cloudstation?" Madison repeated. "What does that mean?"

"A satellite floating in low orbit," Jaxrill said. "*Very* low orbit, among the clouds. Cloudstations are easily reachable from the ground compared to geosynchronous orbiters. We have hundreds over Kraxis 9. And . . . " His mouth fell open, and he stared for a moment into space. "And so does Dradus Mox. These creatures . . ."

He started pacing in a small circle, holding the red tag in one hand and the wormhole wand in the other.

"These creatures didn't rise from the wastelands of Dradus Mox at all. I'm guessing they came from this cloudstation—Rabeium 234—possibly some kind of medical facility, or a morgue, or both. These Mox are different; everyone knows that. The Draduns assumed they rose from one of the toxic regions, like undead mutations, but this red tag suggests otherwise." He looked at Liam. "You might have given us the answer we needed."

Liam felt a surge of pride. "I *knew* that tag meant something."

Madison gestured at the glowing aura that still hovered across the corridor. "So did the Nyx."

"So what now?" Ant asked. He said his next words with a degree of apprehension as he looked at the wraith. "We send them back to the cloudstation?"

The wraith glowed stronger, withdrawing its tendrils.

"I think that's a yes," Liam said.

* * *

Opening a wormhole to the Rabeium 234 cloudstation apparently involved getting authorization from officials on both Kraxis 9 and Dradus Mox. Liam couldn't help feeling a little bemused. Up until now, his experience with wormholes had been simply to point the wand and open one—no authorization needed.

But that, as Jaxrill pointed out, was illegal.

Thinking back, Liam's own wormhole-opening antics had been while using a robot body supplied by the Ark Lord, a villain who wouldn't have cared about such things as "official approval" and "proper channels."

Liam supposed there had been both authorized *and* unauthorized visits to Earth. The Kraxins turned out to be law-abiding citizens of the galaxy. He doubted the Draduns could claim that—at least not the small group he'd met.

He waited with his friends in the brightly lit corridor as Jaxrill spoke with someone far away—a sort of air traffic control officer in one of the major cities on Kraxis 9. They in turn spoke with Dradus Mox, and after some conferring, the mission was greenlit.

"The Draduns are very interested in this," Jaxrill said. "They're sending their own people to the cloudstation to investigate. If Rabeium 234 is indeed the source of the undead problem, then it will be dealt with very quickly and quietly. All we need to do is send these Mox patients to the cloudstation—back to their wards."

"So the Draduns have no more need to send giant bugs to Earth!" Ant exclaimed. "Lucky we came here, then. Without us, you'd never have figured it out."

Jaxrill grunted in agreement.

As the Kraxins emerged from hiding and set about dealing with the undead Mox—both the frozen and those still shuffling around at the back—Liam couldn't help pondering his friend's flippant remark. Lucky?

He'd stolen the wormhole wand from the Draduns, so it wasn't a huge surprise they had Kraxis 9 programmed into it; they probably had the coordinates of all the neighboring planets. Still, it seemed awfully coincidental the wand had brought them *here*, to this hidden scientific research facility, which in turn had led them to the cloudstation—the supposed source of the Draduns' problems.

Was that luck? Coincidence? It didn't seem likely.

His attention was drawn to the low moaning and grunting farther along the corridor behind the frozen Mox. Those unaffected by the stasis grenade seemed eager to forge a path through to the front and continue the attack. Yet they did not.

"Why don't they push past?" Liam wondered.

Jaxrill pointed. "*This* is why."

Four of the Kraxi scientists gathered around the first of the frozen corpses and bent to pick him up. It was like hoisting a statue into a horizontal position. Clearly the Mox weighed a lot judging by all the perspiration and grunting.

"They're not normally so heavy," Jaxrill explained. "It's a side effect of stasis. They're locked in a fixed position in space."

Liam remembered how the Mox outside in the snow had frozen in mid-step, impossibly balanced.

But that wasn't all. Amazed, he watched as the creature was tilted forward—and then released while the scientists stood back to rest. The Mox hovered there, face down, utterly still, frozen in midair.

After a while, the scientists started pushing his feet, and the statue slid through the air. He stopped moving the very moment the scientists eased up.

"That's bizarre," Madison muttered.

"Like a levitation magic trick," Ant agreed. "All the magicians on Earth have obviously been using a stasis grenade."

Madison smiled. "Obviously."

As more and more of the Mox were tilted forward or backward into a horizontal floating position, Jaxrill opened a wormhole to the cloudstation. He aimed very carefully to make sure it spanned the corridor instead of being half embedded in a wall. Then it was a case of shoving the Mox into the wormhole. They shot off like Olympic swimmers, some face down, others up, all with arms at their sides.

One of the Kraxins lobbed another grenade, and the remainder of the corpses were frozen. Then it was safe to deal with the rest.

Liam, Ant, Madison, and Jaxrill stood with their backs to the wall as the creatures were pushed past and into the wormhole, where they went spinning off into the distance. Jaxrill sighed with relief. "Just a few more to go and we're done here."

"That's it?" Liam said. "We just send them to the cloudstation?"

"They'll end up floating around a room on Rabeium 234 until they wake in an hour, at which point they'll hit the floor. The rest is up to the Draduns. Their cloudstation, their people, their mess."

"Fair enough," Liam said. Still, he needed *more*. "When will we find out if the Draduns fix whatever's wrong there?"

"Oh, not for a while. Put it out of your mind. All we need to do now is generate a wormhole to the vacuum of space in the Nyx system. We'll just send the wraith through."

But they had to wait for the last of the Mox to depart before the wormhole could be closed. They stood and watched as the Kraxin scientists maneuvered the last two into position. Both frozen creatures were laid out flat on their backs, suspended in midair at about waist height.

"It's like Han Solo when he was frozen in carbonite," Ant said, his eyes gleaming and a smile on his face.

Liam laughed. "I was thinking the same thing!"

"Nerds," Madison muttered. After a pause, she said, "See, I was thinking more of a water slide. The wormhole actually looks a bit like rippling water, so—"

Liam and Ant cracked up. After the claustrophobic darkness of the underground complex, and the horror of unstoppable zombies, the image of these statue-like creatures being tossed down a slippery water chute in a theme park was just too funny. Madison joined in, her laughter a little more reserved.

Jaxrill and his fellow Kraxins looked bemused.

The hilarity quickly turned to panic as a long-haired rotund scientist barked a warning and fumbled in her pocket. "Grenade!" she yelled.

It took Liam a second to figure out *why* they needed another stasis grenade. Then he yelled and pushed his friends away from the wormhole, squeezing past the scientists and the two floating Mox so they could escape along the corridor.

Three Mox came spinning back through the wormhole.

And they were very much awake.

Chapter 22

The three new arrivals tumbled out of the wormhole and crashed into the scrambling crowd of Kraxin scientists.

Liam, Ant, and Madison paused to watch from a safe distance.

There were four scientists alongside Jaxrill. As the newly arrived Mox sprang to their feet, one of the Kraxins pulled out a grenade—but before he could twist it, an undead creature grabbed him around the neck. The scientist immediately fell limp and started turning grey. Then, abruptly, he dissolved into a cloud of dust, his clothes dropping to the floor.

The other Mox attacked in unison. As three more Kraxins crumbled into piles of fine dust, Jaxrill staggered away from the confusion.

"Run!" he yelled to Liam and his friends.

"You too!" Madison shouted back. "They're right behind you!"

Jaxrill put some space between him and the Mox while studying his wormhole device. With trembling fingers, he fiddled with it and glanced over his shoulder to watch the wormhole flicker and break apart.

More Mox spun into view—five of them, apparently eager to kill. But it was too late. The swirling tunnel sputtered, and just as the first of the spinning Mox looked like he might make it through, the wormhole collapsed around him. In that moment, the blackness of space swallowed him up, and he was gone, replaced with an ordinary corridor stretching deep into the bunker.

That still left three Mox, though. Plus the two floating patients, who might wake up at any moment. And small piles of dust and clothing on the metal floor.

"Run!" Jaxrill yelled again, this time breaking into a jog to escape the shambling undead.

Liam felt Madison's hand gripping his wrist as she pulled at him. "Come *on*," she hissed.

After a breathless but short sprint, they wound up once more in Jaxrill's rounded chamber. He stood there a moment, glancing from doorway to doorway. "Mechanical room . . . Sector 3 living quarters . . . storage . . ." He clicked his tongue. "There's nothing secure at this end of the station. All the doors are lightweight. The Mox will get through in no time."

"How about an armory?" Ant said.

If he meant it as a joke, Jaxrill took it seriously and shook his head. "This is a research facility, not a military base. And guns do nothing."

"They must do *something*," Ant argued. "Got any more stasis grenades?"

Jaxrill instinctively patted his pockets. "Not here." He studied the tripod in the middle of the chamber, then sighed. "I think an unauthorized wormhole is in order."

"Ya think?" Liam scoffed.

He could already hear the Mox in the corridor, shuffling closer. He tried to relax. They were slow-moving creatures, just like in most zombie movies. That gave the heroes a chance to think their way out of situations. It would be far worse if the undead Mox were crazed homicidal sprinters.

"So get us out of here," Madison urged.

But Jaxrill simply tapped the wormhole device against the palm of his hand, his forehead etched with a deep frown. "I have a better idea. A simpler idea."

Without a word, he set off at a brisk march along the main corridor, heading away from the Mox.

Liam, Ant, and Madison hurried after him.

They passed the observation room where a Mox had once been laid up. Glass crunched underfoot. Though the door was buckled, the window had been far easier to escape through. Inside the room, the restraining straps had been snapped and tossed aside, and a recharged stasis weapon hung above the gurney. Liam wanted to wrench it loose and use it like some kind of hastily attached robotic weapon-arm.

"Where are we going?" Ant demanded.

Jaxrill hurried ahead, past Steeg's communications room and up the sloping, rock-floored corridor.

"We're going outside?" Madison said, sounding a little peeved. "We're going to run around in the woods playing hide and seek with these things?"

Liam glanced back. It would be a while before the Mox caught up—assuming they didn't turn around and head back into the station. He half hoped they would . . . but he suspected he knew what Jaxrill had in mind.

An icy chill blasted them as they approached the open doorway ahead. On the floor just inside were Steeg's clothing and his ashes. Jaxrill very carefully stepped over the mess, his gaze lingering before he growled and marched on.

At the door, he hurried outside and up the steps. As Liam, Ant, and Madison went to follow him out, he came back in again. "Let's hold up here for a while," he suggested. "Warmer inside. We'll see the Mox coming and just step out when they get here."

He pulled the door shut but left it unlatched.

With nothing else to do for the moment, they huddled together in the corridor and waited.

"We're going to use the stasis gun, aren't we?" Ant asked in a flat voice. Obviously he'd caught on to the idea by now as well.

"We don't need to do anything but run outside," Jaxrill said. "The power's on, and I can see the weapon is enabled. The system will do its job. It'll detect our movement as we leave but will ignore us because we have heartbeats and normal body temperature. Not so with the Mox. It will put them in stasis as they follow us out."

Liam fished in his cargo pants pocket and pulled out his wormhole wand. "Will you fix this, please, while we're waiting? Set it to Earth?"

"Same place as before," Madison quickly added. "That cemetery where you dug up a body."

Jaxrill quietly took the wand from Liam's fingers and studied it. When he pressed the button, it lit up in a fierce blue and remained vibrant. "Fully charged. Mine is, too. The Nyx restored our power and then some."

Liam tried to contain his excitement as the Kraxin rock dwarf gently twisted the end while narrowing his eyes, a combination of manual adjustment and some kind of psychic power. Half a minute later, he handed it back.

"It's set. The log file shows a recent hardware error and emergency shutdown due to excessive cold." He raised a bushy eyebrow at Liam. "You can't go throwing these devices around in the snow, you know."

"It fell out of my pocket!"

"Yes, well, my advice is to go home and *stay* home."

"Copy that," Ant said, sounding relieved.

Madison nudged Liam's arm and grinned. "Beats customs officers and CIA interrogations. We might even be able to sneak home and act like everything's normal."

That got Liam thinking. How long had they been gone? They'd crawled out of bed and waited for the Draduns to arrive at 3:11 AM, used the wormhole, tackled the Draduns and their giant bugs on their home planet, then jumped back into another wormhole and ended up in London on a Monday morning, around 9 AM local time. How long had they been on Kraxis 9? It felt like forever but couldn't be more than . . . five or six hours?

He pulled out his phone. It was fully charged again, and he powered it on. But even before it booted, he knew the device would be totally confused. Was it on London time? Eastern? Somewhere in between?

"It's gotta be mid-morning back home," he finally reasoned. "Maybe lunchtime already. That means our parents know we're missing."

"My parents will be on the way back from New York . . . but I betcha they know we're skipping school already," Ant said, his eyes wide.

Madison shook her head. "They probably shut schools down today with those bugs that were on the loose. They're dead now, but there might still be giant bug warnings out."

Liam had to agree. "Yeah, just a hint of snow will bring the country to its knees. Imagine what giant killer bugs from space will do. People will be storming to the grocery stores for emergency supplies of bread and milk."

Ant nudged Liam and lowered his voice to a whisper. "You know, we could just . . ."

He nodded at the wand, then gestured with his thumb as if to say, *"We're outta here."*

Madison shook her head. "Let's wait a bit longer. We can't just desert these people."

"You don't have your pet Nyx," Liam suddenly realized. "I guess it won't matter. When all this is over, Jaxrill can open a wormhole and send it home."

Jaxrill had been standing quite still, facing back along the corridor. Hearing his name, he turned his head. "They're coming."

Chapter 23

Though the sound of the shuffling corpses made Liam's skin crawl, he gripped his wormhole wand tightly, feeling confident. He had a way to escape to Earth if necessary, plus Jaxrill had a wand of his own. And neither would be needed if the stasis weapon did its job. *We got this*, he thought.

The undead appeared around a corner—three at first, then another two a little way behind. All shuffling and stumbling. Tattered grey clothing hanging off their grey skin. Gaunt legs and arms. Cold, dead eyes.

"Time to step outside," Ant said with a nervous laugh.

Madison shoved the door open, and the icy wind blasted them. Liam almost wished he'd thought to pick up Steeg's fur coat. He *could* go get it right now, since it lay just ten feet away . . . but the thought of all that ash lining the collar . . .

He shuddered as they all hurried outside and climbed the steps. Jaxrill was last out, and he shouldered past the group and headed into the open where the weapon high above could easily see him.

The red light blinked. The watchful device swiveled to look down at him, and rotated again as Liam, Ant, and Madison walked out. Then it resumed its vigilance on some distant place in the trees.

Shortly after, the Mox appeared. They gathered on the tiny stoop outside the door but didn't ascend. They looked a little trapped and bewildered.

Liam watched the stasis weapon. It hadn't detected the Mox yet. "Come on, come on," he whispered, feeling Madison's hand in his. He wasn't sure who had grabbed whom.

One of the Mox finally took a step up. Buoyed by its success, it climbed to the next, then the third. As it trudged onto the snow and focused on Liam's group, it let out a hungry groan and raised its arms—and at that moment, a bolt of energy froze the creature in place with a soft *phut*.

The stasis weapon was angled sharply downward now, and it swiveled slightly to zero in on the other Mox. One of the undead raised a foot to step up, and the dazzling flash came again.

Two down, three to go, Liam thought with glee.

The next two were a little different. They stumbled up the stairs together, then abruptly veered off in opposite directions, their dead gazes fixed on Liam and his friends as they attempted to circle around in some kind of orchestrated pincer movement.

It was a valiant effort, but the stasis laser quietly spun and zapped them both, freezing them in an instant.

The last of the Mox watched from the safety of the steps. Then it retreated inside the doorway.

The stasis weapon high above swiveled and whirred, its red light blinking furiously as it tried to detect movement. But the Mox had vanished from sight.

"Uh . . ." Ant said. "It went back in."

Madison backhanded him. "Thank you, Captain Obvious."

A dull clang sounded.

Liam swallowed. "And now it's locked us out."

Jaxrill sighed. "Despite what I might have told you, they do show tiny signs of intelligence from time to time. That one we had on the gurney, for instance; when it woke and broke loose, it could have gone in either direction along the corridor. These things can smell us through the woods and across the valley, and it certainly could have smelled us along a corridor. Yet it came out here and opened the door to let others in."

"So they're smart zombies," Ant grumbled. "And now what? We're stuck outside."

Jaxrill started fiddling with his wormhole wand. "We'll take a short cut."

Another flash of light—only this time it didn't come from the stasis laser. The thick, pure-white bolt froze in midair just a few paces away and expanded into a shimmering disc. It then plunged inward to form a swirling tunnel, and as the wormhole stabilized, Jaxrill pocketed his device and stepped in.

Watching him tumble away into the distance, Liam was struck by the intense weirdness of it all. The wormhole could stretch for billions of miles through space, yet it would loop around and end just under the ground nearby. On the flipside, Ant and Madison had once allowed a ball of string to play out along the length of a wormhole, and it had proved the tunnel was only eight hundred feet long . . . and yet it opened up in another galaxy.

"Let's just go home," Ant suggested.

The three of them stood there, undecided. "Arguments for going home right now?" Liam said.

"It's dangerous in there," Madison said.

Ant added, "And it's not our fight."

"Jaxrill has it in hand, right?" Liam reasoned. "He can easily go grab a stasis grenade. There's only one Mox walking around now. Plus these out here. He just needs to keep that one inside frozen until the Draduns sort things out."

"We're done here," Ant finished.

Still, they stood there looking into the wormhole.

"Aw, man," Ant complained. He was staring at Liam. "You have that look on your face."

"What look?"

"That look where you're about to do whatever the heck you please no matter what we agree."

Madison sighed. "I don't feel right about just leaving. Let's pop inside, make sure things are under control, and then get out of here."

Liam could have hugged her. "If you say so," he said, putting on an exasperated tone. "Come on, Ant—the boss says it's not over yet."

With that, he leapt into the wormhole.

* * *

He ended up exactly where the last wormhole had begun.

It made sense. When Jaxrill had opened a gateway to the cloudstation, the coordinates at both ends had been logged forever. The previous starting point now served as a destination.

Liam almost fell over the briefcase, then grimaced at the sight of the scattered clothing and remnants of ashes. Worse, he realized much of the dust was swirling in the air, sucked into the vortex as he emerged. He jerked sideways to avoid it, then warned his friends as they came tumbling out.

Jaxrill deactivated the wormhole, and they waited for it to sputter and collapse. Madison picked up the briefcase and stood there holding it like she wasn't certain it was her responsibility. *It's not*, Liam thought. *Leave it for Jaxrill to get rid of.*

But maybe she'd become attached to it. It wasn't a thing anymore. It was a creature. A sentient, strangely caring, completely remarkable space jellyfish.

When the wormhole had gone, Jaxrill led the way along the corridor. "Need to fetch a grenade. Some of us carry them for emergencies, but I'm out."

They came to a steel door. Jaxrill opened it and stepped through into a room—a kind of antechamber where various passages led off in different directions. Just how big *was* this place?

Another steel door led directly ahead. That had to be the third barrier Jaxrill had talked about earlier—*three steel doors between us and them*. He headed that way, pulling the door open and waiting while Liam, Ant, and Madison stepped through into an oddly darkened room.

"Huh," Jaxrill said, coming in after them. "Lights are off. They must be somewhere else."

They all heard the noise at the same time—a scuffling nearby.

"Lights," Jaxrill barked.

They came on immediately, brightening like a sunrise in fast motion.

"Oh no," Ant whispered.

Liam took in everything at once: bench seats lining the stone walls of the rectangular chamber, a few metal cabinets standing at the far end, tables in front, seven wheeled gurneys pushed against another wall—and probably a dozen Mox standing there in silence, perfectly still.

The isolation ward was empty except for the Mox . . . and a floor strewn with clothing.

Liam knew immediately what had happened. How could he not? But it seemed Jaxrill had a mental block for once, a serious case of shutting out the obvious. "Where *is* everyone?" he wondered aloud.

But he got no further. Liam jerked in horror, and he heard Madison cry out.

The Mox were standing there in silence . . . *almost* perfectly still.

They started shuffling, raising their hands and moaning, reaching for the small group.

"Here we go again," Jaxrill muttered. "Let's get out of here."

They turned and dashed from the room, and Jaxrill slammed the door shut. He couldn't bolt it from this side, but maybe the undead creatures didn't have the smarts to turn the handle.

"There's more!" Madison shouted, making Liam jump.

The creatures shuffled from one of the doorways— then from another—and another. They were everywhere.

"How is this *possible*?" Jaxrill roared. "How are they even here?"

Same way they arrived on Kraxis 9, Liam thought. *By magic.*

The four of them ran from the antechamber back into the long stretch of corridor. Ant turned and slammed that door, too. Liam knew a lone Mox was busy shuffling its way toward them from the entrance, but that seemed a small concern right now.

Madison still had hold of the case. Liam couldn't help scowling at it. *Either it's glued to her hand, or she's forgotten she has it. Just throw the thing away!*

They jogged until they reached the discarded clothes of Jaxrill's colleagues. Seeing these, the rock dwarf slowed, panting. "The grenades were in the isolation room, in a cabinet at the back." He huffed and scowled. "I don't understand where the Mox are coming from. There's no wormhole. I know it's still a mystery how they just showed up on Kraxis 9 in the first place, but . . . so many in one place? There are more here now than ever before."

Liam reached for his cargo pants pocket. "I think it's time we—"

"And where is everyone?" Jaxrill demanded. He turned to face them all, and it was only then Liam spotted tears in the rock dwarf's eyes.

"There's nobody left," Madison said gently, her voice full of sorrow and dread. She had her hands to her face, and suddenly she stepped close to Jaxrill and half hugged him, burying her face in his broad shoulder.

Chapter 24

Jaxrill stood quite still. His mouth worked up and down, like he was trying to say something but couldn't get the words out. Liam felt horrible. All of the Kraxins in the station—*dead*. Turned to dust by the creepy, zombified Mox.

Abruptly, another appeared. It simply blinked into existence ten feet away and stood there with its back to them.

From the expression on Jaxrill's face, this was the first time he'd seen one simply materialize. *There you go, mystery solved*, Liam thought. *Now we know how they've been showing up on Kraxis 9. They just teleport. It's obvious, really.*

Liam and his friends stood perfectly still, knowing that one sound would cause the Mox to swing around. They had seconds before it would anyway. Meanwhile, Jaxrill quietly slipped a hand into his pocket and pulled out his wormhole wand.

Again, Liam reached for his own. If there was ever a time to head back to Earth . . .

But then the Mox could leap into the wormhole and follow.

Or worse . . . they could somehow lock onto Earth's coordinates and beam that information back to base, and then they'd *all* start teleporting to Earth.

Liam trembled in his shoes. Had he just figured out what was happening here? These things—patients on the Rabeium 234 cloudstation—had somehow developed the ability to teleport. Popping up randomly on Kraxis 9 might have been a wild stab in the dark at one time, becoming more practised later . . . but then Jaxrill had opened a wormhole to the cloudstation, to the *source*, and it was like sending them a beacon. Some had come through the wormhole and tasted blood, and now *all* of them were teleporting in, homing in on the coordinates . . .

He swore under his breath as the Mox slowly turned to face them. He'd have to think about his theory-in-progress later.

"Hurry," Madison told the dwarf.

Jaxrill activated the wormhole wand just as three more corpses popped into existence. The tunnel formed at a maddeningly slow pace in the same place as before—

But the Mox stood in the way.

"Uh-oh," Liam said. "How are we—?"

Blocking their escape, the four undead creatures shuffled toward them.

"Do another one!" Ant shouted.

So close, yet so far, Liam thought as they backed away.

If the swirling vortex would only suck the creatures in, all would be fine. But, although their raggedy clothing whipped about, they remained on their feet and staggered away from the wormhole, pursuing the group.

"Can we drop-kick them?" Liam wondered aloud.

"I can whack 'em with this briefcase," Madison snarled. "It has a tough shell."

"Don't touch any part of their skin," Jaxrill immediately warned. "We're not sure yet if—"

One of the Mox creatures broke free of its zombified shuffling and lurched at Jaxrill, arms outstretched. He backpedaled in alarm, then tripped on the fur coat of one of his colleagues. As he fell flat on his back, his wand flew from his hand and skittered across the metal floor.

Liam, Ant, and Madison bent to help him up, then cried out in unison as the lurching Mox practically fell on the helpless dwarf.

"Jaxrill!" Ant shouted.

It was too late. The Mox flattened him to the floor and placed his hands on Jaxrill's face. A second later, the dwarf fell limp—and collapsed into a pile of dust, his fur coat and pants sinking flat on the floor, and his boots turning onto their sides with dull thuds.

"No!" Madison screamed.

It was almost too much to bear. They hadn't known Jaxrill for long, but after Steeg, then all the other scientists, and now this—Liam felt suckerpunched, sick to the stomach, on the verge of tears yet ready to explode in anger.

A small gap opened near the wall while the shuffling creatures had their attention on their latest victim's remains. With a yell of rage, Liam dashed forward—and threw all his weight into the one closest to the wall, battering it as hard as he could to create a gap large enough to squeeze past.

It was like trying to shoulder past a cow.

He almost bounced off, but the Mox staggered just a little, enough to widen the opening—enough for him and his friends to slip through.

"Go!" he gasped.

They ducked and weaved, and Madison lashed out with the hard briefcase. Then they were through, with nothing between them and the wormhole. Ant and Madison wasted no time and leapt straight in.

Liam almost followed them, but something vital occurred to him in the blink of an eye, and he faltered. As the Mox swung around and renewed their lurching, he dropped to the floor under their outstretched arms and grabbed Jaxrill's wormhole wand.

Then he rolled, sprang to his feet, and allowed the wormhole to suck him in.

As he tumbled and spun, he focused on one thing only—the wand. He'd done this before. Closing wormholes was easy. He just had to . . . to . . .

To what?

He thought back to that moment in the alley in London when the Draduns had followed him through. He hadn't had time to figure it out then, and he had very little time now. He *had* deactivated a wormhole before, though. When he'd been one of the Ark Lord's robot soldiers, he'd had full wormhole-creating capabilities, with a database of coordinates and everything. He imagined that was what having an implant was like—a tiny, highly portable version of a robot shell.

But he didn't have a robot body now, and he didn't have an implant. He had only his fumbling fingers.

All four Mox leapt into the wormhole after him.

Already far ahead, his friends twisted and yelled back at him. Not that he could do anything to speed himself up or slow down the Mox. They all traveled at the same rate, just spaced apart.

He gripped Jaxrill's device in both hands and wrenched it back and forth, sweating with the effort. He felt it bend, but it didn't break. He tried harder, aware that he was attempting to destroy something worth a fortune on most planets and was utterly priceless on Earth.

"Arrrgh!" he yelled in frustration. "Why can't I have an implant like—"

He felt something pop in his hands. When he opened his fists, he saw a slightly bent wand but with a split down the shaft. Just for a second, he saw a miniature lightshow, which quickly fizzled out. The blue light on the end flickered and dimmed.

He had no idea if breaking the wand was the same as deactivating the wormhole. Dropping it in the snow had done the trick, though. Maybe a short in the wiring would send a signal . . .

Gaping, he could see the end of the wormhole, and he could see Ant and Madison tumbling into a pure-white room. But around him, the swirling vortex strobed and flickered, and patches of black, starry space showed through.

"Yes!" Liam shouted, raising a fist at the Mox to his rear. They simply stared back, emotionless, twisting and turning in the distance.

Through the glimmering wall at his side, Liam saw the stars. Then a green planet filled his vision, and he caught sight of a cloudy sky . . .

And slammed onto a hard white floor.

He slid to a halt. Dazed, he focused on the wormhole, which was sputtering like crazy and sending out the usual fireflies and arcs of light. In the last half-second, Liam saw the four Mox suddenly spin outward and away from the confines of the tunnel. Then the wormhole was gone, nothing but a display of pulsing glows.

Liam and his friends sat there for a while after that, gasping at first, then just allowing a calm to fall on them. They hardly dared hope they were safe, but this room they sat in—this pure-white circular room with two hospital-style beds and a post hung with monitors and machines— offered them safety for the moment.

As long as no Mox appeared out of thin air.

"Poor Jaxrill," Madison said at last.

She sat up and pushed her hair back off her tear-stained face.

Ant crawled over to Liam and gave him a hard look when he saw the bent, busted wormhole wand. "Please tell me—"

"It's not mine. It's Jaxrill's. Mine is in my pocket."

Ant closed his eyes and gave a sigh.

"So we can go home?" Madison asked, sounding almost doubtful.

Liam grinned and took out his wand. "We can. Look, it has power. I can open a wormhole right now if you want."

"I want," Ant said.

"Me too," Madison said. She gestured vaguely around the place. "This is probably the cloudstation Jaxrill kept on about, and there might be Draduns and Mox everywhere."

Liam jumped up in alarm. She was right. All the Mox had been sent up here—

But then they'd beamed themselves back down to the bunker on Kraxis 9.

He let out a relieved sigh.

Still, if the Mox could teleport at will, what was to stop them coming straight back again?

"You're right," he said to Madison. "We don't need to be here. Let's go."

Madison picked up her briefcase. Liam solemnly held up the wand and jabbed the button on the end. It powered up. "Now, Jaxrill set the destination to Earth, so I don't need to adjust anything—I just need to activate it."

"So activate it already," Ant urged.

"Wait," Madison said. She held up the briefcase. "We should . . . I mean, don't you think we should do something about the Nyx? It's trapped in here."

"We don't have a way to find the Nyx system," Liam said, feeling like he was explaining something to a five-year-old. "I'm not going to mess with this wand and ruin our chances of getting home. Even *I'm* not that reckless."

Madison nodded. "I know, I know. Well, I guess . . . I guess we'll just have to leave it here? Or take it home? What should we do?"

It's not some cute puppy you found on the side of the road, Liam thought, anger stirring. *It's a highly intelligent being. It'll find its own way home.*

But would it, though? It hadn't yet.

He felt his hope deflating like a balloon. "What the heck, Maddy?" he griped. "We can't hang around here. Just bring it. We're going home."

He held up the wormhole wand again. But as he did so, he found he had a tendril of yellow energy looped around his wrist. Ant and Madison noticed at the same time, and their gazes followed the tendril to the briefcase. Despite it being firmly shut and hanging in Madison's hand, the Nyx energy had snaked its way out.

Maybe it could escape the case after all—it just didn't want to. There was nothing here for it. The Nyx system was too far away.

Liam realized something that sent a chill of horror down his spine. The light had gone out on the wand. And when he thumbed the button on the end, nothing happened.

"Guys . . ." he said in a shaky voice. "I don't think the Nyx wants us to go home yet."

Madison's spare hand flew to her mouth.

"What are you saying?" Ant demanded, though his stricken expression suggested he already knew.

Liam swallowed. "The wand is dead. We're stuck here."

Part Three

STASIS ERROR

Chapter 25

Ant's first impression of the Rabeium 234 cloudstation was of a cold, heartless lab.

The two hospital-style beds in the center of the brightly lit circular room told him it had to be a tiny ward rather than an operating theater; apart from a few monitors hanging from a post, the place was devoid of surgical equipment, ventilators, tools, and everything else he'd seen a million times in movies.

Yet it was a little too sparse and clinical for an outpatient ward. Where was the bedside table with a bowl of grapes and a vase of flowers? The wall-mounted TV?

This isn't Earth, he reminded himself. *We're in another galaxy. And anyway, it could be a psychiatric ward. Or some kind of experimental lab.*

When the power in Liam's wormhole wand faded, it seemed pretty obvious the Nyx energy wasn't ready to go home yet. It wanted something.

"So now what?" Ant asked, staring with suspicion at the glowing tendril circling Liam's wrist as he grasped the wand. The fact that the ghostly energy protruded from a closed briefcase confirmed it had no substance whatsoever. "What does this thing *want* from us?"

"Don't call it a thing," Madison muttered.

Ant opened his mouth to argue, then shut it again. Maybe she was right. Clearly it understood what was going on. "What does *it* want, then?" he corrected himself.

When the Nyx energy retreated into Madison's briefcase, Liam tapped the wand on his palm and spoke quietly while pacing back and forth. "I've been thinking about this." He frowned at Ant. "Remember when you told Steeg it was lucky we showed up?"

Ant shrugged. "I guess. So?"

"So I don't think it's luck at all. I think the Nyx brought us here."

If Liam expected a response, nobody obliged.

He lowered his voice. "Okay, so we stole the briefcase from the Draduns, right? We didn't know it, but we saved this strange, glowing space-alien from its nasty captors. And we stole this wormhole wand. Right?"

"Right," Ant agreed, wishing he'd get to the point.

"I think the Nyx programmed the wand and brought us to Kraxis 9. That can't be a coincidence. We showed up and somehow solved the mystery of the Mox popping up undead in random places. Well, we didn't *solve* it, but we figured out they're coming from here—from this cloudstation."

"And?" Ant prompted.

"And, for whatever reason, it now wants us to save the Mox."

Ant sighed. "That's kind of a stretch, buddy."

Madison knelt by the briefcase. "Is it, though? It's definitely sentient. It doesn't have a way to communicate with us, so it's guiding us however it can—by programming the wormhole wand, by shutting off the bunker's power so we could get inside out of the cold, then restoring power when it thought we finally understood what it wanted us to do . . . then cutting it again when Jaxrill said he'd send the Mox back to their wastelands . . . and back on again when Liam mentioned the red tag . . ."

At that moment, a crack of blinding light shone all around the briefcase. It faded at once.

Madison smiled and shook her head. "If that's not a sign, I don't know what is."

Ant moved toward the monitors between the beds. They were off, but a tiny green light showed on the bottom of each. *Standby mode.* The rectangular boxes below had dozens of lights and buttons, all meaningless. The translator in his chest identified letters of the alphabet along with numbers, but they were probably abbreviations. *Medical jargon.*

"Why is the Nyx still with us?" he asked as he felt around the monitor's edge for an on/off button.

Liam answered first. "What do you mean?"

"Well, it just stuck a glowing arm out of the briefcase and drained the wand." Ant turned to him. "The briefcase wasn't even open. If it can do that, why doesn't it just escape?"

"Well, because it wants to help us," Madison argued.

"But how was it trapped in the first place?"

Ant studied their faces. Ha! Neither one of them had considered *that.*

"How did the Draduns catch it?" he persisted. "Why did it stay locked in the briefcase if it can ghost its way out anytime it wants?"

"It snuck just one arm out of the joint where the lid closes," Liam said, frowning. "That's not the same as squeezing its whole body out."

Ant snorted. "Isn't it? It's *energy*. If it can squeeze an arm out, it can squeeze *everything* out."

He turned back to the monitor. His searching fingers found a button that brought the screen to life. A series of weird symbols flashed at him before his translator overlaid them with the words *Powering up* . . .

"Maybe I didn't close the lid properly inside," Madison mumbled, opening the briefcase wide and feeling around the slim box nestled within. "I did, though. It's shut." She looked at Liam. "He's right."

Ant's attention was drawn back to the screen as a dizzying display of options spread out before him. "Whoa. Can you make sense of this? Looks like a long list of medical procedures. Or experiments? Look, controlled variables, independent variables, hypotheses . . . What's a quantitative observation? And here it lists the latest trials, treatment groups, casual relationships—sorry, *causal* relationships—cohort analyses, inconsistencies, margins of error, statistical significance . . . And this one, *deviances*, is highlighted in red."

"Jaxrill said this was a medical facility," Liam said. "I guess the patients here were test subjects."

"Test subjects . . ." Ant murmured. He tapped on the highlighted *deviances* label and bent toward the screen, eager to read and understand before Liam and Madison made their way over. But, even with the words seemingly printed in English, none of it made sense—just a bunch of statistics.

"There's a video," Liam said over his shoulder.

Ant spotted the video play button he referred to. He couldn't figure out why a small icon of an eyeball so obviously represented a recording, but somehow he knew his friend was correct. Maybe their translators offered a subliminal layering he hadn't previously been aware of—a kind of gentle suggestion tool.

"Play it," Liam urged.

Ant pressed the eyeball. It lit up, and a window opened on the screen. Playback began immediately.

Three scientists stood looking down on two patients. Ant recognized the twin tails of those standing around the gurney. *Draduns.* The patients had to be Mox, though they lacked the crazed, corpselike features of those who had escaped to Kraxis 9. Instead, they looked gentle and serene, more like alien greys than ever. Not so much gaunt as slender, their faces strangely beautiful in a weird, otherworldly kind of way.

What are Draduns doing with Mox patients? Is that normal?

While the three scientists wore silvery coats that hung almost to the floor, the patients were garbed in simple lightweight vests and pants of a drab pale-grey color. Each had a red tag around his wrist.

"Is this the same room?" Madison whispered.

Ant glanced around. "Maybe. I bet all these rooms look the same, though."

"Shh," Liam said even though nobody on the film spoke.

Both patients had been in a restful state. Suddenly, one bolted upright—or tried to. Straps around his chest and thighs kept him down as he thrashed and strained to free himself, letting out piercing screams. The Dradun scientists stepped backward but seemed unperturbed. One tapped a notation on a tablet. All three waited and watched as the patient fought to escape, his shrieks distorting the speaker output.

Then the Mox changed. His face darkened a shade or two, his cheeks sinking, his eyes bugging out. Each tiny change was subtle but the overall effect dramatic. In seconds, he aged twenty or thirty years. The peaceful, slender figure turned into a monster full of terrible rage, spitting and snarling as he continued to toss from side to side in an effort to break free.

The scientists remained cool, one still tapping out notes. Another said something, but his words were lost amid the noise.

Then, abruptly, the patient vanished.

"Whoa!" Ant exclaimed.

"What—?" Liam said at the same time.

On the screen, it seemed the scientists were just as taken aback. They reeled, shouted, pointed, then rushed to lay hands on the empty bed, pulling at the still-fastened restraints and jabbering at each other.

Meanwhile, the other patient lay sound asleep.

Just then, another Dradun appeared. His words were lost amid the babble of his panicked colleagues, but it didn't matter—Ant's attention was on the gold-colored shoulder plates. "Krun!" he gasped.

The recording ended.

After a while of staring at the frozen screen, Madison let out a breath. "So, whatever happened just then . . . Was it some kind of experiment gone wrong? A virus they were trying to contain?"

Ant hadn't even thought of that second option. He was firmly latched onto the first. "I just assumed they were doing something evil, and it went horribly wrong. That was Krun. Those were the same four Draduns we met before."

"And that's not a coincidence," Liam muttered. He pushed closer to the screen and began jabbing at some of the other options. "Let's see if there's something else. How about the latest trials? Or the inconsistencies? Man, all the answers we need are probably right here in this—"

The door hissed open.

All three of them yelled and clutched at each other, expecting to see a crowd of undead Mox shuffling their way into the room.

Instead, they found an armed Dradun framed in the doorway, a weapon drawn and pointed in their direction. One of Krun's henchmen.

"Don't shoot!" Liam blurted. "We're unarmed!"

The three of them held their hands high. Ant couldn't help feeling that endless TV westerns and cop shows had driven this automatic stick-'em-up motion into them. It probably wasn't necessary. Super-advanced aliens most likely had implants or other tech that instantly warned them when their enemy was armed.

The Dradun eased into the room. He wore a puzzled frown, and his twin tails flicked back and forth as he circled the group to see what was on the monitor.

"So, you understand," he rumbled at last.

The Dradun holstered his weapon. And a good thing, too. It looked like a cross between a Magnum and an Uzi, probably much worse; it no doubt spat terrible laser fire able to cut people in two.

"U-understand what?" Ant stammered.

The Dradun scowled at him. "Why the Mox must be purged."

"I'm not sure we understand *anything*."

Ant saw Liam open his mouth to retort and quickly elbowed him. Now was not the time for mouthing back. They needed answers.

Ignoring his friend's surprised look, Ant swallowed and moved toward the Dradun, lowering his hands as he went. "Seriously, we don't. You experimented on the Mox and . . . what? Something went wrong? They started vanishing? Tell us what's going on."

The Dradun shook his head in obvious disgust and gestured toward the door. "This way."

"Where are you taking us?" Liam demanded.

"We're not going anywhere," Madison added.

Out came the weapon. Ant was impressed by the alien's speed—a regular quick-draw cowboy. "Whoa!" he cried, dismayed at the way his hands automatically shot into the air above his head. He forced them down to his sides again. "We'll come with you. We just want some answers first."

The Dradun narrowed his eyes, raised the weapon higher—and fired off a shot.

Chapter 26

The oversized handgun made a sound like it had a silencer screwed onto the end, a dull thud, more of an implosion than an explosion. A burning smell filled the air, and Ant looked sideways at his friends, almost expecting one of them to keel over with a gaping wound.

All three were unharmed, but the wall behind them had a fist-sized hole punched through it, and a scorch mark as big as a soccer ball. Amazed, Ant couldn't help edging closer for a better look. He could see into the next room.

"Point well made," Liam muttered. "We'll go with you."

He and Madison led the way, and Ant hastened to catch up, aware that the Dradun thudded along behind, his weapon hanging loosely at his side.

"Which way?" Madison asked when they arrived in the corridor. Ant noticed she'd brought along the briefcase. He had no idea why. It annoyed him that she held onto it so dearly, like it was some kind of pet. If it wasn't for the Nyx, Liam could have used his wormhole wand and got them home by now.

"Left."

The cloudstation had to be circular judging by the way the corridor curved. Well, it didn't *have* to be circular, but Ant felt sure it was. He imagined he was walking around the set of a *Star Wars* movie: metal grid flooring, smooth white walls, ceilings stuffed with pipes, conduits, and strip-lights . . . Bulkhead doors hissed open as the group approached, then hissed shut again after they'd passed through.

They arrived in a large chamber with archways all around. The Dradun ushered them onward to the far side. Ant stumbled as recognition flashed in his mind. "Wait a minute . . ."

"We're *here*," Liam exclaimed.

In the center of the room stood a micro-thin telescopic stand with five equally thin legs splayed flat on the floor. Its purpose might have been lost on anyone else, but Ant and his friends knew immediately it was something to attach a wormhole wand to.

Several minifridge-sized crates littered the room, all of them open, their lids standing upright in triangular sections. Ant shuddered at the memory of Nyx-infused bugs being released from these very crates, on this very cloudstation, and sent to Earth. He scrunched up his nose at the weird feeling of *déjà vu*. This was the second time they'd revisited a chamber where a wormhole wand was propped in the center!

They passed through an archway into the darkened corridor beyond. Lights illuminated as they marched. They came to another chamber similar to the first, though this one had what looked like observation cells rather than archways leading to more corridors. The Dradun pushed them out an exit to their left, where they resumed their dizzying journey through the maze of interconnecting passages. Everywhere he looked, Ant saw doors, hatchways, control panels . . .

And an elevator.

"Stop here."

They halted.

The Dradun shouldered past, reached out with an oversized, seven-fingered hand, and jabbed at a button. *Going up*, Ant thought.

The elevator was like any other, but so smooth it hardly seemed they'd ridden between floors at all. The Dradun stepped out first, then turned and waited.

This room's lighting, unlike everywhere else, remained dim. *We're in the Emperor's chamber*, Ant thought. *This is where a hooded figure tells us to turn to the Dark Side, and when we refuse, he blasts us with blue, crackling energy from his fingertips . . .*

Computers surrounded the circular room. Above the terminals, windows looked out onto a night sky—stars, several moons, wisps of cloud, and a colorful streak of light that suggested a form of aurora borealis.

The elevator had risen dead center of the chamber, so when Ant stepped out, a complete three-sixty turn was necessary to take everything in. The other three Draduns were present. Two sat at computers, but the third, wearing golden shoulder armor, hobbled on a crutch. He had a rough bandage around one knee, the silvery pant-leg ripped open so that his purulent flesh showed.

Ant grimaced. The scorpion had done some damage. The leg was obviously infected. He wouldn't be surprised if an amputation was in order.

The Dradun leader eyed Madison's briefcase and smiled. "Thank you for returning what you stole."

"It wasn't intentional," Madison said, sounding a little shaky. She gripped the briefcase tighter against her side.

"Still," Krun rumbled, "the extinction event may now resume. This is the day the Mox cease to be." The limping Dradun stopped before them and studied each of their faces in turn. "The story we release to the public, days from now, will not be far from the truth. It is well known that the Mox practice the dark arts of sorcery in the wastelands they call home. That sorcery will be their undoing. For years they have sought *immortality*. Instead, they found the opposite—instant aging and death, their bodies flung through the vortex of space and *reanimated*, then returned as mindless killing machines. Their reckless dabbling into black magic has led to an outbreak of *undead mutations*, a scourge of teleporting monsters bent on cold-blooded, unrelenting extermination!"

Ant rolled his eyes. The Dradun had a flair for the dramatic. "Except that wasn't their magic, was it? It was *you*. You did something to them right here on this cloudstation. You were experimenting on them."

The Dradun leader smiled a thin, creepy, alien smile. "As much as I like the idea of creating monsters, I am not lying. The Mox did this to themselves. I have worked on this cloudstation for many years, participating in various research projects above the wastelands, and we always have Mox subjects in our wards—for their own benefit, I might add." He pointed out one of the windows. "Do you see the dead moon?"

Ant squinted. He saw several enormous disks in the night sky, each at least ten times bigger than the moon back home. "The white one?"

"No, that's Kraxis 9. I mean the—"

"Kraxis 9?" Liam blurted. "We just came from there! It's really that close?"

"It's a *moon*?" Madison said, her eyes narrowed in what looked like disbelief as she studied the sky. "But . . . we walked around outside . . ."

Liam leaned close and whispered, "Ever heard of Endor?"

"No. Should I have?"

"Uh, hello? Where the Ewoks live? That's a moon, too, full of forests. Moons don't have to be cold and dead like ours. Moons are just natural satellites orbiting planets."

"What are Ewoks?"

Liam looked aghast. "What?" But then he saw a faint smile on Madison's face and rolled his eyes.

Ant glared at them both. "Are you done talking about Ewoks? Krun was saying something important." He put on his most attentive expression. "So if Kraxis 9 is just a moon . . . what's it orbiting?"

The Dradun leader had a look of annoyance and disgust on his face. "Kraxis, obviously."

"Oh."

"Kraxis is the fourth planet orbiting Zutrillon and is home to nine trillion Kraxins in four hundred populated sectors. Kraxis 9 is its ninth moon."

"So . . . the people on Kraxis 9 are just called Kraxins?" Ant asked, thinking that was more likely than Madison's made-up name, Rock Dwarves.

"Until they name their moon, yes. It's not the most hospitable world, used mainly for research. Settlements there are sparse." He pointed, and this time Ant ignored the white moon and focussed on the brown one beyond. "That is Kraxis 7, the dead moon, named Mox. It has been empty for a thousand years."

"And where are we right now?"

Krun drew himself up. "In the clouds above Kraxis 8. One of the oldest moon colonies. We named our world Dradus, and we became Draduns . . . but then we rescued the Mox from a deadly volcanic ash cloud and gave them a new home here. Our world was subsequently renamed Dradus Mox."

Krun sounded like he'd eaten something nasty.

"They are primitive, and the very best of their medicine is based on generations of homemade recipes. It is pathetic. In the eyes of the public, it is the Draduns' responsibility to help our backward neighbors—the same way we care for pets."

Ant felt like he'd had all his self-righteous thunder snatched away. So the Draduns *weren't* responsible for the undead Mox epidemic?

Still, he felt a need to accuse them of something. "So you're . . . what? Like animal vets? You treat the Mox on this cloudstation like they're sick pets?"

"Indeed." Krun looked surprised by the accusation. "They are not our equals. If they were, we would treat them in regular hospitals and not these research facilities."

"But that video we saw," Madison argued. "There were two Mox, and they were fine until you did something. One died, then disappeared. He turned into one of those undead monsters. *You* did that!"

Krun shook his head. "They were not *fine*. And we simply administered what we believed to be a cure. These subjects were aging rapidly for an unknown reason— perhaps the result of meddling in dark magic."

"The rock dwa—I mean, the Kraxins don't believe that."

"Then they are fools. Dark magic exists."

This surprised Ant, but he said nothing. Krun seemed keen to talk, as he had from the first time they'd met him. *Typical supervillain.*

"To halt the rapid aging, we put the subjects in stasis while we worked to discover the cause."

"You were actually trying to *help* them?" Liam said, sounding doubtful.

"Why not? I am primarily a scientist. Also, what if the same mysterious affliction spreads to the Draduns in the surrounding cities? Of course I tried to help." Krun gave Liam a hard stare. "But if you think for a moment I cared for each individual Mox life, then you are mistaken. I cared only for the science, for the test results."

"And the video we saw?" Madison asked again.

Krun gave a shrug, his golden armor rising briefly. "That was a new occurrence. We administered the trial drug and awakened the patient to record the outcome. He deteriorated and expired . . . but then he *vanished*. He was the start of the undead Mox scourge."

"So your trial drug made him vanish!" Ant accused the Dradun.

"Again, you are wrong."

Ant, Liam, and Madison watched as Krun limped his way back to them.

"Shortly after, the station alerted us of a stasis error in the wards. That was where the real trouble began. The Mox woke, aged rapidly, and vanished—*without* the use of our trial drug. This proves that my drug trials had nothing to do with it. Something else caused them to vanish."

"They showed up on Kraxis 9," Ant said, feeling weak.

"Indeed. They attacked a settlement there, and it was noted how extraordinarily strong they were all of a sudden—and how their touch turned the residents to dust. It was at that point I decided to take action—something my people should have done long ago."

Ant felt self-righteous anger stirring again. "Giant bugs."

Krun offered a thin smile. "Eventually, yes. There has never been a more appropriate time to rid this planet of the Mox once and for all. Of course, our elders are too weak-spined to sanction genocide, and so . . ." He gestured to the briefcase standing alone in the middle of the floor. "I devised a plan."

"Giant bugs," Liam said, repeating Ant's exact words.

Krun continued as if Liam hadn't spoken. "The world shall see that the Mox's irresponsible spellcasting not only brought them a terrible death by aging, but it also unleashed a plague of *mutated insects* straight from their own forests. These relentless monsters gorged on the Mox until nothing remained but bones. An absolute tragedy brought on by their own foolishness."

The Dradun smiled again, his beady eyes like pinpricks of yellow light.

"You could try harder to help them," Ant said through gritted teeth. He glanced at his friends, who wore expressions of utter disgust.

"Why?" Krun raised his voice and looked upward as though addressing a hidden camera. "They are but a blight on our planet's surface, a single region of wasteland surrounded by superior Dradun civilization. We brought them here as refugees from a dying planet; our elders, in their *infinite wisdom*, extended the hand of friendship and gave them a home. But this is *not* their home."

Ant glanced at his friends. The Dradun was becoming unhinged, trembling and apparently shouting at the ceiling.

"Soon," Krun boomed, clenching his fists, "at first light, swarms of deadly insects infused with Nyx energy will descend on the wastelands and attack every living creature in their path. The Mox—"

"They'll attack your city as well, then," Liam interrupted.

"Not with the ultrasonic transmitters and electromagnetic pulses we use. We haven't had insects in our populated areas for decades. Not even these Nyx-infused giants will venture near. And why should they? They have a feast directly below. The Mox will be stung, bitten, ripped apart, stripped of flesh, and obliterated! Finally, I will bring our deadly plan to fruition and—"

"And fulfil your destiny to become rulers of the galaxy?" Ant blurted before he could stop himself. He clapped both hands over his mouth.

The Dradun's exuberance suddenly turned into a snarl of anger, and his eyes blazed. Nearby, his gun-wielding colleague stepped closer and raised the weapon.

In an effort to distract the towering alien, Ant just started babbling, saying whatever came to mind. "You'll never get away with it! Everyone on Kraxis 9 knows about this cloudstation! They'll come snooping, and they'll find out you work here, and they'll ask questions and look at old footage, and they'll ask why you have a Nyx wraith in a briefcase! How will you explain *that*?"

His tactic worked. Krun paused and tilted his head. All his anger evaporated, replaced by the more familiar scorn and the need to explain. *Typical supervillain ego.*

"It is true an outpost on Kraxis 9 alerted our elders of this cloudstation—but our elders already knew what we were doing here. They diplomatically thanked Kraxis 9 and assured them the issue would be investigated. And so it will. Our esteemed commander and wise elders will be arriving tomorrow afternoon with an entourage of official investigators, some of them from Kraxis 9—"

"So you're in big trouble," Ant interrupted. "The problem started here because you couldn't cure a simple aging disease. It's your fault," he added for good measure.

Because of the way Krun had turned toward him with fire in his eyes, Ant had detached himself from his friends and now stood apart from them. He looked longingly over their shoulders at the elevator. Its door stood wide open. If only . . .

But that weapon! It could punch a hole right through him.

"The real problem is below, in the wastelands," Krun rumbled. He seemed to be talking more to himself than anyone else. "Whatever is causing the Mox's rapid aging and turning them into murdering monsters that can teleport between worlds—it has to be stopped. So we will destroy the Mox at dawn before any more can turn."

"And these humans?" his colleague asked, raising the weapon a little higher. He aimed it straight at Ant's head.

Krun turned away and gave a dismissive gesture. "Dispatch them. Dispose of their bodies. Leave no evidence they ever existed."

Ant yelled and bolted for the elevator.

Chapter 27

Flinching at the dull thud of the oversized handgun, Ant felt the air behind his head crackle as he ran. The blast punched through the center of a window on the opposite side of the room, and though the surrounding glass remained intact, the sudden whistling gale was a strong reminder of the cloudstation's high altitude.

Ant felt like time slowed. He could see out of the corner of his eye the Dradun's arm swinging around to fire again. Just ahead, Liam and Madison yelled and swung around. Beyond them, the elevator door stood wide open.

"Don't fire in here, you fool!" Krun roared.

Still expecting a second shot to tear him in two, Ant almost barreled through his friends in his haste. The three of them stumbled and weaved into the elevator.

He turned to jab at the buttons, but Liam was already doing it, so he pressed himself against the side wall with Madison and waited for that dreaded second shot to punch a hole through his gut.

It never came. Instead, the Dradun's heavy footsteps pounded closer. The door shut just in time, and Ant distinctly heard a bark of anger from the leader.

"Get the Nyx!"

Astonished, Ant noticed Madison had the case. He felt like wrenching it from her hands and tossing it out.

Then the elevator car dropped.

"I can't believe you still have that!" he complained.

She swallowed. "Nor can I."

For a few seconds, the only sound was panting as the three of them trembled against the walls.

"Where are we going?" Ant said, watching the levels light up on the display as they descended.

Liam jabbed again at the last button. "All the way down. As far away as possible."

There was no faulting his logic. But what was at the bottom of the cloudstation?

Madison clutched the briefcase tighter under her arm. Ant gritted his teeth and pointed. "It's that thing they want."

"Right," she said through equally gritted teeth, "and they're not having it. Without this, they don't get to send an invasion of giant bugs."

"But that's not our problem," Ant argued.

He knew immediately he didn't mean that. Plus, handing over the Nyx energy to the Draduns wasn't going to stop the maniacs from killing them. They might not use that awful weapon, but they were strong enough to strangle them or bash their heads against the walls.

The elevator hit bottom and opened.

Ant, Liam, and Madison rushed out into a room full of doors—at least twenty in a perfect circle, surrounding them.

"What *is* this?" Madison murmured.

Ant turned slowly, confused but with a glimmer of hope. "This could be good. We can choose one and hide. If the Draduns follow us down—"

"It could take ages to find us," Liam finished. He grinned. "This place is a maze."

Behind them, the elevator door closed.

Ant chewed his lip. "It's going back up. Those psychos will be here any minute now. Let's move it."

They picked a door at random. A keypad to one side looked complicated at first, but when Liam pressed a large button, the single narrow door hissed open.

Beyond the doorway, Ant saw what looked like the inside of a futuristic subway train—a compartment of about the same size, with seats lining both sides. "What the heck?" Madison whispered.

Ant had a flash of understanding. "Escape pod!"

Liam let out a sigh. "Escape pod," he agreed, nodding. They all stared in silence.

"So," Madison said, "where are we supposed to hide? The Draduns just need to open every door one at a time. They'll find us easily."

"Maybe the seats lift up," Liam said, darting into the escape pod. He tried the first seat he came to, to no avail. "Luggage space, maybe?" he added, dropping to his knees and poking around at the panel under the seats.

"Luggage?" Ant said, hardly able to contain his scorn. "You think escape pods have luggage space? Luggage is the *last* thing you take on an escape pod."

"Well, maybe they're not *escape* pods," Liam argued, still working his fingers around the panel. "Maybe they're just . . . I don't know, passenger transporters or something . . ."

The sound of the elevator door opening caused them all to jump and swing around. The Dradun leapt out, his weapon pointing straight at them.

Liam, already inside the compartment, whispered at them to get inside. Ant was closer to the door than Madison, and he tugged at her shirt from behind. She backed up, holding the briefcase like a shield as the Dradun stalked toward them.

"Put it down," he growled at her.

"If you shoot, I'll—"

She had no chance to continue. She'd managed to back inside the doorway, but the Dradun quickly holstered his weapon and reached out with both hands. In one violent action, he grasped the case and shoved hard, smacking Madison in the face with it and sending her tumbling backward—but he maintained his grip and yanked it from her hands as she fell.

Ant saw red. He rushed at the Dradun with his shoulder forward—but it was like hitting a padded lamppost. He bounced sideways against the keypad on the inside of the door, and purely by accident, the door hissed shut. Just for a second, the briefcase was jammed between the door and the frame, preventing it from closing and causing a groan of protest. Madison moved toward it—but the Dradun snatched it clear, and the door slammed shut.

A near-silence fell, again filled with frantic panting.

The Dradun thumped his fist once on the door. The sound was muted and distant.

"Get ready," Liam whispered, adopting the stance of a football player about to launch himself at his opponent. "As soon as the door opens, we run him down and stamp on his head. Go for his gun and grab the case. Whatever it takes, guys. We can't just let—"

The floor began throbbing, and electronic displays flashed and beeped into life. A countdown on a screen commenced, accompanied by a low-pitched *dong* sound.

The door remained shut.

"He's . . ." Liam muttered.

Madison glared at him. "He's what?"

"He's launching the lifeboat." Liam turned toward the seats. "We'd better strap in."

"Launching us *where*?"

Ant and Liam shared a glance as if to confirm each other's thoughts. "Straight down?" Liam said. "We're in the clouds above Dradus Mox. Where else would an escape pod go but straight down to the ground?"

Fear hung in the air like invisible Nyx energy, an almost tangible feeling that prickled Ant's nerves and sent waves of nausea through his body. This was really, really serious. They might actually die. And if they didn't die from the descent to the world below—escape pods were designed to land safely, after all—there was always the bug invasion to look forward to, or whatever fate the Draduns were soon to unleash on the poor Mox.

"Buckle up, Ant," Madison told him. Blood had trickled from her nose, and her bottom lip was swelling up on one side.

Ant fumbled with the clasp, shocked at how slick his trembling hands were. Just as he got the belt secured around his waist, a terrific clunk and thud filled the cocoon—and his stomach rose to his mouth as the escape pod plummeted.

He imagined it being released from the bottom of the cloudstation and simply dropping like a stone. How far to the planet below? When would the rockets kick in and slow their descent? *Would* they kick in? What if there was a malfunction . . . ?

Gripping the seat to stop himself rising out of it, he looked across at Madison. Her hair floated like she was underwater. Her green eyes were wide, her teeth bared in a grimace.

Two seats to his side, Liam had plastered himself back against the headrest and had his eyes shut tight. Ant could see his jaw wobbling.

"Liam!" Ant shouted over the noise. "The wormhole wand! Does it work?" The idea of a miraculous last-minute escape—ironically from an escape pod—excited him so much he forgot to be scared. If its power had been restored, and if a wormhole could be generated fast enough . . .

But Liam simply kept his eyes shut tight.

Ant would have reached over and shook him if it hadn't meant letting go of his seat. He held on.

Then the engines roared into life with a deafening *bang-bang-bang*. Their shuddering upward thrust forced him into his seat so hard he felt like he might fold in two. His head nodded forward, and then he couldn't lift it again, so he ended up staring at his own shirt while the escape pod slowed its descent.

Just when he thought the pressure couldn't get any worse, or the noise any louder, it all ended with a jarring thud as the vessel touched down. All three of them yelled out and sat up, gasping. Ant felt very light all of a sudden.

As the engines died away, leaving an eerie silence, they each unbuckled their seatbelts and slid to the front of their seats, not quite ready to stand up.

Ant swallowed. "We've landed, guys."

Madison reached out and smacked his leg so hard it stung. "We *know* that, you idiot!"

The narrow door they'd entered through hissed open, and a blast of cool air rushed in. Outside, the high-tech circular room in the cloudstation had been replaced by a forest under a night sky.

The three of them stared into the darkness. Ant heard a croaking sound somewhere, and the high shrill of some insect or other. In the distance, a howl lifted into the air.

Liam licked his lips and spoke in a trembling voice. "So, uh . . . I vote we stay inside for now."

"I'll see if I can shut the door again," Ant agreed.

As he fumbled with the illuminated pad on the door frame, he thought he saw a pair of gleaming eyes staring at him from the nearest shadowy bushes. The door hissed back into place, blocking out the creepy vision.

Ant shuddered. "Check your wand again, buddy."

Liam pulled out the wormhole device. They all watched with bated breath as the end lit up blue . . . and then dimmed again.

He shook his head. "Nope."

Chapter 28

No windows adorned the escape pod, but Madison found a screen showing the view immediately outside the door. A set of buttons allowed her to flick from one angle to another—front, back, sides—but there wasn't much to see, just bushes and trees crammed up close.

"Ideas?" Madison said.

She absently wiped blood from her nostril and gingerly touched her swollen lip. Ant wanted to find a cold, damp cloth to dab at her with . . . but something stopped him. She was Liam's *future wife*. Definitely off limits now.

"What if . . ." Liam started. Then he sighed. "Naw, scratch that."

"What if what?" Ant prompted him.

"Well, I mean, I walked around in the snow at night on Kraxis 9 and found a bunker, and that basically saved our butts. Maybe if I walk around in the woods at night on Dradus Mox, I'll save our butts again."

Ant snorted. "Go for it."

He looked over Madison's shoulder at the array of buttons and switches. Nothing suggested manual control of the escape pod's rocket engines or some way to turn it into a land vehicle; the dials and readouts were most likely for communications and analysis. This vessel had one job, and its job was done.

Madison stared at the controls, deep in thought. "This is an escape pod, right? It must have a beacon or something—like a distress call, for when it falls out of the sky? I mean, an escape pod would only be used if there was a disaster on the cloudstation, so there must be some kind of automated system in place to alert rescue crews. Right? We could just wait for help."

Liam shrugged. "That's way better than my plan. Except . . . the Draduns are about to unleash giant bugs on the world. I hate to just sit around and wait."

"It's not happening until shortly after dawn," Ant offered. "That's what they said, anyway."

The silence that followed told him they felt as uneasy about waiting as he did.

"So . . . we go outside?" he said. "Into the forest? In the dark?"

Liam moved toward the door. He reached out and tapped the pad to open it, and when it hissed aside, the cool air rushed in again. They stood together, peering out. The gleaming eyes had vanished, but that didn't mean nothing lurked in the darkness. This was an *alien planet*. Literally anything could be out there.

Since neither Madison nor Liam shifted an inch, Ant steeled himself and took a step outside, feeling for the heavily shadowed ground. His foot immediately sank into a marsh, and he yanked it bank, cringing at the feel of wet mud soaking through his sock. He squinted, looking for a dry patch of ground, but it seemed the escape pod had plunged them into the boggiest place on Dradus Mox.

"Okay, that's it," Liam said. "We can't go anywhere in this. It's bad enough being dark out, but marshy as well? We could get sucked under."

Madison sighed. "Let's wait, then."

With nothing to do, they stretched out on the padded seats and stared at the ceiling. Ant slipped his muddy shoe off, hoping it would dry out. His sock smeared gunk all over the seat, but he didn't care.

He wasn't sure how long the three of them lay there. Despite everything, the pod was warm, peaceful, and relatively safe, and Ant ended up dozing off.

He jerked awake at the sound of a low-pitched beep from one of the control panels near the door.

Liam and Madison were asleep. Ant quietly got up, struggled to put on his damp shoe, and went to inspect the array of controls. A pulsing blue light accompanied the beeping. Ant read a message there: "It is safe. You may exit."

He stared at the message for a long time. Was it the computer saying that? More likely a long-distance instruction from Dradus Mox authorities. Or . . . from somebody standing outside. Either way, when he squinted and looked sideways, he could see the alien symbols lying beneath the translated text. It reminded him of a slightly off-kilter 3D image.

"Guys," he whispered. He raised his voice and went to jostle his friends awake. "Guys, look at this."

The viewing screen showed that dawn had broken. He jerked in surprise. Where had the time gone? He hoped the bug invasion hadn't started already!

The forest looked nowhere near as foreboding in the daylight, but it wasn't a stroll in the park either. Hairy vines hung everywhere, twisted around moss-covered trees and branches, and intermingled with pervasive ivy that reached in all directions. The trees themselves had dense canopies high above, and the ground looked as marshy as it had felt. A trek through the forest promised to be a real struggle.

Nobody could be seen on the viewing screen—until Ant changed the angle. Standing outside the door was a group of Mox.

He stared in fascination. They were the same as the undead corpses in the bunker . . . only *different*. They didn't look as dead and murderous, for one thing. They weren't dressed in those grey rags, either. Instead, they looked serene and wore the sort of togs associated with stone age caveman.

Liam and Madison joined him, still yawning. They soon woke at the sight of their welcome party.

"Just like you said, Maddy," Liam murmured. "They must have an alert system for when an escape pod drops into the woods. This has to be a rescue team." He grinned. "I say we open the door."

Ant sighed, knowing they had absolutely no choice.

Liam activated the door, and it hissed open.

The Mox had gathered on a dry mound sticking out of the marsh. Five of them, all dressed in furs and leathery skins. Each carried a knobby wooden staff.

Aside from their clothes, they had a strange beauty about them that was completely at odds with the forest setting. Ant could picture them quite easily in a science lab or on the flight deck of a UFO, but here in the dense woods they look misplaced, like they'd crash-landed a while back and had learned to survive in the wild.

"Are you here to help us?" Liam asked.

"The real question," the leader of the group said, "is why are *you* here? Who are you? What are you doing in an escape vessel from Rabeium 234. Would you care to explain?"

Before anyone could open their mouth to speak, the leader held up his hand.

"But not here. Walk with us. We shall feed you."

"Feed us to what?" Ant muttered.

Luckily, only Madison heard him, and she grimaced.

The Mox set off through the waterlogged undergrowth, and even though the escape pod had landed in a fairly random place, somehow they picked out a submerged pathway inches below the murky, slimy water as if they had the entire region mapped out. Ant shuddered as he squelched along. In front of him, Madison gasped and batted at a brightly colored bug as big and round as a golf ball that buzzed around her face.

Giant bugs, Ant thought. *We have to warn them.*

* * *

"I am Obram," the lead Mox said.

Ant frowned. His translator hesitated a fraction of a second before spitting out a word he could make sense of. Behind the name, he heard a guttural sound that matched the Mox's lip movements.

Obram suited him just fine. "Nice to meet you," he said, feeling a little awkward.

They walked single-file through the trees, most of the time wading through stagnant water up to their ankles, sometimes rising above, forever weaving, occasionally taking large steps across breaks in the pathway. Obram led the way. Ant, Liam, and Madison followed close behind.

At the rear, four more Mox trailed them in what seemed to be a respectful silence. They reminded Ant of monks.

They ducked under some thick vines. "Mind the nest," Obram whispered, pointing.

To their left, a bright red wasps' nest clung to a twisted, ancient tree trunk. As they passed, keeping their wading as silent as possible, a few wasps emerged and stared at them. Their shiny black bodies and vivid red stripes left no doubt; these were critters to steer clear of.

"That's like the one we passed in the wormhole," Ant whispered over his shoulder to Liam and Madison. He faced front again and called out to Obram. "We have to tell you something. The Draduns are planning an attack on your people."

After a brief moment of contemplation, Obram slowed and looked back over his shoulder, his alien-grey eyes glinting in a rare slant of sunlight. "My people? The Shuntaar settlement?"

There again was that odd hesitation in translation. "I don't know what Shuntaar is," Ant said, "but I mean all of you—your entire species."

Obram halted and pivoted on the narrow log he'd been traversing. "My entire species? Come now. The Draduns have shown their distaste of us for centuries, and it is true that their loathing has deepened in recent times due to the perplexing issue of our dead returning to life—"

That's some issue, Ant thought.

"—but to suggest they're planning an attack on our entire species . . ." The corners of Obram's mouth curled up. "If that is true, these are the rantings of a small faction. Not to be underestimated, to be sure—but hardly a cause for concern where our entire species is concerned."

He turned and continued on his way through the woods.

"You don't know what they're planning," Liam called from over Ant's shoulder. "They've been testing some giant bugs on our planet. Not just giant bugs, but I mean *giant* giant—like genetically supersized."

Again, that silence. And again, Obram slowed and turned around, this time knee-deep in a pool. The rest of the procession hadn't made it off the end of the log. "Genetically supersized?"

His skepticism was hard to miss.

Madison spoke up. "They used a Nyx wraith. They stole one from . . . well, from the Nyx system, and brought it to Dradus Mox. They've been leeching a little bit of energy at a time and putting it into some of your bugs, like those wasps back there, and those bugs have grown to the size of a house. They plan to unleash an army of them on the Mox—like some kind of *terrible accident* they can't do anything about."

Obram nodded, a smile still on his lips. "Ah, the so-called calamity wishers—those who publicly embrace diversity on the surface but secretly long for a natural catastrophe to extinguish us. Some of them are fanatics. I suspect you have been watching illicit propaganda footage."

Ant frowned. Weren't the Mox supposed to be primitive? They sure didn't speak the way their attire suggested.

Hearing a splash, Obram looked down at the pool. Several dark-brown eels eased toward him. When one sniffed at his ankles, a sharp *crack* caused the creature to jerk and skedaddle. One by one, the others did the exact same thing. The whole time, Obram simply stared down at them.

"Are those things dangerous?" Ant asked, looking for a way around the pool.

"Not if you're generating a small electrical charge," the Mox murmured. He glanced up at Ant. "Dradun technology contained within these carved wooden staffs." He waded out of the pool, finding his footing on a ledge buried under a slurry of leaves and mud. "Step quickly."

Ant grimaced at the pool, seeing a few of the brown eels sliding beneath the murky surface. Taking a deep breath, he splashed down off the log and stamped his way toward Obram.

Behind him, Liam and Madison did the same, each with the same frenzied haste. The four Mox at the tail end took their time about it.

"They harnessed the power of the Nyx, you say?" Obram called back as he ducked under a vine and pushed aside a thin, protruding branch. "And they're on Rabeium 234? Why?"

Ant wished Liam or Madison were walking alongside instead of trailing behind so he wouldn't have to explain everything himself. He did his best to cover the events on Kraxis 9—how they'd arrived, found the frozen Mox, taken refuge in the bunker, met Steeg and Jaxrill and the rest of the team, and dealt with an invasion of the undead.

Obram moved slowly the whole time, clearly hanging onto every word. When Ant got through, the Mox said nothing at first. He led the way onto drier land where the woods opened up. Here, Liam and Ant were able to catch up and walked abreast of Ant.

"I think I have frogs in my shoes," Liam complained.

"And leeches squirming around my knees," Madison said.

All three of them were caked in mud up to their thighs. Ant made a point of stamping as he walked. "Definitely feels good to be on firm ground again. Now I just need something to eat. I'm starving."

Madison pointed ahead. "I think we've arrived, guys."

Ant peered through the trees and saw flashes of light, the sun glinting off shiny metal or glass.

"Arrived where, though?" he muttered.

Chapter 29

It turned out the flashes of light were some distance away—a city beyond the forest. Ant gazed in amazement.

The gleaming city towered over the treetops, thousands of highrise buildings reaching for the clouds. Two early morning suns glared between the structures like the blazing eyes of a god, their fiery rays striking the rooftops. Ant made out an intricate network of slender rails meandering between buildings, probably crisscrossing throughout the metropolis.

A monorail, he thought with excitement. *This is like a 1950s vision of the future!*

He tore his gaze from the cityscape and focussed on the wooded lowlands before him. He and his friends stood in a clearing the size of the entire Brockridge High School grounds, where dumpy wood and stone cottages littered the landscape. Grass had long ago given up trying to grow here; the ground was all mud and rocks. Smoke lifted from several chimneys. The Mox milled about everywhere, some pushing small carts, others toting baskets . . . It looked like a day at the market in a medieval English town.

Except they were aliens.

Ant couldn't get over the dramatic difference in landscapes. He and his friends had crash-landed in a depressing marshy forest full of nasty critters and had trudged their way to an equally depressing muddy village—yet a vast, futuristic city towered just beyond the forest, *surrounding* the forest. It was like being in Central Park in the middle of New York City, only on a much grander scale. The contrast was breathtaking, two worlds superimposed.

"There's the cloudstation," Liam gasped, craning his neck to look skyward.

Ant twisted around and shielded his eyes. A disk hung high in the sky above the clouds. It looked even stranger to him than the extra sun. The cloudstation. A research laboratory in the sky. Just hanging there, defying gravity.

"It is lower than normal," Obram commented as he joined them in peering upward. "It is descending."

Ant looked harder. "Is it?"

"Slowly, yes. They do so on occasion when external repairs are needed. It is easier to work on in normalized pressure."

Ant glanced at Liam. "They're coming to release the giant bugs."

Still, he wondered how the four fanatic Draduns would get away with such a stunt. The city would see the cloudstation descending. The populace might even see the bugs being released. They would know the giant bug invasion came from the Dradun cloudstation. How could Krun possibly lie his way out of that?

Easy—because it's a lie everyone wants to believe.

"This way," Obram said, resuming his light-footed walk toward a small, rounded stone cottage. His colleagues matched his step. "We shall eat and discuss our options."

Ant and Liam automatically started to follow, but Madison hung back. "We don't have time to eat and talk," she said. "We have to do something *now*. You need to evacuate."

Obram turned back and spread his hands. "Evacuate to where? Look around. This forest is home to seventy-two thousand Mox, the very last of our species. We, the Shuntaar clan, are a small community at the very center of the forest, but there are many other clans. We have plenty of space here, more than we need, yet the forest is a minor enclave amid the sprawling Dradun civilization. Our people have a legal right to enter the cities, but that right extends to a relative handful at a time. Since the city surrounds the forest on all sides, a mass exodus from our enclave would be seen as a breach of our boundaries, an invasion into Dradun territory."

"I understand that," Madison said, her face reddening in frustration, "but if you stay in the forest, you'll be invaded by giant bugs and will *die*."

The Mox tilted his head and blinked his bulbous eyes at her. "This is why I wish to gather all the details of the matter in order to put forth an informed objection to the Dradun elders. We must appeal to their—"

"Their elders *know* about this!" Ant blurted. "They're planning to turn a blind eye and let you be wiped out before rushing in to help."

Obram and his four silent colleagues, standing shoulder to shoulder, shared a few expressionless glances. Their leader placed his hands together and tilted his head again as if about to explain something to a child.

"You said four Dradun scientists on Rabeium 234 had unleashed experimental insects on your own planet, and I believe you. I might even be persuaded to believe that they will attack the Mox with such insects." He smiled.

"However, a handful of insects, large or otherwise, could never jeopardize the entirety of our species."

Liam opened his mouth to retort, but Madison cut him off. "These bugs aren't just large. They're *gigantic*. They're bigger than your houses. And there'll be more than just a handful."

All around, the Mox had gathered to listen. They'd appeared so silently that Ant hadn't noticed until just now. While the men were bald, he saw women with thinner faces, larger eyes, and faint, wispy hair. There were children, too—they looked wily and strong, crouching like they were coiled springs, able to leap onto rooftops if they wanted to. Every single Mox watched with interest, some nudging and whispering.

He couldn't believe nobody was taking the threat seriously. He pointed skyward. "Look at the cloudstation. It's *descending*. Krun is getting ready to drop a ton of bugs out of the bottom. They'll come buzzing down here to the forest while they're still growing. They'll be too small for anyone to notice, but they'll be massive by breakfast time and looking for food. And *you're* the food."

He couldn't think of a clearer way to put it. Madison shot him a half-smile and nodded.

"That's exactly right," she said to Obram. "You have to evacuate."

Obram didn't exactly have eyebrows, but he managed to raise one anyway. "And if we evacuate to the city—what then? These oversized insects you speak of will simply attack us there, will they not?"

"No," Liam said. "Krun mentioned some kind of ultrasonic bug repellent across the city? He said they'll stick to the forests."

"Ah," Obram said. Still, his skepticism filled the air. "I appreciate you bringing us this news. We will converse with the Dradun elders and draw their attention to the potential incursion from the cloudstation. I have no doubt Krun and his associates will be investigated in no time, and whatever foul experiment they are planning halted in its tracks."

"But—" Madison started.

The Mox turned and headed into the rounded cottage, ducking slightly. They looked like a procession of monks entering an abbey.

Ant, Liam, and Madison were left alone in the muddy clearing. The Mox onlookers sidled away, apparently unconcerned.

Madison shook her head. "This is ridiculous. They're not taking us seriously."

"It's almost like we need a giant bug to attack before they'll do something," Liam agreed.

Ant remembered what Krun had said from the outset when asked why he didn't just test the giant bugs on the Mox: *Not until we're certain of our weapon. We must hit the Mox hard and fast with a swarm of the most efficient killers, not poke at them with tests until we get it right.*

One giant test bug would alert the Mox, and they'd be straight on to the Dradun elders demanding answers. But a swarm all at once . . .

"We have to get out of here," Ant said. "Liam, see if the wand has power."

Liam looked irritated as he took it from his pocket. "I'm telling you it doesn't. Look, see? It lights up, then dims. It won't take a charge until the Nyx fixes it again."

"So we need to find another wand."

Madison nodded. "And if we can't find another wand, we'll have to get back up to the cloudstation and find the Nyx so it can repair ours. And it won't repair the wand until we save the Mox from imminent death."

Ant clapped his hands together. "Good! Right, then, let's get to work, team. What's first on the agenda?"

He realized he was being unhelpfully sarcastic, but neither Liam nor Madison seemed to notice. Liam actually pursed his lips as if thinking about it.

"We need to get back up there," he said, jerking his thumb toward Rabeium 234. "Sneak in, sabotage the experiment again, and save the Mox. Then steal the Nyx. Question is—how do we get back up there?"

Ant couldn't help himself. "Wow, one tiny hurdle and you're stumped."

They all stared up at the cloudstation. It was definitely a little larger now, descending at a slow, steady pace.

"If only we had the wormhole wand," he murmured, "we could actually get up there quite easily."

"If we knew how to program it," Madison said.

Ant clutched his head. *Too many impossibilities. There's no way we can do anything to help.*

Suddenly impatient, he ran toward the rounded cottage and crashed through the doorway. Inside, Obram and his colleagues sat around a sturdy wooden table facing a bright-blue glowing sphere the size of a soccer ball. *A crystal ball*, Ant thought absently as he stomped closer.

He was vaguely aware of traipsing mud onto the weird, piecemeal rug of leathery skin and matted hair. *Gross!* He tore his gaze away, taking in chests of drawers, bench seats, and small tables crammed around the walls. This wasn't so much a home as a tiny town hall.

Ignoring his noisy entrance, Obram spoke in a calm voice to the shimmering figure within the glowing orb. ". . . shed light on such a disturbing report?"

The orb crackled and hissed, then steadied. Inside, an elderly Dradun hunched there with ornate, bronze-colored armor hanging over his shoulders and chest. He wore a curious snakelike crown that curled around his head. "I thank you, Obram, for bringing this to me. Rest assured I will look into it . . ."

As Liam and Madison appeared beside him, Ant remembered why he'd come barging in. "Excuse me," he said loudly. "Obram?"

The Mox leader twisted around to give him a glare of mild annoyance.

But Ant wasn't in the mood to wait. He had a home to get back to. Even *his* parents must have noticed by now that he was missing, assuming they were back from New York. "Shut that thing off, would you?"

Obram's glare hardened. "Young human from Earth, we—"

"Shut it off!" Ant yelled.

All five Mox recoiled somewhat. Then Obram turned back to the orb. "We shall resume in a moment. Please do excuse me."

As the Dradun elder bowed his head, Obram waved a hand, and the orb promptly vanished. He stood up and approached, grasping his staff as if he wanted to club Ant over the head. "I do not appreciate—"

"We need a wormhole wand," Ant interrupted. "Or a way to get up to the cloudstation. Those people, the Draduns, are not going to help you. Only *we* can help you."

"Yeah, especially since you're not going to help yourselves," Liam muttered.

Madison chimed in. "So give us what we need, and we'll take care of it. Do you have a wormhole wand?"

Obram looked puzzled. "A what?"

"A wormhole wand," she repeated. "A device that opens wormholes."

The Mox smiled. "We do not possess that sort of technology. The Draduns do, of course."

"So how about a . . . a small spaceship, then?" Madison said. "Anything that flies. We need to get to the cloudstation."

"I'm afraid that is beyond our capabilities. Now, if there is nothing else . . . ?"

Madison let out a frustrated yell and stormed out.

Ant and Liam trailed after her. She paced back and forth in the mud, muttering something about trying to help idiots who didn't want to help themselves.

"We're gonna die here," Liam said, craning his neck again to look skyward. "Torn to bits or stung to death by rabid monster bugs from the cloudstation."

Ant heard the tremble in his voice. Things had to be *really* serious for Liam to be scared. "I thought you said you couldn't die," he complained. "All that time telling us you would live to a ripe old age, that you saw yourself in the future as an old man, and it was all a big mistake?"

Liam slowly turned to stare at him with narrowed eyes. "No, actually, you're right—I *did* see myself as an old man in the future. Sometimes I forget. I couldn't even die in deep space; the universe brought me back." He grinned. "It'll be all right. We'll get out of this somehow. We just have to . . . to . . ."

He trailed off, his smile fading.

Ant became aware his friend was staring past him. So was Madison. He felt a shiver go down his spine, and he spun on the spot, expecting to find a gigantic spider or monstrous scorpion scuttling toward him.

Instead, he spotted an undead Mox shuffling out from the trees.

Chapter 30

"It's just a slow-moving zombie," Ant said quietly as they backed away. "We can outrun it. Heck, we can out*walk* it."

To their horror, another appeared—not just shuffling from the trees, but materializing out of thin air. Both wore the shabby grey garments of a patient from Rabeium 234.

All around, the living Mox began yelling and alerting others. They let out eerie wailing sounds that carried across rooftops like sirens, quickly spreading the news. Their alarm was evident, yet they still managed to move about with dignified monklike grace, *making haste* rather than sprinting for cover.

Ant doubted that *making haste* would help them when the giant bugs arrived.

Seen in broad daylight, the undead Mox seemed even more aged and rotten than before, vastly deteriorated in comparison to the living—gaunt faces, sunken cheeks, skeletal limbs, that deathly gaze . . . and their unrelenting shuffle and outstretched arms as they targeted their next victims.

Both undead corpses zeroed in on Ant and his friends. He wasn't sure which of them was *the* target, but it didn't matter.

"Don't let them touch you," Ant warned.

Liam sighed. "Thanks, buddy. I don't know what I'd do without your infinite wisdom."

"I'm just saying."

They backed up some more, and the undead pursued them, groaning and moaning as they stumbled through the mud.

"What do they *want* from us?" Liam grumbled.

Madison's answer was short and to the point: "They want us dead."

"Yeah, but why?"

Nearby, Obram and his four colleagues stepped out of their rounded cottage. Ant almost snorted with derision at their somewhat irked manner. He couldn't bring himself to feel sorry that they'd had to cut short their conference call with the Dradun elders in light of the most recent deadly threat to their peaceful community.

The undead were still focussed on Ant and his friends as they shuffled closer.

Obram strode forward to catch up with the invaders. Approaching from behind, he held up his staff and swung it, hitting a shoulder. A crackle of energy burst from the end of the makeshift weapon.

The undead Mox flinched and paused, then slowly turned to face Obram. Undeterred, he swung the staff again, whacking the creature on the side of the head. The energy crackled again, and this time the Mox went still.

By now, the second corpse was almost upon Ant, Liam, and Madison. They continued backing up together, side by side, but they were running out of clearing. Ant glanced behind, seeing no easy way into the dense woods. Thorny bushes, thick vines, low branches—it would be impossible to struggle through that mess.

"Guys," he whispered. "I hate to state the obvious, but we'll have to make a run for it."

His friends grunted their agreement. "Go!" Liam yelled.

They made a dash to one side, and the creature lurched after them in a surprisingly fast move, reaching with long arms. But it had no chance in such a wide-open space. Spinning around, it resumed its slow lumbering, tirelessly stalking them where they joined Obram.

"When these unfortunate souls first appeared in our midst," Obrab said softly, "they were easy to handle. Now they're indestructible. They took several of our people before we learned to maintain our distance. Touching them is death."

"We know," Madison said.

"Does your staff put them in stasis?" Liam asked, amazement in his voice as he peered at the frozen corpse.

"Dradun technology," Obram said. He held up the wooden staff and turned it on end so they could see the tiny metal nub poking out. "We simply had to tune to a different frequency and amplify the signal."

Liam leaned over it. "And how do you tune it?"

"We don't. The Draduns do it remotely."

"Guys, this is fascinating," Ant said, "but we need to move."

They retreated a little more, but Obram held his ground, waiting with his staff held high while the creature stumbled toward him. It looked like easy pickings.

Too easy, Ant thought as the undead Mox glanced from Obram to the frozen corpse. *These things . . .*

As Obram swung, the undead Mox suddenly reared backward so the staff missed its head by inches. The creature snatched at the staff and yanked hard, and Obram staggered. And, an instant later, after a single touch, the leader of the Shuntaar clan crumbled into a pile of dust in the mud.

"No!" Liam gasped.

Ant stared in horror. *It learned. Just like outside the bunker on Kraxis 9. They're not as dumb as they look.*

Obram's colleagues circled the creature, raising their own crude weapons. The undead Mox might have figured out the staff's threat, but that didn't mean it could avoid four attacks at once.

Sure enough, after several crackling blows, the creature turned into a motionless statue. The staff-wielding Mox nodded with approval and gently prodded its inert, scrawny flesh.

"Well, two down—" Ant started.

Four more undead Mox appeared out of nowhere.

Then another three.

"Okay, time to go," Madison said, gripping Ant's arm. She tugged him and Liam away. "This way. Come on."

Ant felt bad about leaving the staff-wielding Mox alone with the newcomers, but what else was there to do? The undead were unstoppable.

With Madison leading, they weaved between cottages. The place was deserted already. Had the Mox hidden away inside their homes? If so, the undead might sniff them out and easily crash through those flimsy wooden doors.

Running as fast they were, it was no surprise that they caught up with a mob of villagers *making haste* ahead. Madison had no choice but to slow down since their way ahead was blocked by a wall of Mox crowding along a narrow alley between low buildings.

"We don't *have* to stick to the same streets," Liam panted.

They took a sharp left turn and bypassed the crowd. Why were they sticking together anyway? Where was the sense in clustering together like that? A few undead corpses could dispatch them in no time!

Liam stopped at a small barn and leaned against the rickety wall. A grunting came from the other side, suggesting some kind of piglike animal resided within. Maybe more. Ant kept an eye on the loose-fitting boards.

"Oh, for a wormhole," Madison said with a sigh. "If I could just go to sleep and figure out where the next one will be . . ."

She had an interesting point. "You slept in the escape pod earlier and didn't dream anything," Ant told her.

"I didn't have a notepad and pencil."

"You have your journal, though, right?"

Madison shook her head. "I don't carry it everywhere. It's too bulky. Don't have a pencil, either."

Liam pointed at the squelchy ground at their feet. "Take a nap right here. You can draw in the mud."

"Sure, I'll get right on it," Madison said in a voice that suggested nothing remotely like that would be happening anytime soon.

Ant's mind was working overtime. "So . . . the fact that you haven't predicted a new wormhole for us isn't something to worry about?"

She shook her head. "It's not a hard and fast rule. Even if I had a really good nap right now and slept for eight hours with a notepad by my side, that doesn't mean I'll predict our way home."

"You're useless," Liam snorted. Then he grinned and nudged her. "Kidding. You're awesome."

They considered their options and came to the conclusion they had none. They literally had nothing to do but chew their fingernails in anticipation of being turned to dust by undead corpses, or attacked by swarms of lethal monster-bugs.

"We could maybe head for the city," Liam said, looking toward the distant treetops.

It was a fairly short distance to the far side of the clearing—they'd already made it most of the way through the Shuntaar village—but the forest stretched for miles beyond. The idea of traipsing through marshes, ducking under endless branches, getting tangled up in thorny bushes, and running into genuine forest-dwelling nests of creepy crawlies . . . It just didn't seem like a feasible plan.

Plus, it wouldn't help the Mox, and therefore the Nyx would never help *them*.

Liam let out a gasp and jerked away from the barn wall. A twitching snout was pushing its way through the gap, hairy and snotty and disgusting. Liam grimaced at the slimy stuff on his sleeve.

Howls of anguish filled the air.

The three of them clutched at each other. The screams came from the crowds of Mox they'd just left behind. Maybe more of the undead had materialized in the middle of them.

"This is a nightmare," Ant moaned. "What are we going to do?"

He glanced up at the sky. The cloudstation was definitely closer. He could see a series of rings, the largest at the top. Set among those rings, numerous blocky shapes protruded downward as though part of the Dradun cityscape had been dug up, turned over, and launched into the sky. Other blocks poked out to the sides and upwards, a curious mishmash of conjoined structures. How the cloudstation floated in the air was a mystery.

His mouth dropped open. "Uh, guys?"

He sensed them looking first at him, then skyward.

Madison let out a groan. "Is that what I think it is?"

Nobody answered. All three of them stared in silence as a fuzzy dark-grey cloud spilled from one of the rings. It looked rather like the cloudstation had developed a leak and was oozing smoke into the atmosphere—or perhaps wispy, vaporous oil—but they knew without a doubt it was actually a swarm of bugs.

The cloud spread like an ominous portent.

Chapter 31

More howls filled the air.

The undead corpses were teleporting in from somewhere—probably from Kraxis 9 where they'd last been sighted—and were attacking the Shuntaar clan. And above, a swarm of bugs descended on the forest.

Ant had to assume they were infused with Nyx energy, which meant they were already growing. How much energy had they absorbed? How much had they left behind? Was the Nyx still alive?

He couldn't make out what kind of bugs they were. Flying ones, naturally. But even that might not be true. Critters could fall from great heights and survive, especially with the Nyx energy to toughen them up. He knew that all creatures reached terminal velocity no matter their size; smaller creatures naturally fell slower than larger ones. In fact, he seemed to recall that mice could survive falls from any height. That meant bugs certainly could.

"There could be spiders and scorpions and ants and beetles," he muttered. "Not just dragonflies and wasps."

"Krun was after the ultimate killer, though," Liam argued. "Hopefully he'll just send one type."

Madison swung around to him. "And that will help us how? Guys, we have to—" She broke off and looked lost for words.

"We have to hide," Liam said, staring at Ant. "That's all we can do. We have to hide and . . . just wait it out."

Wait it out. Let the Mox die. Then plead the Draduns for a wormhole wand so we can get home. Because the Nyx sure won't help us if we fail.

They headed for the nearest building, a cottage just like the rest with sturdy stone walls but what looked like a flimsy roof. They burst in and slammed the door shut. In the wan light, they made out layers of rugs on a dirt floor, walls of lath and plaster, drapes hanging everywhere, wood furniture, and faintly glowing lamps. The place smelled of some kind of leafy incense—a little strong but not unpleasantly so.

They stood and waited, an unspoken agreement that someone might be here. The heavy drapes across the room acted as dividers, and they had flaps pinned back like tent openings. Ant tiptoed toward one of three inner rooms and peered within. A couple of low bunks. *Bedroom.* The next was jam-packed with clay plates and bowls, metal pans, and various iron pots. *Kitchen?* And the third— Ant scrunched up his nose at the smell. This room was tiny, no wider than the tent flap opening and not much longer. A narrow bowl stood on the floor. *Toilet.*

"Nobody here," he said after his inspection.

Liam and Madison nodded and visibly relaxed.

Ant studied the underside of the roof. He couldn't see daylight through it, but he knew the rafters wouldn't hold much weight. If a giant bug landed on top, it would crash straight through.

His friends had obviously noted the same. "We either find someplace else," Madison remarked, "or we cower under the bunks and be completely still. Maybe the bugs won't find us."

"Can they smell their prey?" Liam wondered aloud.

Nobody had any idea. And besides, these were *alien* bugs.

Ant went to the door and opened it an inch. He had a fair view of the bug cloud. "They're close. We don't have time to go hunting around. We're just gonna have to hide and pretend we're not here."

With trepidation, they hurried to the bedroom and, one by one, scooted under the bunks. There were only two, and since Madison picked one and Liam the other, Ant suddenly found himself making an awkward decision. He wanted to squeeze up next to Madison, but . . . would that be weird? Especially as she'd eventually marry Liam!

"Get in here," Madison hissed at him.

That settled it. Madison wanted company. Or someone to shield her from an attacking bug. He chewed on that as he slid under the bunk and wriggled sideways away from the edge, pressing up hard against her shoulder.

Wonder why Liam didn't choose this bunk, he thought, turning his head sideways. He could see his friend staring back from the shadows with narrowed eyes, probably wondering the same thing.

They waited.

In the distance, more howls. The undead corpses were still shuffling about. Or worse, appearing in the middle of the crowds and taking out lots of Mox at once. Maybe they were hopping from place to place—disappearing from *here* and materializing *there*. Could they do that? Did they have that sort of control?

Ant closed his eyes. This was quite possibly the worst experience of his life. He wished he were back home, safe and sound, watching a B-movie with his dad. Or . . .

"My mom liked cycling," he whispered.

After a pause, Madison said, "Huh?"

"My mom. She used to cycle everywhere. She taught me how to ride, and when I was big enough to manage without training wheels, we rode down the trail that leads into the woods near the house we used to live in. These were nice woods, though—all trimmed back, mowed grass along the edges of the trail, bluebells and daisies and other wildflowers everywhere—really pretty. In the spring and fall, we'd ride early when mist was rising off the river, and the sun would shine down through the branches and create these amazing golden rays . . ."

He knew he was babbling, but he didn't care. It was better thinking about that than monstrous bugs.

Just then, he heard a low drone from outside. It grew louder, amplified across the forest as the swarm descended.

Ant felt Madison's hand touching his, and they clasped. Her grip was painfully tight.

"My dad was always rich," he went on in a hushed voice, "but then he got *really* rich, and my parents hired a nanny, and cleaners, and other staff, and we moved into that huge house we're in now. They got busy. My dad still let me watch movies while he worked, but my mom stopped cycling. She made sure I got a new bicycle every Christmas, though. I guess it was her way of—"

"You got a new one every Christmas?" Madison interrupted with a whisper directly in his ear.

He heard a thud outside, then a crash of glass. A chittering sound filled the air, and Ant knew whatever kind of bug it was had to be *big* already.

He glanced sideways at Liam. His friend put a finger to his lips and mouthed "Shh."

Ant held his breath. Staring straight up at the underside of the bunk inches above his head, there was absolutely nothing to do but wait to see if they would all die or not.

Or rather, to see if *he* would die.

Bitterness welled up deep inside. He didn't want to be angry that his friends would come out of this alive no matter what, but he couldn't help it. How come *he* was fair game for the bugs and they were not?

Thudding footfalls on the roof caused Madison's fingernails to dig deep into the flesh of his hand. Ant couldn't tell if the bug on the roof had landed there or clambered up the wall, but he didn't like the sound of the creaking rafters and the dust pattering on the tabletop. The creature scuttled—no, *stomped*—from one side to the other, and the roof creaked even more.

But the noise of one monster on the roof was quickly drowned out by the arrival of dozens more. Their incessant clicking and stomping, the buzz of their wings, the thuds and crashes as they turned this way and that, the collapse of nearby structures as the rafters gave in . . . Ant felt a new terror: that of being crushed under stone and heavy beams. That could be as bad as being torn apart by massive mandibles, or stabbed with a stinger the size of a swordfish.

When the rafters above cracked and splintered, and debris rained down, Ant felt like his life was just about over. It could be that the place collapsed, pinning him to the ground while Liam and Madison crawled to safety. The bitterness and anger he'd felt a moment ago evaporated; now he just wanted them to be safe even if he wasn't.

The nightmarish cacophony outside rose in volume and intensity. He could sense the ravenous hunger of the giant critters as they foraged for tasty morsels within the stone buildings. The buzzing gave him the creeps. The constant thumping of multiple legs against doors and windows scared him to death. The hissing and clacking and chittering nearly drove him screaming from the cottage—which would be a disaster.

Hiding under bunks, he thought as a hint of scorn joined his rollercoaster of emotions. *Might as well hide under the sheets for all the good it'll do.*

With a tremendous crack and squeal, something ripped the roof apart. Ant knew instantly what had happened because the darkened room suddenly lit up, and bits of wood and plaster and chunks of rocks thudded down on the ground inches to his side. The bunk bounced and splintered as well, and he took back his cynicism from moments before. Sheets wouldn't have protected him from this deluge of damage, but this sturdy wooden frame had.

Still, the weight of rocks on the bunk pressed it closer to his face. He could feel Madison's claws digging deeper still into his hand, and he heard her pants and occasional whimpers. He fought to control his own hammering heart and turned his face toward her. "You're gonna be okay," he whispered.

An insect's foot slammed down between the bunks. Was foot the right word? Ant had no idea, but he stared in horror at the hideous, pale-brown appendage that had to be as thick as his arm. It dug heavily into the rug, into the ground below, and teetered from side to side as the creature—whatever it was—sprawled across the cottage and twisted about, obviously searching for food.

Where was its head? Ant tried to get a better look, squirming to see out of the tent flap of the bedroom—but the tent flap was no more, because the walls were gone and the drapes bunched up in piles on the ground. He could see nothing but the bottom of his bunk and Liam's frantic expression a few feet away.

Abruptly, the leg lifted away, and the giant crashed through and over the remaining walls. Dust tickled Ant's nose and throat, and he clapped a hand over his mouth and bit down on the cough that wanted to erupt.

The buzzing and chittering and clacking was far noisier now that the roof had collapsed. Ant risked a careful peek, looking up at the open sky. Monstrous shapes darted about everywhere. He ducked back under with a shudder. "Dragonflies and wasps. They're the size of cows."

Liam said hoarsely from across the aisle, "And that was a spider just now. Krun sent the whole lot of them down here."

"Shh!" Madison hissed. "I hear something."

"Ya think?" Ant retorted—but he winced when she elbowed him.

"Listen!"

He listened, confused. What else was there to hear except the ghastly sound of gigantic bugs tearing the Shuntaar village to shreds? Crashing, creaking, ripping, chittering, clacking, buzzing—the sounds would haunt him forever.

"I don't—" he began.

But then he heard it. A moaning and groaning, the shuffling and scraping of someone dragging their feet over debris. He edged sideways to peer out.

Oh no.

He shoved himself up against Madison. "Undead Mox!" he hissed.

Chapter 32

As if the bug invasion wasn't enough, now they had a corpse scouring the ruins for fresh meat.

"Where is it?" Madison whispered.

"In the living room."

He didn't need to explain that the living room, if indeed it could be called that, was now just a space filled with rubble and splintered rafters. But the undead corpse was there nevertheless, tripping and stumbling over the mess.

How is it still here? Why hasn't it been taken away by dragonflies or chomped in half by giant spider mandibles?

He looked again. The undead Mox stood there, peering around with those awful cold eyes. Above, one of the cow-sized wasps buzzed down and hovered, its wings a blur, the shiny black body gleaming in the sunlight, red stripes vivid in the dusty ruins. Its hideous legs hung loosely, twitching as the creature turned and tilted.

It suddenly dive-bombed, maneuvering so its stinger pierced the Mox directly through the chest. The corpse barely moved an inch despite the force of the attack—but the wasp abruptly exploded into dust, showering the ruins and coating the Mox's head and shoulders.

Ant stared in amazement. For the first time, he felt a sense of relief at the sight of one of these lifeless Mox creatures making a kill. But his relief turned to astonishment as a foot-long, wispy, pale-yellow glow floated down from where the wasp had hovered moments before. It flickered and pulsed, twisting like an eel in water.

Nyx energy.

The undead Mox didn't seem to notice as the faintly illuminated entity crackled and stretched, becoming as thin as a ribbon. It snaked between the remaining wall sections and undulated away.

"Did you see that?" Ant whispered hoarsely to Liam.

Liam shook his head. The angle was all wrong for him. And Madison certainly hadn't seen anything.

The undead Mox, unperturbed by the hole in its chest where the wasp had struck him, and unaffected by any venom that might have been injected, turned and shambled off. Above, numerous dragonflies and wasps buzzed closer, hovered for a moment, and moved on.

"What happened?" Liam urged.

Ant explained as quietly as he could—then had to twist around to face Madison and say it all again.

By the time he'd finished, the sky had suddenly gone quiet. He peered up in surprise. He could hear the incessant buzzing in the distance, and he saw the occasional dark shape shoot by, but it seemed the swarm had moved on.

Liam slid out from under his bunk and crawled over the rubble to a half-wall. He watched for a minute, his hand held high to signify that it wasn't safe yet. During that minute, the buzzing grew more distant. But Ant could still hear *movement* in and around the neighboring cottages—the clicking and scrabbling of insect feet.

"Okay," Liam said in a low voice.

Ant released himself from Madison's grip and squirmed out. Coated in dust, he made his way to Liam and peered over the remains of the stone wall at the ravaged village beyond. He felt rather like a soldier in a World War II movie as the Panzer tanks were rumbling by—only the tanks in this case were the enormous dark-green carapaces of a dozen beetles as they marched through the ruins.

Vaguely aware that Madison had joined them, he shook his head in disbelief. "Look, there's the corpse."

The undead Mox shuffled aimlessly, not caring about the dangers all around. *Because its invincible*, Ant thought. *They're more scared of him than the other way around.*

A red ant came around a corner. The size of a dog and probably still growing, it attacked the Mox without hesitation—and turned to dust. As with the wasp, it left behind a wispy, pale-yellow aura that pulsed and stretched, then threaded its way slowly through the ruins.

"Follow it," Ant said, jumping to his feet.

Both Liam and Madison yanked him back down. "Are you *nuts*?" Liam hissed.

Ant glared at him, his heart pounding and adrenaline pumping through his body. "Yes. But what else can we do here? Nothing! That Nyx energy—where's it going? You know it's not just gonna evaporate into thin air. It's going back to the—the Nyx wraith." He pointed skyward. "It's going back up there. That's where we need to be."

Madison shook her head, and dust flew off. "That—you're not—how can—"

"You're nuts," Liam said again. But he stared at Ant and nodded. "I think you're right, though. It's better than doing nothing."

"No," Madison said, digging her fingers in both Ant's and Liam's arms, "it's not. Hiding here has saved our lives so far. Let's wait a bit longer."

Ant pointed at the marching beetles, then toward the distant swarms. "The Mox are dying while we wait here. Look, the Nyx energy is heading *that* way. The bugs are marching in the other direction. The swarms are already gone. We just need to watch out for beetles and ants as they pass."

Liam stood up. "I'm game. Let's go."

Ant climbed to his feet, took a quick look around, and slid over the low wall. Liam quickly joined him.

Grumbling with irritation, Madison was just a few seconds behind.

Ignoring the undead Mox, even when it spotted them and shuffled their way, Ant, Liam, and Madison stayed low and hurried single file from one ruined building to another, peering around corners, over rubble, and through sections of demolished roof on the lookout for deadly bugs. They froze at the sight of a pale-brown spider poised on top of a round cottage; its roof was gone, and the arachnid had taken its place, absolutely still as it watched for its next victim.

It had plenty to choose from. Ignoring the tank-like beetles, it leapt on top of a red ant and immediately began chewing. The attack was sudden and vicious, and the ant didn't stand a chance.

Then a wasp came down and stung the spider. The giant spun around, tried to fend off another stinging, and ended up on its back with eight legs wriggling wildly before curling up. The wasp then flew off.

With two new dead bugs, another couple of foot-long, glowing yellow ribbons snaked their way clear. These two immediately joined together and flashed briefly, then meandered lazily through the ruins in the direction of the first.

Ant glanced sideways at Liam. "See?"

His friend nodded. "I don't know what this means exactly, but yeah—it means *something*."

They hurried on, worried the glowing ribbon would get away from them. Their haste made them careless, and they very nearly ran into a scuttling scorpion, stopping just in time as it raced past. The deadly stinger was arched high as it clambered over one dwelling after another.

"There!" Madison cried, pointing.

The combined Nyx ribbons caught up with the first, and they merged with a flash. Now thicker and stronger, the snakelike energy continued onward, weaving back and forth. Ahead, Ant spotted more yellow glows—dozens of them—all headed in one direction.

They were now nearing the edge of the clearing, and many of the cottages in this area were untouched. Looking back, Ant felt his stomach lurch at the idea of hundreds of Mox hiding in those homes directly beneath the swarm. The angry black cloud had found them; it had smothered the structures already, and the sounds of rooftops being ripped apart carried across the forest.

He looked up. The cloudstation continued to descend—and now a fresh wave of bugs were spilling out, staining the sky. "Guys," he said, pointing.

"Oh!" Madison gasped. "Just when we thought it couldn't get any worse."

Liam picked up the pace. "We've left our giant bugs behind. That new lot are headed somewhere else."

He was right. The cloudstation had rotated and was pumping them in a different direction. They'd be on the next village within minutes. And the bugs from the Shuntaar community would be done here soon, and would move on to someplace else, heading out across the forest hunting for food. How many other waves of bugs would there be? How many thousands had the Draduns collected?

After the bug attack on Earth, Ant had done a bit of research and found it was easy to obtain a hundred spiderlings from a single sac. A queen wasp could manage a hundred in a day. A queen ant, on the other hand, could lay thousands.

A dragonfly's clutch might hatch into fifteen hundred aquatic nymphs with voracious appetites, although they'd spend years underwater before ever spreading their wings and flying. Had the Draduns collected up that many adults? Or had they been breeding them? If so, that suggested they'd planned this for a long time.

Or maybe they'd raided an insect zoo.

Despite his recently morbid fascination for bugs, and his ironically insectoid name, Ant would be glad never to see another for as long as he lived.

A Mox appeared in a doorway. "This way! Quickly!" This one was female. Her voice gave it away far more than her appearance.

"Thanks, but we're good," Liam called to her as they passed. "Get inside and hide under your beds."

Lame advice, Ant thought. Yet the bunks had probably saved their lives.

The Mox lady looked flustered as she backed into her home. "The day of reckoning is upon us. The Ragnarons have brought death to our doors. We will not survive this night." With that, she slammed the door shut.

The fringes of the forest stood just beyond her home. There were no more structures this far out; this was the end of the line. The mud gave way to grass and bushes, and it felt good to run across the lush, springy meadow following numerous streaks of yellow light.

This is a like a weird dream, Ant thought. *We've found the end of a rainbow, and there's going to be a pot of gold, or a unicorn, or something.*

The narrow ribbons of Nyx energy converged in one particular spot—a seemingly random spot just short of the first line of trees bordering the forest. Each glowing streak wriggled and swam through the air and plunged into a tiny stationary orb that flashed and pulsed with vibrant life. No larger than a soccer ball, and hovering a few feet above the grass, it rotated like a miniature sun at the center of the solar system, pummeled by fiery comets from afar.

Ant and his friends approached cautiously. The ribbons of light kept coming, but less frequently now. One streaked by inches from Ant's arm, and he felt a prickle of energy that caused goosebumps.

"The wormhole wand," he said to Liam.

Liam extracted it from his zipper pocket and held it up with a shaky hand. The three of them moved closer. Ant could feel a tingling sensation all over his skin.

"This isn't gonna work," Liam murmured. "I'm telling you, the Nyx won't repair this thing until we've saved the

Mox and defeated the Draduns. But we *haven't* saved the Mox, and we *can't* defeat the Draduns while we're stuck here. We're useless."

He held the wand out anyway, pointing it at the fiery ball.

More glowing ribbons streaked into the orb, causing it to flash and pulse.

"Please," Liam said. "We can't do anything here. We're not superheroes. We're just kids. We want to go home."

The orb brightened so much that Ant had to squint. When it returned to its former pulsing state, Madison nudged Liam and said, "See that? It heard you." She addressed the orb herself. "We want to go *home*."

Again, the orb brightened.

"It wants to go home, too," Madison said softly.

"Well, why doesn't it just go, then?" Ant demanded, suddenly annoyed. He raised his voice. "Why don't you go home? You can easily escape from that briefcase. You reached all the way around the Earth to suck the energy out of those test bugs, so why don't you do the same here?" He jabbed a finger at the cloudstation. "You're right there! Just reach down and take your energy back! You can kill those bugs in seconds, and you can save the Mox—and then you can fix our wormhole wand, and we can come get you, and you can program the wand to take us to the Nyx system, and we can release you back into space—if you really need us to help you with that."

He flung his arms out to his sides and started pacing.

"Seriously, the Nyx doesn't need us at all. It can fix *everything* without us. It doesn't need to be here, and it could wipe out those giant bugs in a heartbeat. I'm sick of this!"

Snatching the wormhole wand from Liam's outstretched hand, he thrust it forward himself, only much closer to the orb, so close that yellow energy crackled around the end of the device.

"Give us our wormhole wand back!" Ant yelled.

Without warning, the orb expanded and engulfed the wand along with his hand, and as he jerked backward in surprise, it flowed all the way up his arm.

"Ant!" Madison cried.

He opened his mouth to say something—and everything went black.

Chapter 33

Ant blinked and rubbed his eyes, then wished he hadn't. Somehow, he'd been yanked into a wormhole and dumped into deep space, and now he was floating in a vacuum. He clamped his eyes shut again and struggled to remember what he knew about spacewalking without a spacesuit. *I have fifteen seconds max . . . and that's only if I expel all the air from my lungs first . . .*

He breathed out and waited, shaking all over. But what was the point? He had no suit to climb into, and nobody to rescue him.

This is it. I'm dead.

But nothing happened. He just floated there, unharmed.

He opened his eyes, realizing he wasn't ice cold and could breathe just fine. "Where am I?"

His voice echoed, which didn't seem right. He shouldn't have a voice at all. How was he even alive?

"About time you showed up," a familiar voice grunted.

Ant jerked his head around to find a rock dwarf staring back. "Jaxrill!"

A rock dwarf. Floating in space with him.

"How is this— What's going on? Where are we?"

"We're echoes," Jaxrill said. "Well, *you* are. I'm just in your mind. An echo of an echo. This is your head, your body. Your spirit, if you want to think of it that way."

"Huh?"

"You know all this already, but you're having trouble processing the information, so I'm here to help you along. Sometimes the mind does that. It splits in two, gives you someone to reason with, to interpret things."

"I don't understand."

"Of course you don't."

Jaxrill sighed. He folded his arms and continued to float there in deep space, with stars all around.

Ant tried to move. He could wiggle his feet and flex his fingers, but he felt like he was deep underwater. Yet when he spoke, his voice was clear.

"Where are we?" he demanded.

Jaxrill paused before speaking. "For the moment, we are one. You and I, Anthony Carmichael of Earth, are at a crossroads. You have a choice to make."

Ant stared with suspicion at the rock dwarf. "You don't sound like Jaxrill. And I doubt I'd be that sinister if I were talking to myself."

"Ah, very astute. I could wear a different face if you prefer . . . ?"

"How about your own face? Who *are* you?"

"The spirit of the skies. The mind between moons. The great intelligence of the stars."

Ant frowned. The last thing he remembered was sticking his hand out toward the glowing orb and being engulfed by its aura. His mouth fell open. "You're the Nyx!"

With a heavy sigh, Jaxrill nodded. "That, too."

"So . . . we can finally talk to each other! Can you help us? All we want to do is go home. If you could just fix—"

Jaxrill shook his head and rolled his eyes. "And what do I get out of this bargain?"

"Barg— What? Are you serious?"

The rock dwarf's eyes glowed in a manner that suggested he was anything but a rock dwarf. For a moment, Ant was reminded of a Dradun. Their eyes glowed occasionally, too.

"Tell me, young Anthony, what exactly do you want? To go home? Is that all? What about the chaos around you? Do you care what happens to the Mox?"

"Well, sure, but there's nothing we can do about it. Not from down here, anyway. In the forest, I mean. Maybe if we were back up on the cloudstation . . ."

"What if you could change history?"

Ant sensed the Nyx was about to make a rather large point in a roundabout way. He played along—for now. "That would be awesome."

"What would you do? Close your eyes and think about it."

He did as he was asked. After a moment's thought, he settled on one simple change that would make everything better. To his surprise, when he opened his eyes, the deep space all around was blurring. He tried not to freak out. None of this was real. As far as he knew, he was still in the forest clearing with his friends, either standing there with his arm outstretched while the Nyx encompassed him, or lying in a heap on the grass. This was nothing but an extremely detailed vision.

"The Mox have risen from the dead," Jaxrill said, offering a little recap of the scene opening up before them. "They have begun teleporting, and have attacked a settlement on Kraxis 9. Krun and his henchmen are taking action. Action that they and possibly their superiors believe is necessary but will never be sanctioned. They must act quickly, but in secrecy."

Ant almost yelled out as he materialized in a snowy landscape under a dusky sky. He floated a few feet above the ground, and before him stood three figures.

"That's . . . that's *us*."

He saw himself, Liam, and Madison facing the bunker. A camera was trained on them, its red light blinking. Madison pointed down at the open briefcase and shouted in an oddly faraway voice.

"We want to trade! This case of . . . of magical energy has to be worth something. It's yours if you let us in." After a quick nudge from Liam, she added, "Oh yeah, and we have a wormhole wand—I mean a device—whatever it's called. But there's something wrong with it. If you let us in and help us, you can have this briefcase. It's a fair trade, right?"

Fascinated, Ant watched the events unfold exactly as he remembered. The Nyx energy shot out, disabling the camera and indeed the entire bunker. After a while, Steeg emerged and allowed them entry.

Ant felt a pang of sorrow for the rock dwarf. For Jaxrill, too. For all of them. They'd all died in that bunker.

Anger stirred. "If you hadn't taken out the power," he said to the Nyx, "none of this would have happened."

Jaxrill floated into view. "Is that so?"

Behind him, the scene had switched to chaos within the bunker—rock dwarves filing along corridors, a steel door being slammed shut, the undead Mox pounding on the metal . . . His view was a little more omniscient than he'd experienced in real life. As an echo, he could move freely from one side of the door to the other.

"You could have restored power anytime," Ant growled. "If there had been power, Jaxrill—the *real* Jaxrill—could have used stasis grenades. He and Steeg wouldn't have died, and everyone else would be alive as well."

"So change it."

Ant ground his teeth together and concentrated. With very little effort, he rewound the scene to the beginning.

Outside the bunker once more, he stood with his friends in the snow. Madison had the briefcase open at her feet and was talking to the camera on top of the pole. As before, the Nyx energy began to flow from the briefcase.

Feeling like a ghost trying to manipulate the living, Ant floated closer and reached for the briefcase. "No!"

The Nyx tendril quivered, recoiled, and snaked back inside the case.

"Well, that was easy," Ant muttered. "But this is just a dream."

Dream or otherwise, the red light on the camera remained on. And after a while, Steeg emerged anyway. The dwarf scowled, then huffed and gestured. "Inside."

Again the scene changed. The lights were on inside the bunker, and the frozen corpses remained in the snow, unmoving. Everything was fine.

"This is much better!" Ant exclaimed. "So in this alternate version, everyone in the bunker is okay?"

Jaxrill spoke softly. "It's not real—but yes, you changed things. Go forward and see my prediction of how things worked out."

Ant gently urged himself forward through time, watching as he and his real-life friends traipsed around after first Steeg then Jaxrill, exploring the bunker with the lights fully on, and with the Mox test subject firmly in stasis. All was calm. No attack from outside, no need for Steeg to rush to the entrance and die, no steel doors busted open, no massacre in the corridors or in the rooms at the far end of the bunker. No wormholes, no nothing, just a calm, peaceful tour of the facility.

"This is way better," Ant said. "And all I did was stop you from taking out the power."

"Small changes can be powerful," Jaxrill murmured. "Keep going forward."

Ant's interest increased. "This is all so . . . uneventful. Look, Jaxrill is programming the wormhole wand for Liam. Is that so we can go home?"

The wormhole opened in the usual way. Ant, Liam, and Madison—all smiling and waving at the throng of rock dwarves seeing them off—leapt into the swirling tunnel. Ant felt a strange tugging and allowed his echo self to follow.

The real-life friends arrived in Ant's bedroom, safe and sound. Mission accomplished!

Right?

Ant shrugged. "So? Look, this version of history is way better than the other, but I know it's not real. What's the point of this?"

"I think you know. What do you suppose happens next as a result of your small change?"

With a sigh, Ant played it through in his mind. A completely uneventful time in the bunker, with no attack from the undead Mox, meant . . . what? He focussed on the scene and sped forward. Seeing himself at school, he scowled and forced a location change.

Several weeks had passed in the bunker. Jaxrill, Steeg, and the other scientists were hard at work on a cure for the Mox, a way to keep them properly dead instead of returning as teleporting murderers. For a moment, Ant was confused as to why the rock dwarves were still working on this problem when the Rabeium 234 cloudstation had already been identified as the source. Then he realized. Without the Nyx stealing the power, and without the attack from the undead, Ant and his friends never would have made the connection to the red tag around one of the corpse's wrists. In turn, the rock dwarves never would have pinpointed Rabeium 234 as the source.

"So what does *that* mean?" Ant muttered, looking closer.

Madison had left the Nyx briefcase with the rock dwarves. This meant the Draduns didn't have it, and therefore the bug attack could not occur. That was good, right?

Yet the undead corpse problem continued.

Ant changed the scene.

The Shuntaar settlement, deep in the forests of Dradus Mox, was in turmoil. Mox screamed in terror as their own people—decomposed and gaunt, yet impossibly strong and relentless—shuffled about claiming victim after victim, turning them to dust. And when there were none left around them, they teleported a short distance, materializing in the middle of a crowd and reaching out with their death touches.

Ant fast-forwarded. The attacks weren't restricted to the forests. The undead Mox started teleporting into the

Dradun cities, and then to Kraxis 9. A few shuffling corpses were one thing, but a legion of them leaping from place to place at will was terrifying. The epidemic spread, an ever-growing army of undead, almost unstoppable warriors showing up in unexpected places and taking lives in the blink of an eye. Nothing but stasis fields halted their advance—and stasis fields were temporary.

As Ant watched in growing horror, Draduns began to rise from the dead also. The disease had hopped species. The massacre continued unabated until, finally, a massive region of Dradus Mox was hit with a hundred warheads from the gigantic planet of Kraxis. The epidemic had to be halted, and this was the only way . . .

Ant shut off the vision and floated in darkness for a while.

"So," he said eventually, "if I'd stopped you from switching out the lights in the bunker, a quarter of Dradus Mox would end up getting nuked?"

Jaxrill spread his hands and shrugged. "Ripples in a pond. So, you see, Krun and his henchmen are saving the world by wiping out the Mox today."

Ant shook his head in disgust. "Says you. I can't believe there's no other way. How about tackling the disease itself? If you're the great intelligence of the stars, figure out a way to *cure* the Mox instead of letting them be annihilated."

Jaxrill smiled. "And there it is."

"There *what* is?"

"The point I had to make. That no matter how things had transpired in the bunker on Kraxis 9, the result would have been tragic. Whether it's five billion Dradun and Mox lives across a quarter of the planet, or a mere seventy-two thousand Mox lives in the forests, both outcomes are unspeakably awful."

"Right," Ant agreed, confused. He had a nagging feeling he wouldn't like where the Nyx was going with this. "So . . . what's the answer?"

"The answer, as you said, is to tackle the disease itself. Or at least stop the undead from teleporting. A few shuffling corpses can be contained, agreed? That's something I can help with."

Ant waited.

Jaxrill floated closer. The look on his face was deadly serious.

"I needed you to understand the stakes. I had to let you stand on the brink of destruction. And here we are. Now it's all down to you, Anthony Carmichael."

"Me? Me how? Why?"

"Why? Because you brought this on us, my boy."

"M-me? What . . . ?"

"You and your friends. Especially Liam Mackenzie."

Jaxrill's face fuzzed out. His short, stout body grew taller and slimmer, much taller than Ant, and his face slowly began to reform—only this time into someone different.

Someone familiar.

Ant let out a strangled gasp.

"Ah, now you see me," the figure said with a chuckle. "Now you know who is wreaking this havoc on your behalf."

The creepy, detached, doughy face appeared to have been slapped onto a smooth, robot skull. Under the flowing black cloak, the gangly body resembled a mechanical skeleton. Black tubes wove in and out of artificial bones like eels feasting on rotting flesh . . .

Ant found his voice at last. "Y-you *can't* be the Ark Lord! He's *dead*."

"I'm no more dead than you, Anthony Carmichael of Earth."

With a wave of a hand, the scene reverted back to the vacuum of deep space. This time, what looked like ethereal manta rays eased through the darkness, ghostly yellow light streaming behind. There had to be at least fifty of them.

The Ark Lord—or was it the Nyx?—spoke softly.

"The Nyx and I are the same. We have become one. I've toyed with you from the beginning—from the moment Krun and his henchmen captured me from the Nyx system."

"B-but—*captured* you? You were dead! What do you mean? You're not a Nyx—I mean, you *weren't* a Nyx—"

"What, do you think nobody ever survives in a vacuum?"

An impossibly long, thin, glasslike tube streaked through deep space, passing close to the school of glowing manta rays. All at once, the creatures turned to study the anomaly.

"What's that?" Ant whispered, fascinated despite himself. He knew it was just a vision, but he also knew it was accurate, one of the Ark Lord's memories.

The tube flickered and broke apart, and Ant recognized it as a wormhole. Like a trail of gasoline-soaked tissue paper, its entire length burnt up in a single hot flash, leaving spots of light floating in space . . . along with three people. Two wore spacesuits. No, they *were* the spacesuits. Liam and Sandrina, whose nanobot blood had given them temporary robot bodies, were at this point reverting to their natural forms.

And with them floated the Ark Lord.

"I was always more machine than flesh," the skeletal figure said from behind Ant. "I remained alive longer than most. And of all the places in deep space to dump me, Liam accidentally chose the Nyx system."

As he spoke, the phantom mantas eased closer. One reached out with several tendrils of light, circling the three motionless figures. Abruptly, Liam and Sandrina vanished.

"The Nyx saved him and that female from Glochania. Oh yes!—returned them to my Ark on the basis they had a future ahead of them. They gleaned this information in an instant, and they sent them back. But me? No, they wouldn't extend me the same courtesy. Instead, they absorbed my life force into their own and left my body floating. I ended up as one of them, nothing but a mind hitching a ride with a ghost."

Ant couldn't believe his ears. "You *became* a Nyx?"

"But they couldn't silence me!" the Ark Lord said with a laugh. "In the end, they enjoyed my conversation. And I learned from them. Once, my host teleported into a dying spacecraft and sniffed about the place, finding several dead crew and one remaining survivor of a ship malfunction. He expired shortly after, and my host absorbed his life force before it could dissipate. That pilot was weak. I heard his confusion, his desperate pleas for help, but the Nyx overcame him in moments." The Ark Lord drew himself up. "Not me, though. I am *strong*, and I became a companion to the Nyx, traveling with her, watching, learning . . ."

"Her?"

The Ark Lord chuckled. "I like to think so, yes. Now, *watch*."

Ant twisted around to see a sleek spacecraft approaching. It looked like a flattened speed boat, dull-grey in color. It cruised among the Nyx and slowed, a needle-thin beam of white light projecting from an aperture in its side. The beam jerked this way and that as if trying to aim, and the Nyx swam around it like curious sea creatures sniffing at bait.

"A crude tractor beam," the Ark Lord said. "Naturally, I insisted on being captured."

As he spoke, the beam played across one particular glowing Nyx and intensified, dragging it in.

"These idiots from the nearby Zutrillon system put my host and I in a durrelium-lined *briefcase*, of all things. My host wasn't impressed, but I urged her to stay put. Watch and learn, I told her."

Ant sighed. "I *knew* the Nyx could get out whenever it wanted . . ."

"And you know what happened next, young Anthony. With the Mox rising from the dead, Krun grew anxious and pleaded with the Dradun elders to take action. What if this disease, this curse, spread to other species?"

Vague visions played out, with Krun's golden armor shining as he entered a magnificent palace and stood before a semicircle of aloof Draduns, their regal garments and weird snakelike headpieces suggesting they were the ultimate authority on the moon.

"Krun outlined a plan—one that used the insects of the forest infused with Nyx energy, an attack that could be blamed squarely on the Mox's irresponsible dabbling in the dark arts . . ."

Now you sound like Krun.

"All Krun needed was a place to test out the infused creatures. A Class D planet, perhaps. That certainly got my attention! But the elders held back, not ready to intercede. They suggested Krun and his colleagues continue their good work on the cloudstation for now."

In the vision, the elders shook their heads at him, and Krun swung around and stomped away in anger.

"Krun was furious. But, rather annoyingly, he obeyed. He resumed his work trying to find a medical cure for an entirely magical curse. The height of futility! However, I saw an opportunity. He just needed an extra push."

Ant clenched his fists. "I don't want to know."

The Ark Lord patted him on the shoulder, and Ant flinched. "Of course you do. It was at this point I decided to assert my presence. I, uh, borrowed some of my host's energy and slipped into one of the patients. When that patient awoke from stasis, I teleported to Kraxis 9. Or rather, the Mox did. It's hard to tell sometimes whether I'm here or there. Being a Nyx is liberating."

"You did that," Ant said in a monotone. It wasn't a question. Nothing about this story surprised him anymore.

"I sent others to Kraxis 9 shortly after—a horde of undead empowered by Nyx energy. I didn't want them dispatched with ease, so I made them stronger—and hungry for energy. Suddenly, the undead Mox were far more of a threat than before. They went after a local community, killing everyone in sight. You see, I needed

Krun to understand how deadly this so-called disease could be. He wasn't to know his own Nyx energy had enhanced the very patients he'd been tasked to cure.

"To my delight, he decided enough was enough. He set out to exterminate the Mox with armies of oversized insects. To test his weapon, he targeted a Class D planet in a faraway system. Of course, the planet he chose wasn't Earth. Not originally. I made sure to rectify that. This was the opportunity I foresaw."

Echoing laughter reminded Ant he was in the presence of an evil supervillain. "*You* brought Krun to Earth?"

"Absolutely! The Draduns had giant killer insects! Why would I *not* point them straight toward your little town on Earth? Krun didn't seem to care. It wasn't Bur'Ghum 4 as they'd expected, but it was still a Class D planet."

Ant said nothing for a moment, preferring to seethe quietly rather than let the madman see his reaction. He couldn't hold his tongue for long, though. He puffed up and said, "If you expected to kill us with bugs, you failed."

"Oh, that was just a precursor. Something to get you *here*. And it worked; to the cloudstation you came, just as I'd hoped." The Ark Lord couldn't help chuckling again. "I obliged you and dealt with the giant bugs. Just a little reward for working so hard. Aren't I kind? And when you thought you would all try to hop home afterward, it took the most *casual* adjustment to send you to Kraxis 9 instead, where you met my puppets standing around in the snow. Phase Two."

We carried the Ark Lord around everywhere, Ant thought miserably. *All that time, thinking it was some kind of intelligent, caring entity that wanted to help the Mox . . . and it was the Ark Lord toying with us.*

"And here we are, in Phase Three," the Ark Lord said with a self-satisfied sigh. "I've had fun nudging you here and there, but soon I will leave all this tomfoolery behind and go on my merry way. And for that I need your help, young Anthony." He leaned forward, his fake rock dwarf eyes gleaming. "Would you like to help? Would you like to save the world and your friends?"

"Do I have a choice?"

"Of course! But . . . well, no, not really." He smiled. "Perhaps you'd like to see another vision, this one not so much a prediction as . . . a *warning.*"

Ant reeled backward as the scene abruptly changed again. He felt giddy, floating high above a gigantic house in the middle of an expanse of land covering many thousands of acres. *My home*, he thought with a chill. "Why are we—?"

He didn't get to finish, because all at once a colossal laser bolt from space blasted the house to smithereens, sending chunks of the structure in all directions and leaving an enormous crater. A black cloud mushroomed up, turning the sky dark and staining the hills grey.

"My mom and dad!"

But the nightmare didn't end there. The scene fuzzed and switched to Liam's and Madison's houses. Fast-forwarded action took place as though the Ark Lord were bored and wanted it over with. Ant glimpsed a small spacecraft landing. Hovering droids streamed out. They attacked the houses hard and fast—laser blasts, screams, smoke—it all happened in a few blinks of the eye, and Ant wrenched his gaze away.

The Ark Lord chuckled. "I'm not finished. Watch."

Appalled and frightened, Ant squinted as the droids emerged from the ruins dragging Liam and Madison kicking and screaming into the small spacecraft . . .

Once more the scene changed, and this time their faces swam all around him, twisted in agony, their shrieks deafening. Dizzying images flashed before Ant's eyes, and he spun away from the gruesome sight of limbs being plucked from their bodies—

"Enough!" he yelled.

The scene dissipated, drifting away like fog.

"I cannot kill your friends," the Ark Lord said in a soft voice, "but I can torture them. And your parents are easy pickings." He sighed. "I am, however, a man of my word. None of what you saw will occur . . . if you do what must be done."

"Is this all because Liam left you in space to die?" Ant whispered.

"That's part of the reason. But not the *whole* reason. Now, do you agree?"

Ant said nothing.

The Ark Lord shrugged. "I will show you what needs to happen. And then you will decide."

Chapter 34

Ant jerked awake.

This time he stared up at a partly cloudy sky where Rabeium 234 was still spilling swarms of bugs into the air. Liam and Madison leaned over him, and he realized they were shaking him vigorously and yelling.

"Wake up! Ant!"

"Are you okay, buddy?"

He sat up. The yellow Nyx orb was gone.

Seeing how he stared at the empty spot, Liam gestured and said, "It whizzed off to the cloudstation to join up with the rest."

Ant climbed slowly to his feet. His voice felt dry as he spoke. "Don't worry about the Nyx. It'll take care of the bugs when it's ready."

Liam blinked at him. "Huh?"

"Like it did when Krun was sending them to Earth." He looked at Madison. "Remember when you opened the case, and the Nyx reached out and snatched its energy back? The bugs dried up and rolled over, dead. That'll happen again soon—to *all* the bugs. But only when the Nyx is ready. When the bigger problem is taken care of."

Madison grabbed his arm. "*Bigger* problem? What are you talking about?"

Ant looked back toward the Shuntaar settlement. So many homes destroyed . . . But it wasn't too late. "We have to hurry. The Mox are holding out in an underground chamber. That's where most of them were headed. Every clan has one, a kind of safehouse in case the Draduns ever attacked."

Liam's eyes widened. "Wait, what? The Nyx told you this? So the Mox are safe?"

"For now. The bugs will get in eventually, though. We have to hurry."

Madison retained her grip on his arm. She peered at him closely, and he took a moment to gaze into her beautiful green eyes. He might not get the chance again. "Hurry for what? What are we doing? What else did the Nyx tell you?"

Ant gently disengaged. "Let's go find us an undead Mox."

He marched off, his heart thumping and nerves jangling, torn with uncertainty. He doubted he could go through with this, but for now he'd play it out as the Nyx had shown him. Maybe another solution would reveal itself.

"What happened?" Liam demanded.

"I don't want to talk about it."

Madison gripped his arm again. "Ant, come on. What did the Nyx do to you? Did it speak to you? What did it say?"

He gently shook her off. "These walking corpses are bad, but they can be dealt with if they're all in one place, shuffling about in the forest, easy to knock down like they were when they started out. If they keep leaping to other planets, though, being super-strong and turning people to dust . . . then things will get *really* bad around here. We have to stop them from teleporting and take away their power."

"And how are we supposed to do that?"

Ant didn't answer. He hurried across the grass, re-entering the muddy lanes between stone cottages, retracing his footsteps from earlier. Not too far ahead, the black swarm cloud had dropped to ground level, smothering the buildings. He could see individual dragonflies and wasps buzzing about, and many more squatting on rooftops and piles of rubble, while armies of green beetles and ants clambered over everything. The spiders and scorpions were the biggest, and they reared up in random places, snatching whatever prey they could from the swarm.

"Don't work with spiders next time, Krun," Ant muttered. "They're not helping your cause."

He heard a crashing, splintering sound and knew another roof had collapsed. How long before these critters found their way into the underground chamber?

"There's one," Liam said, nudging Ant.

They stopped and watched from a safe distance. An undead corpse shuffled through the rubble of a house, his arms dangling as he leaned forward to peer under fallen rafters.

"That'll do," Ant said.

"For *what*, Ant?" Madison shouted as she gripped his arm for the third time. "So help me, I'm gonna throw you to the ground and stand on your neck if you don't tell us what we're doing."

He couldn't help smiling at her irritation. She probably *would* do that, too.

Behind her, the undead corpse suddenly spotted them and let out a moan loud enough to be heard over the distant racket. It awkwardly climbed over the nearest low wall and began a slow shuffle toward them.

Ant guessed he had less than a minute to explain. He took a deep breath, then let it out in a rush. "It was the Ark Lord. He's not dead. At least, not completely. He's out for revenge." He avoided Liam's gaze, looking instead at the ground. "Someone royally ticked him off."

It seemed both Madison and Liam stared at him hard enough to burn holes in his skin. Ant rubbed his face, feeling suddenly tired. Not just physically, but mentally, too.

"The Ark Lord is out to get us. He's the Nyx. The Draduns accidentally rescued him from space." He shot Liam a glance. "Where you left him."

Liam sputtered like a goldfish, but no words came out.

Ant checked on the approaching corpse and knew he'd better speed up a bit. "Of all deep space to dump the Ark Lord to die, you happened to pick the Nyx system. Not your fault, but . . . well, a Nyx absorbed his essence, or his spirit, or whatever. And that would have been the end of it, except the Nyx liked talking to the Ark Lord and kept him around." He sighed. "And then a Dradun spaceship came along and netted a Nyx wraith. Guess which one? The Ark Lord made sure it was *him*. And so he ended up on the cloudstation, in Krun's briefcase."

Madison had her hand over her mouth like she was going to be sick. "Our Nyx was the Ark Lord?"

Ant nodded. "Up until then, the undead Mox were just like normal zombies, but not as bity. You could knock 'em down without a problem. They couldn't turn you into dust, and they couldn't teleport. It was the Ark Lord who made *that* happen."

"What do you mean?"

As quickly as he could, Ant explained how the Ark Lord had given one of the comatose patients a special gift and created a mutation. Soon, all the undead Mox were teleporting, knocking down doors, and turning people to dust. Then Krun got started on his diabolical giant bug scheme. "The Ark Lord pretty much held our hand the whole time, nudging us to do this and that so we ended up here. Pretty brilliant, really."

And all to get back at you, buddy.

"What's brilliant about it?" Liam muttered, visibly shaken and whitefaced.

Ant didn't want to be mad at him. He took a deep breath before letting loose with some cutting remark he might regret. "Nothing. It's just that he blames *you*. You and your robot friends. He sent you on a mission to capture a Gorvian time grub, and you all betrayed him— and then you and lizard-girl—"

"Sandrina," Madison said somewhat icily.

"—dumped the Ark Lord into space."

"I had to!"

"I know, I know." Ant forced a smile. "It's okay, I get it. You had to. But anyway, the last thing the Ark Lord saw before he died was your ugly mug—or your robot one, anyway—and when he cheated death and ended up with a chance to make you pay, well . . ." He shrugged.

The shuffling corpse was close now, just twenty paces away. Ant had a few more things to say, though, so he gestured for them to move to a safer distance.

He wasn't ready to go just yet.

Madison shook her head and closed her eyes. "You're saying the Ark Lord caused the walking dead to teleport?"

"With the Nyx's help, yes."

"The Ark Lord survived," Liam whispered, staring off. "I can't believe it."

"The Ark Lord's more machine than anything. He's cheated death all his life." Ant narrowed his eyes. "So have you. *Both* of you, most likely. You two have a future; Liam's seen it. That means you can't die. If you threw yourself into the jaws of one of those dragonflies, you'd escape somehow." He looked at Liam. "What was it you said when you miraculously escaped from dying in space?"

"The universe wasn't through with me yet," Liam mumbled.

Ant rubbed his hands together. They were strangely cold. Was Death standing nearby, silently waiting?

Liam wasn't done asking questions. "Why do the undead kill?"

"For energy. Any kind of life will do. Like here, today—the teleporting corpses have come to join in the fun and festivities of the bug battle." Though his friends failed to smile, he couldn't help piling on the flippancy. "Krun put a tiny bit of energy into every bug. Everytime the undead kill one, the Ark Lord gets that energy back *and* absorbs the bug's supersized life force while he's at it. Mox, rock dwarves, humans, even bugs—it's all the same, a bit like filling up on gas. With the bugs, he gets back more than he put in. And all those Mox together underground . . . it'll be like a banquet. It all adds to the Nyx, strengthens it. Or in this case, strengthens the Ark Lord so he can live again."

"Oh, Ant," Madison whispered.

"So here we are," Ant said with a gesture toward the approaching corpse. Its moaning had intensified. "This is what it comes down to."

"Where *what* comes down to? What are you talking about?"

"The only way out."

Liam thrust his hands forward and gripped Ant by the shirt. "Ant, what are you talking about? Stop talking in riddles!"

Ant said nothing until Liam slowly released his grip. But then Madison put her hands on his shoulders and turned him toward her, asking the exact same question as Liam but in a softer voice.

"All this will end in a minute," he told her, grateful for one last close-up gaze. Liam would be a lucky man one day. "Just do me a favor. Tell . . . Tell my mom and dad I love them."

Her eyes widened further and immediately filled with tears. They broke free and ran down her cheeks. "Ant, what— No. Stop this. Whatever you're planning—"

"Either I do this," Ant said, trembling, "or he comes after us all, including our homes and our parents. He won't stop. It's just best if I go with him."

Madison's grip tightened. "Go *with* him? Go with him how?"

"I need to . . . to leave my body behind."

He couldn't bear the gasps his friends let out.

Meanwhile, the moaning, groaning, and shuffling was closing in again. They could easily outrun the corpse, but what was the point? Besides, time was pressing. The swarm of bugs would be finding their way underground shortly. And there were dozens of other clans across the forest, too.

He gently pulled Madison's hands off his shoulders. Though he was in a cold sweat, somehow his resolve was strong. Plus, it wasn't the end for him. Not yet, anyway.

"Guys, it's been fun. Please don't worry about me. And Liam, buddy . . ."

He studied his best friend's face, wishing now that he'd tried harder to hide every ounce of bitterness. If Liam went through life blaming himself for this, the Ark Lord would have won. But saying 'Liam, none of this is your fault' would sound exactly like the opposite was true.

Instead, he whispered, "Liam, come look for me in the Ghost Realm."

Abruptly, unable to face them any longer, and afraid his resolve would break, he pulled away and ran toward the shuffling corpse.

As his friends screamed at him to stop, and the undead Mox raised his hands to welcome his death, he couldn't help letting out a sob, which angered him.

Some hero I am.

Chapter 35

He didn't feel anything when his body crumbled to dust.

In fact, he thought for a second nothing at all had happened. But when he got himself turned around and refocussed, he looked down at his own clothes lying in a pile amid a sorry smattering of grey dust. He wished his underpants were a little better hidden. He hated for Madison to see that.

His friends were yelling and screaming. He looked up at them and realized his hands were stretched out ahead. Not *his* hands, though. The hands of the undead corpse whose head he now occupied.

The compulsion to keep shuffling forward and take the life energy from his friends was strong, but not *that* strong. He imagined it would be harder to resist after a day or two stuck in a rotting corpse like this. Still, as much as he willed himself to turn away, his new body wouldn't cooperate. It remained there, poised, hands outstretched.

This wasn't the deal, he yelled—completely in his head. *You said you'd let them go and end this!*

If he'd simply trusted the word of the Ark Lord, he never would have done this. He'd seen with his own eyes what would happen if he did not, and he believed it. Of course, the vision was just that—a vision. It could easily be another Ark Lord lie.

But Ant reasoned the *only* way forward was to take that chance. The Ark Lord wanted Liam to live out the rest of his life in guilt and misery, and Ant felt that was better than some of the awful things offered as an alternative. As if letting billions of Draduns die wasn't enough, the Ark Lord would have taken the three of them away for imprisonment, torturing them and worse. Ant probably would have ended up dead after all—murdered in front of his friends just to spite them.

Liam and Madison couldn't die, but they could still suffer. If they were to get home in one piece, Ant had to sacrifice himself. This was the Ark Lord's ultimatum.

But with that sacrifice came a tiny glimmer of hope, something called the Ghost Realm. "A not entirely unpleasant place," the Ark Lord called it.

He tried again to turn away from his grief-stricken friends who had fallen to their knees in dangerously close proximity. His undead host remained frozen.

You couldn't turn them to dust if you tried, Ant said to the Ark Lord through gritted teeth—or imaginary teeth, anyway. *They're invincible! So turn this rotting Mox around and do what you said you'd do.*

He thought he heard a distant, echoing chuckle. To his surprise, his Mox host body lurched backward, turned, and set off toward the mass of giant bugs.

Yeah, that's right, let's end this. The Mox go home, my friends go home, you go home—everybody goes home. No more teleporting, no more turning people to dust. The Mox get to clean up their own mess and reverse the dark magic or whatever nasty spell they cast.

Again, that distant chuckling.

He imagined stalking into the crowd of monster critters and touching each and every one, turning them to dust and releasing the Nyx's yellow energy. Would he also absorb the bug's life force, or did that go straight to the Nyx as well? He shuddered.

As he drew near, flashes of light above caught his attention. He saw numerous ghostly tendrils shooting through the air and latching onto flying insects. The monsters started dropping out of the sky—huge wasps twisting and falling, and dragonflies dive-bombing the ground and smashing down. All of them left behind faint yellow auras.

The same phantom streaks shot down to the ground, causing massive beetles to act like they were gagging on something. As the Nyx energy left, they dried up and caved in, all their essence gone, their shells withering into semi-transparent husks as though they'd just shucked off their skin.

Enormous spiders and scorpions turned on their backs and spasmed wildly. Ants the size of sports cars reared up and toppled over backwards, falling against each other before expiring.

"Ah," the Ark Lord whispered. "So much energy. Enough for what I need."

With hundreds of supersized dead bugs rolling about and wriggling, walls toppled and roofs fell, and the dust cloud made it difficult to see much of anything. Ant still remembered the vast mess left by the warp giant on Glochania. The mess on Dradus Mox was probably worse—especially with multiple swarms across the forest and wastelands.

Out of the dust came the undead Mox, shuffling aimlessly. Ant found he had a little control over his limbs now, though he had nowhere to go. The hunger he felt for new life, a source of energy, was as strong as ever, and he wondered where the Mox's underground chamber was located. He started scouring the rubble, hoping to find a trapdoor or maybe a raised entrance with steps leading down . . .

He and his fellow corpses stumbled around for a while, searching. There had to be twenty of them now, all converging on one spot. He imagined others across the forest, using whatever brain cells and memories they had left to seek out the hidden chambers. Ant found it took an awful lot of willpower just to make his legs stop moving. Whatever drove these dead creatures had far more strength than he could muster on his own. He was nothing but a puppet.

And the Ark Lord was pulling the strings.

His hapless comrades found the entrance to the chamber. It resided inside a cottage, which had collapsed, leaving a single stone column in the center. It had a door set into it, and the undead crowded closer and started pounding on it.

Ant joined in. Being one of the first there, he found himself at the front of the mob, hitting the door as hard as the next corpse. He couldn't help it. If he tried hard enough, he could halt his fist from smashing against the sturdy wood, but only for a moment. Then he resumed, and the power behind his fist startled him.

He imagined a sledgehammer buried deep inside his arm. He pulled back and slammed it down, and the wood splintered and cracked like it was a thin, delicate layer of veneer. It took all of ten seconds for the mob to rip the door to shreds, and then they pushed through onto the staircase leading down into darkness.

Ant was probably third or fourth in line. He felt others pushing him from behind, and he shoved at the ones in front. There was a strong danger of tripping, but how much would that hurt a corpse? He stumbled and staggered his way down the steps, jostling with his comrades, seeing a faint glow of light below.

Stop this, he growled in his head. *Ark Lord, keep your end of the bargain. You wanted to see Liam get home safely so he could live out his life blaming himself for my disappearance. Well, you won.*

He considered again what kind of fate would have befallen his friends if he hadn't given himself to the Ark Lord like this. The evil villain had the power to annihilate their houses from space, or perhaps drop monsters on them if he wanted a chuckle. He could shut them away in one of the cells on his Ark. He could do anything, and they'd never be rid of him. In the meantime, he'd have let this onslaught continue, allowing billions of Draduns and Mox to die.

Ant thought about his parents. The idea of them being pulled into any kind of orchestrated alien invasion or sinister UFO abduction—all because he and his friends tinkered with wormhole wands and nosed around where they shouldn't—left him cold with terror. They didn't deserve that.

The sickening thing was, the Ark Lord still might do all that even now . . .

Ah, but that would mean reneging on a deal, a distant voice echoed in his head. *As it happens, I am finished with this game and ready for the final step. And do you know what the final step is, young Anthony?*

Ant knew full well, but he said nothing as he shuffled through tight corridors toward the glow of lamps ahead. He could hear yells of alarm and panicked footsteps.

The final step, my young friend, is life. How ironic is that? All this death around us, and yet my goal is life. You can help me with that.

The mob of undead emerged into the first in a series of connecting rooms. The place was jam-packed with panicked Mox, and there was absolutely nowhere to run. The nearest cowered and squirmed, wishing they could melt backward through the crowd and let others be up front.

Although Ant kept shuffling forward with his hands outstretched, with his equally relentless mob alongside, his inner voice screamed at the Ark Lord to stop.

This, the Ark Lord murmured, *is what's called a crossroads. Or perhaps a line in the sand. Do I cross it? Do I break my agreement with you and slaughter them all? Allow the annihilation I predicted to come to pass? Or . . . should I stop now and honor our deal? Retract the Nyx energy in one fell swoop and return the undead to their former pitiful and harmless state? What say you, Anthony? Should I move on with a clear conscience, satisfied that dear Liam will spend his life regretting what he did to me?*

Ant reached for a Mox. The crowd shrank back, terrified and helpless. Even in the poor light of the bobbing lamps, he could see his own horrible reflection in their bulbous eyes.

There was no point pleading with the Ark Lord. The supervillain would do whatever he wanted no matter what. He'd already made up his mind and was toying with him.

As Ant's fingers curled around the throat of a delicate Mox woman, and his dead comrades reached for victims of their own, the Ark Lord gave an audible grunt as if his moment of triumph had reached its natural conclusion.

Enough, he said, sounding tired.

Ant's fingers had touched the woman's throat—but she didn't turn to dust. He felt something leaving him. The room lit up with snaking ribbons of yellow light, and a sense of startled wonder filled the place as, just like that, the crisis ended.

His corpse host felt weak. Ant staggered backward, jostling with the other undead as they fought to stay upright. But he felt something else, too—like he was fading, his senses leaving him, memories drifting away.

All at once, the crowd of terrified living Mox surged forward and attacked the undead. Ant went down, pinned to the hard floor by at least four determined Shuntaar villagers. But the sounds of the struggle dimmed in his rotting head. He felt displaced, like he was no longer in that body.

He was floating, carried in the glowing yellow arms of a phantom.

Goodbye, Anthony Carmichael, the Ark Lord whispered. *Enjoy the Ghost Realm.*

Epilogue

Liam sat on a low wall, turning the wormhole wand over and over in his hands while staring at a sprinkling of grey dust on the ground nearby.

Ant exploded into dust right there, he thought, still unable to believe it.

He would never forget the moment his friend had sacrificed himself and lunged at the undead corpse. Madison's tears had flooded out, and she'd clung to Liam as though he might throw himself at the shuffling Mox as well. But he hadn't. They'd sunk to their knees together, wailing and shouting for Ant to come back.

When the undead creature had turned and lumbered away, Madison had stifled her tears, climbed to her feet, and stalked off muttering, "He's not dead, he's not dead." And since then, clearly in denial, she'd been wandering about the village, surveying the damage, and talking to the Mox as they emerged from their underground chamber.

Liam had knelt there alone for what seemed like ages, unable to accept what had happened. The world around him had become muted. He couldn't say for sure when Madison had stomped away; that was more of a vague memory than anything. Shaking and moaning, on hands and knees, he'd leaned over the ash-sprinkled mud like he was retching and watched his own tears fall, trying to make sense of it all, trying to wake up from his nightmare. Ant was dead! He was *dead!*

But even then, a nagging voice in his head told him it wasn't so. That voice grew stronger, offering clues to suggest why Ant might not be dead after all, that though his body was ashes, his spirit lived on.

Liam's tears had finally dried up, and he remembered leaning back on his haunches taking long, deep breaths as the world slowly came back into focus around him. Only then was he conscious of Mox walking past, offering him sad looks and muttered condolences.

He'd migrated to the low wall where he now sat to ponder a future without Ant. How would he inform Mr. and Mrs. Carmichael that their son was dead? Not only that but explain *how* he'd died, and where his body was now? The idea of such a task mystified him. It was impossible.

Ant's muddy clothes sat in a pile next to him. All that remained of his best friend was the trampled ash and endless memories. And his final words: *Come look for me in the Ghost Realm.*

Those weren't the only words that still rang in Liam's head. *I need to leave my body behind . . . Tell my mom and dad I love them . . .*

Ant wasn't coming back. Yet, as his inner voice kept telling him, his friend had also said, *It's best if I go with him.* What did that mean? Go with the Ark Lord into death? Or go with him someplace else? Was this a clue that he might be alive somewhere?

But the ashes . . .

Liam sighed. He supposed it was always possible that Ant's mind, or his spirit, survived in some other realm— this Ghost Realm he'd mentioned. Stranger things had happened to Liam. Like swapping minds with a group of other kids. Turning into a robot. Seeing himself in the future. Meeting an eight-year-old boy who could create an entire world. Carrying a briefcase full of sentient energy while undead aliens battered their way through steel doors.

Yes, when he really thought about it, *much* stranger things had happened. Ant's body was a pile of ashes, but so what? Beyond Earth's limited technology was a universe where building new bodies was child's play: flesh and bone, mechanical, a bit of both—anything was possible. The main thing was that Ant's mind could still be intact. He could be somewhere safe.

Alive.

Liam felt something settle deep inside. In a long battle between anguish for his friend's death and a seemingly futile hope that he might still be alive, it appeared hope had just won. Maybe Madison had come to the same conclusion already. Ant was alive and in the Ark Lord's clutches. It was time to stop moping and find him.

He had pins and needles from sitting there so long. He stood and stretched, looking around for Madison. She was close by, talking to a Mox woman.

In the past few hours, the Mox had emerged from their underground chamber and spread about the village in astonishment and dismay. So many homes destroyed! So many enormous, dried-out insect and arachnid carcasses blocking the streets and lying across ruined structures!

Liam imagined a handful of towns on Earth likely resembled this chaos; once the Nyx had shot out tendrils of energy and sucked the life from the test bugs, they'd dried up and died in the same way. Images of their monstrous, inert bodies no doubt filled every TV screen, and would be the primary topic on every social network for months to come. There had to be a *lot* of head-scratching going on right now.

From the snatches of conversation he'd caught from passers-by, a dozen or so Mox lives had been taken in addition to Obram and his colleagues. Their remains—piles of clothing and scattered ashes—had been respectfully cordoned off so their loved ones could mourn.

And those undead corpses . . . They were still undead and shuffling about, but all of them were locked up in the underground chamber. They were weak now, easy to restrain. The Nyx had left them, and they were nothing more than reanimated corpses.

Something for the Mox to figure out. If they'd created the problem by dabbling in the dark arts, they'd just have to figure out how to undo the curse.

As for other clans throughout Mox territory, it seemed the bug attack had been a monumental failure as far as Krun was concerned. Liam imagined him up in his cloudstation, looking down in anger. "What happened?" he'd probably screamed at his scientist colleagues. "Where did the Nyx energy go?"

It's gone, Liam thought. *Gone to the same place as Ant, I guess.*

The Nyx was the Ark Lord, and the Ark Lord was the Nyx. They'd become one and fled, taking with them more energy than they'd started with. The Nyx had fed well, and the Ark Lord was in control. But why? Nobody had an answer, especially not the Mox.

"Magic," one elderly alien had said in a wavering voice as he bent over his staff. What this one-word explanation meant was anybody's guess.

Liam studied the wormhole wand again. It had power now. He wasn't sure why. Had the Nyx fixed it? Or the Ark Lord? Was it still programmed to go to Earth?

"Are you about ready?" Madison said, stepping around some scattered stone blocks.

She looked tired. Her face was pale, her eyes heavily shadowed. She'd attempted to smooth out her long, black hair, but it needed some serious detangling. She had smudges of dirt on her cheeks, a bruise on her chin, and a small split on her bottom lip. Her clothes were a mess— dried mud on her knees and anywhere she'd wiped her hands. Liam's own clothes were worse.

"I'm ready," he said. "What's the news?"

The moment he said that, they heard a grating roar in the sky, like a jet fighter taking off from a nearby airstrip. They spun around and spotted a flat, oblong craft lifting above the trees, heading for the cloudstation, a wispy black trail in its wake.

"*That's* the news," Madison said grimly. "Remember Krun said the commander and some investigators were on their way? Well, that's them. He was supposed to have wiped out the Mox by now, but—" She barked a laugh. "—all that kind of fell flat, didn't it? There are plenty of people here left alive to explain to the world what really happened."

Liam pursed his lips. "And what exactly do the Mox think happened?"

"An attack by a small group of Draduns from above. I told that woman over there. She's the leader of this place now that Obram's gone. She's already put a report in. The commander will be arresting Krun in the next few minutes."

Liam shook his head with disgust. "Bet they wouldn't have arrested him if he'd wiped out the Mox. With nobody to report what really happened, the Dradun elders would have turned a blind eye and pretended it was a side effect of dark magic."

He looked for the Mox woman, but she'd disappeared. She was in charge now despite her ordinary appearance— as ordinary as an alien woman can be, anyway.

Madison gestured at the wormhole wand. "So . . . it has power, right?"

"Ant stuck it straight into that floating ball of Nyx. It must have been fixed then, either accidentally or . . ."

"Or what?"

Liam frowned. "Why would the Ark Lord fix it, though? It must have been the Nyx he's sharing his mind with." He thumbed the end, and a blue light illuminated strong and bright—and stayed on. "Anyway, we have power."

"Let's find someplace quiet," Madison said. "Too many eyeballs around here."

Too many alien kids, too, Liam thought as a group of them came running around the corner, squealing in an unearthly way. They headed back down an alley, then leapt onto the dried-out husk of a giant, upside-down ant just visible beyond a partially collapsed dwelling. The group clambered up all over its bent and twisted legs like monkeys in trees. It was surreal to watch them. The young Mox were far more agile than humans.

"Liam?"

He shook himself. "Sorry."

Seeing no real point in bringing Ant's clothes with them, he left them on the wall. They found a place away from prying eyes, around the far side of the least damaged structure on the outskirts of the village. The forest loomed nearby. Nobody ventured their way.

Liam held the wand out in front of him. The blue light awaited activation.

He paused.

"What if . . ." he started to say.

Madison raised her eyebrows at him. "What if what?"

"What if it *does* take us home? What then? I don't even know what time it is back on Earth, but I bet we're late, or missing, or something. What do we say to our parents? What do we say to—"

He broke off.

Madison's jaw tightened. "To Ant's parents? I don't know. But I know what we should do first."

Liam waited.

"We should dig up the echo wand. Maybe I should have let Ant do that before. But anyway, if we dig it up, we could maybe . . . you know, check into the future a few days? A week? Whatever it takes to find Ant. To see when he's *there* with us again, you know?"

"Oh, Maddy, that's genius." Liam felt a surge of excitement mixed with relief. "Yeah, it's cheating a bit, but we can fast-forward past all the worried parents and search parties and find out when he actually gets back home. At least we'll know. And then, even if it takes us a month to find him and rescue him, we'll *know*."

Madison nodded at the wand. "Do it."

The wormhole exploded into being in the usual way, with a streak of white light that expanded into a swirling tunnel. Once stabilized, its eerie glow reflecting in a muddy puddle below, Liam sighed with relief. It was working. They had a wormhole wand of their own, and hopefully—if Jaxrill had done right by them, and the Ark Lord hadn't messed with it—it was still programmed to take them to Earth.

Madison reached for him. Gripping the wand tightly, Liam took her hand. Together, side by side, they ran at the wormhole and leapt in.

They tumbled and twisted, rushing through the vortex. Ahead, a tiny black hole signified the far end, and it grew rapidly until they could make out a little detail. The inside of a church, perhaps? What looked like a polished marble floor, ornate columns reaching high above, and . . . was that a man on a throne?

Liam and Madison shot out the end and staggered before tripping and falling. Liam grunted with annoyance. Aliens made it look so easy.

He helped Madison up and cast his gaze sideways at the man on the throne. He sat there quite calmly, chin on his chest, wearing an ivory-colored crown that looked like it had been thrown together from bits and pieces—thin rods, wire and string, sea shells, perhaps even bones. Clearly a king of some sort.

A quick glance up took Liam's breath away. All the light in the room came from the ceiling—or lack of. The cathedral columns stretched high above, holding up several arches, but the roof itself was missing, the massive structure open to an orange sky. Something about the sky struck Liam as *off*.

His heart sank. This wasn't Earth.

What about the motionless king? Was he asleep? Liam moved closer. Hidden beneath the crown and almost obscured by the furskin coat wrapped around his neck, the visible part of the man's face was a weird coppery color, all gnarled and wrinkled.

"Liam," Madison warned.

He stopped a few feet from the throne, his heart thumping. "I don't think this is Earth," he whispered. "And I'm not sure, but . . . I think this man is dead."

Author's Note

Did you enjoy *Aliens Undead*?

It occurred to me right after I started the first part, "Target Earth," that Earthlings are starting to see some really weird stuff in the Brockridge area. What with that strange yellow cloud in the first book that ripped the roof off Liam's house, then his house falling into a sinkhole and the subsequent discovery of odd tunnels far below ground, and probably quite a few sightings of aliens popping up at night, I figured it's only a matter of time before the dreaded adults find out what's going on.

I decided to run with that. If you can't go big, go home, right? So "Target Earth" went big—literally. There's no way those giant bugs can be explained away. Colonel Peterson has some investigating to do. The way he sees it, Brockridge was the first place an oversized insect showed up, and there was that crazy chauffeur woman claiming a bunch of kids can predict the opening of wormholes . . . so maybe, just *maybe*, there's something in her story after all. Those kids are involved!

But where are they now?

In the previous book, *Warp Giants*, the three stories were fairly independent. The three in *this* book are definitely crucial parts of a single tale. It's actually the longest of the five Sleep Writer books so far, and it's kind of a turning point for the intrepid trio. Or is it now a duo? I expect you're wondering whether Ant will be rescued from the clutches of the Ark Lord. To be honest, I'm wondering the same thing. What, just because I'm the author, you think I have all the answers?

Anyway, my goal is to keep the gang in space for a few books. Book 6 is pretty well planned out, but beyond that, all I know is that the kids don't get to go home just yet.

Sometimes when I need to invent aliens or creatures, I often find a nice graphic first. It's much easier to find a cool image of an alien or ghoul and write my story to suit, rather than the other way around. That was the case with "Frozen Corpses." But to be honest, that image on the front cover is almost exactly what I had in mind anyway, so it worked out well. The story was originally "Frozen Demons," but my beta readers pointed out (correctly) that the creatures aren't necessarily demonic, just nasty-looking. Demonic suggests evil, and as scary as the undead are, they're really just misunderstood teddy bears at heart. (Okay, that's an exaggeration.)

It was difficult to write the end of "Stasis Error." Ant is not fully dead yet, but he might as well be. His mind, spirit, soul, or whatever you want to call it, will be in the clutches of the Ark Lord for a while, and I'm telling you now that his future is undecided. So don't rest on your laurels thinking, "Oh, but he's a main character, and all is going to be hunky-dory." Remember, only Liam and Madison have predetermined distant futures. Ant does not.

I experimented earlier in 2019 with a serialized version of the books. I split each novel into three parts, meaning my four existing novels became Parts 1-12. This was easy with *Warp Giants*, because it was already in three parts, but it was interesting to see how the first three books, *Sleep Writer*, *Robot Blood*, and *Caleb's World*, split so easily as well, almost as though I'd subconsciously planned them that way.

I then began work on the fifth novel, *Aliens Undead*, which would be Parts 13-15. But I found a few problems when it came to publishing as a serial. While I enjoyed creating the covers, and will continue to write each book in three parts, it's really hard to get readers to pick up a serialized story even on Kindle Unlimited. This is partly because reviews are incredibly difficult to get these days, and the prospect of getting some for each serialized part is daunting. Also, pricing is difficult. Readers expect more than 20,000 words for $2.99 (of which I get 70%). And if I price at less than that, I only get 35% of the price in royalties. Either I lose out, or the reader does.

So I've dropped the experiment. That said, I'm keeping the format of the books as three novellas each and creating covers in the background just in case I ever decide to serialize again, perhaps on a different platform in the future.

Next up? Liam and Madison will be back soon, fumbling their way around the universe in a vain attempt to find Ant and thwart the Ark Lord. Look out for *Dream Phase* in 2022.

Keith Robinson
Sci-Fi and Fantasy Author

Visit http://www.thesleepwriter.com for up-to-date information about this series and other books.

Printed in Great Britain
by Amazon